Prologue

Everyone knows at least one. A place where happiness goes to die. Stepping within it's doors seems to drain every ounce of it. It doesn't take long to notice, the eerie silence hiding whispers of stolen hope and joy. The feeling of utter despair overcoming the happiness once held, destroying hope and decimating dreams. It's an abyss linked to all manner of darkness. A place no one talks about, because talking about it is an admission… an admission of insanity. And it slowly grows. Every day spent within this dark molds it, shapes it, and nurtures it. In the end, the madness seems a welcome escape. This is the story of one such place, a place built to be welcoming… but only to the mad.

I didn't believe them when they first told me. Why would I? Although the mere mention chilled me to the bone, I could lie to myself rather easily. It's just another ghost story, just something to tell around a campfire. But no amount of fire could shake it, no jokes or childish teasing… not even the promise of a happy sunrise the next morning. The second this story was whispered among friends, it was burnt into my brain forever. At first, it was just something to laugh at. A poor attempt to scare the new kid, nothing more. Albeit, I'm only new to the school district. I've lived near here my whole life. After a while, however, it started clawing at my mind. I found myself thinking about it more and more often. Perhaps that's why I now stand here, staring at said place. That's what I tell myself anyway. In all actuality, I was dragged here by my friends. My name is Catori Hashna, the idiot that fell to peer pressure… and this is where my story begins.

The building is only one floor, yet it still seems to loom over me. It's shadow casts an eerie dark that draws the warmth from my body. My knees are shaking, though it's more from the cold. October nights tend to be around here. From behind me, I hear the snickers of my classmates. I forget how we came to be here. The last thing I remember is sitting in front of a television, watching some poorly made vampire movie with my new friends. No doubt one thing led to another, as they often do in the face of boredom. Now, I await the dare that's lain silent for the last five minutes.

"I dare you to go in, Catori," one of the boys says, tone quiet with a hint of fear. "No one ever comes out again, you know. That place is cursed."

"You're such a baby," I scoff. "You know that's only a made up story, right? I bet no one's ever tired. That place looks condemned, we wouldn't make it past the doors without the floor falling in."

"You're just scared."

"Not as much as you, apparently."

With that, I march forward. What started as a determined stride, however, quickly becomes a wary scoot. No one followed me, I'm all alone. There's a flash of lightening and a crack of thunder. It's so real I can feel the electricity on the air. Eyes wide, I gaze overhead... but the skies are clear and the full moon is bright. Shaking it off as my imagination and far too many horror films, I take a deep breath and stand straight. The building is weathered, trapped in its own time as ours passes it by. One door hangs on it's hinges, the other gone missing. As I move ever closer, I see the webbed cracks upon large windows. It was once a store, though I can't say which.

Timid as the fear grows ever more, I let one foot sneak past the threshold. Nothing. With a sigh of relief, I force myself through. At first, I feel nothing but disappointment. I had hoped for a wailing spirit, or walls that bled crimson. Instead, I get silence. Now I have to ask myself if that wasn't the worst thing to have found.

With the quiet of the grave surrounding me, I wander toward a counter. Upon it are still a few coins from the last transaction. One of the registers is jarred, as though someone tried to force it open. Maybe that was the infamous person that never came out. I suppose I'll never know.

All around me, I see a place trapped in the throws of its last moments. There's debris on the floor, the tiles overhead falling with time. With each step, they crumble underfoot. I'm not sure why I walk further in, it really doesn't make any sense. There's nothing here. The curiosity, however, is always insatiable. My heart nearly stops upon a loud clunk off to the side. Eyes darting in that direction, I can see a rusty metal pole. It finally succumbed to years of rust, falling to the floor of its own accord. I take a relieved breath as I chuckle nervously. By this time, I can hear my friends calling from outside. They're not about to come in, no matter how much they feel the need to 'save' me. Rolling my eyes, my feet take me back outside.

"You made it!" one of the guys comments.

"Don't sound too upset," I scoff. "I told you it was all a story. Nothing happened in there, except a pole falling from it's mount. Far from a supernatural occurrence with all that rust."

"Maybe it was a slow night."

"For a haunted building? Seriously?" I frown. "Do you want me to go back in and wait?"

He huffs, as I thought he might, and shakes his head. It's getting late and we all snuck out, so we need to be getting back. As we turn to leave, I glance back at the building once more, surprised to see lights flickering on inside. The power should've been turned off in that place, it hasn't been operational for years. A silhouette stands at the window… and a spatter of blood suddenly paints it. The silhouette still stands, waving 'goodbye'. I don't say anything, just keep on walking. Within me, however, is that growing curiosity. It won't be long, I'm almost positive, and I'll be back inside that dead place. Until that time, I'm happy to investigate far from the decay.

The night is cold, its winds howling aggressively, and we're all huddled together. Our small group couldn't get back fast enough. The streets are so deserted, it gives me chills. So many horror movies, so many negative turns. Most of which start with some such scene. A cat yowls in the nearby alley, knocking a garbage can over. That's enough to get us moving, the lot of us bolting down the street. The night will never be the same for me.

Lying in the darkness, lost within my dreams, it eats me alive. I can hear screams from the past. The endless wails of spirits, left in unrest and trapped in torment. They all call to me. It doesn't matter how far away I get, that place has ensnared me. And I know at that moment... I've joined them.

Chapter 1

Morning doesn't come fast enough, waking me from my nightmares. As I lay beneath the blankets, covered in a cold sweat, the images repeat within my mind's eye. The screaming still echos within, though I can't recall if it was mine or not. There was so much blood, covering every surface and dripping from the ceiling. Hands still trembling, I toss my blankets aside and get up. Last night haunts me still, yet it won't keep me from living. I push it to the back of my mind and head to my dresser.

The morning sun is warm, even cutting through the cold wind. My favorite autumn days are soaked in this sort of sunlight. I take a deep breath, ignoring the stink the cold air gives me, and sigh in content. It hasn't been long since I moved here, so the town is still new to me. With so much to discover, I'm more than happy to give way to distraction.

It's only Sunday, a holiday compared to what lies in wait tomorrow. It may be my last year, but that doesn't mean everything can't go wrong last minute. Considering how last night went, that may be a great thought to keep in mind. Down the street is a bus stop. It's crowded with people looking for a ride. I don't blame them, even I had second thoughts about walking today. Striding past, I make my way down the street. I'm not located in the center of town, but everything is within walking distance.

The library is closest, which works for me. I have so much to learn about that strange place, and everything I need is right here. I take the few steps to the door quickly, not paying any mind to the large lion statues on either side. The heat inside slams into me, destroying the ice upon my breath. Just past the doors is a long desk, a quiet woman reading on the other side. Her mousy appearance is the stereotype for a librarian. It's almost disappointing.

My eyes sweep the place, yet no one is here. Not within my immediate line of sight any way. With only a couple long strides, I'm standing before the woman. Her curly brown hair is in a messy bun, a couple strands falling into her eyes to be brushed aside repeatedly. Her name tag reads 'Sadie'. I clear my throat, the woman glancing up through think black glasses.

"May I help you?" she wonders.

"I'm looking for information on a specific store," I comment. "It's not open anymore, but it has a rather colorful history. I thought it would be interesting enough to get me an 'A' on my assignment."

"I see. Well, the history section is over that way," she points out. "But if you're looking to go in-depth, I suggest the archives. We've stored years of newspaper articles and such, there might be something that can help out."

"Thank you so much! I'll look through the books first, and then the archives."

"Just come get me when you're ready."

I nod, letting her go back to her book. The shelves are so tall, creating a labyrinth all around me. As unnerving as that seems, I don't let it deter me. On a mission, I steel myself and step into them. My footsteps echo upon cool tile, the only sound within this desolate building. If I didn't know any better, I would assume I was the only survivor of an apocalypse. The thoughts are quickly shaken from my mind.

The section I'm looking for isn't far in. It holds so many books, it's hard to choose the first. My fingers trail along their spines, quickly grabbing one with a red cover. After pulling out a few, I sit upon the floor and open them. The words swim around my head. So much has happened in the past here, yet there seems to be so little on the building I seek. With a sigh, I put them back. The archives will likely have more useful information.

Back at the desk, the librarian is setting her book aside. She's ready for me, it's easy to tell. Perhaps, in the back of her mind, even *she* knows what I'm looking for. There's a small key in her hand, brass and antique. That probably should've been my first clue to leave. I probably wouldn't have listened anyway.

"The archives were built when this library was first erected," Sadie offers. "That was so long ago. Since then, the building has been renovated a few times… but no one ever touched that part. I'm not sure why, but I suppose it's because of that 'incident'."

"What incident?"

"A long time ago, when the town was still new, there was a woman that lived here. The whole town feared her. She seemed really nice, but… there was just something about her. She worked here on the weekends, spent her time in the archives. Her day job was at an old store, though. It's not here anymore, that was so long ago," she informs, her tone holding a creeping edge for the tale. "One day, she didn't show up at the store. They looked here, but the archives were locked from the outside and the key was missing. They assumed she locked up and left. After a month of searching, the owner needed something out of the archives. He had a locksmith come in and take care of the lock. When they opened the door, they found her decaying body. She had surrounded herself with books on black magic. A piece of chalk was beneath her, used to scrawl a bunch of symbols on the floor. The owner and the locksmith got sick and died a few days later. That was the last time anyone went near the archives."

"… You're going down there now," I point out skeptically.

"I don't believe in those ghost stories," she laughs. "Along the way, people stopped believing and it was forgotten. The librarians are the only ones that talk about it now. We just try to scare anyone going there, but you don't seem to scare easily."

"Nope. Sorry."

She unlocks the large door, waving her hand for me to enter. That's where she leaves me. I can hear her footsteps retreating, my eyes taking in the room. If anything, I would call it a storage area. There are so many books piled atop each other, strewn about tables, and crammed onto shelves. Obviously, her tale was likely made up. Someone had to renovate down here, because there's a couple computers lit up in the corner. I roll my eyes and sit down.

The internet is rather strong here, which is shocking. I figured it would lag much worse than this. With a shrug, my fingers hit the keys. The search brings up a lot of interesting newspaper articles. Curiously, there aren't many positive ones. A shivers runs up my spine at the contents. So many strange deaths revolve around that store. One states 'Robbery Gone Bad', showing a picture of the woman I saw. She's smiling and happy, so different from the image lying on the floor.

"Shot in a robbery gone bad," I read. "How sad. The thief was never caught. No wonder she can't move on."

Scrolling down, there's another death… then another… and so many more. Beheading, explosions, hangings, dismemberment. My head spins with the amount. If all these people are trapped in that building, it's no wonder they call it haunted! I would've used the word *cursed*! Could that woman from long ago be the cause? She was dabbling in black magic, it's entirely viable. I worry my bottom lip, pulling a small notebook and pen from my bag. The pen's tip touches the paper… and I start making a list. I can look them up at home, but having the names in advance will help greatly.

Chapter 2

That night, I return. Against my better judgment, I go alone. After all the disbelief, I can't bare to tell my friends what I'm doing. It's better kept a secret. No one needs to know I've returned, or they might just call me crazy. With a deep breath, I walk in. The wind blows through a hole in the window, rustling age old signs barely sticking to the glass. It seems there was a sale before this place met its end. Shrugging it off, I travel past the registers. On my right are large changing rooms, one of the mirrors cracked and missing pieces. Between them and myself, are a wide array of metal racks. Some have fallen apart, while others still hold clothing. It may be ragged and moth-eaten, but it's somewhat survived.

As I pass them by, I reach over to grasp a sleeve. The cloth was once cotton, white and likely beautiful in design. Now it's been dirtied and forgotten. A sound in the back of the store catches my attention, just a faded thump in the distance. At first, I step away. It's a move any sane person would make. After a moment's thought, however, I push forward. The title 'haunted' isn't given so whimsically. Something about this place earned it, and I'm going to find out what happened. Shelves on my left hold broken knickknacks and cracked vases, the racks on my right are covered with empty hangers and rags. As my foot meets the floor once more, something slides across the tiles. It's stopped by my sneaker, my eyes watching a moment in surprise. Slowly, searching the area for another presence, I crouch down. It's a book. Not a fantastically spooky one, like something of the occult or witch craft. Not even one on haunted houses. As I go to pick it up, the intercom system screeches to life. My hands cover my ears, teeth gritting at the noise. When it finally stops, I chance listening.

"Welcome to our home," a collection of voices says, the tone gritty and warped. *"It's been so long since we had a guest. We hope you stay longer than the night. This place used to be so lively, filled with customers and team members. We were a happy family. We're always so eager to invite new blood into the pool. We hope we can bring you into the fold, too."*

"… Okay… that's not creepy at all," I murmur.

"You'll love it here, we just know you will. Let us tell you about our home. We're always happy to help. Customer satisfaction is the most important feature here in our home, after all."

"… I think I'll pass for the moment," I answer warily. "If you don't mind, I'd just like to look around a bit."

"Customers are only allowed in this part of the store. Upstairs and in the back are off limits. For your convenience, we'll be keeping those doors locked. Please follow the rules of the store, we wouldn't want you to

get hurt. After all, you'll be joining us soon enough."

"... Well... that's awfully confidant."

For some odd reason, I pick up the misplaced book. The shelves are already full of rotted pages and loose binding, but I replace it anyway. This large area is where I'm allowed to go, so I'll follow the rules... for now. I begin to investigate the store. It's not much of a sight, just more of the same stuff upon entrance. When I walk around the counter, however, I notice a large smear of orange. It appears to have sprayed all over the broken computer, a hole in the cracked screen hinting at a bullet. I shudder to think what transpired. A piece of tape is still stuck to the floor, so I crouch down to see it better. As I get closer, it starts to grow along the tiles and black mat. When it's finished moving, I gasp at the sight of a body outline. It's leaning up against the counter, right beneath the register. Something flickers into existence, my body automatically jerking away. As I lay upon the floor, arms keeping my torso upright, I can see a spirit. They're so lifelike, though pale and transparent. I can almost ignore those differences.

They don't move, don't speak. It's just a picture of a crime scene, locked in a still life... or still *death*, all things considered. I study her, as it's obviously a 'she'. Her body is tall and lithe, darkened to a nice chocolate tone. Black hair down past her shoulders hangs loose. There's a small hole in the center of her forehead, no doubt the point. Cautiously, I stand and move closer. Still no motion. Wary of the dead body before me, I carefully move around to the side. The back of her head is an open mess of blood and brain matter. I gasp, one hand rising to cover my mouth... and a hand grabs my wrist. Dead opaque eyes stare at me, the corpse turned to lock eyes.

"Welcome to our home," she rasps. *"How can I help you today? Are you looking for something new? Or perhaps... you're looking for a new home."*

I jerk away from her, falling back on the floor before crawling away. My heart is thumping so hard, I can feel it in my throat. A feeble attempt at freedom. When I turn back, the ghost is gone. Breathing hard, I try to still my racing heart. I can already tell this is going to be a difficult investigation.

After the near heart attack, I found it best to retire for the night. The walk home is about the same as before, though I'm alone this time. The second I relax, enjoying the cool night air, I catch movement from my right. Probably just another cat. Shaking that off, I try to fall into a serene frame of mind. The moon is beautiful tonight. It's waning light is trying hard to outshine the stars. Those tiny pinpricks in pitch dance about, twinkling with laughter. With a sigh, I stuff my hands in my pockets and hum to myself. My ear catches the wind's whispering. If I concentrate on it, the breeze seems to be calling my name. As unnerving as that sounds, I put it out of my head. A few more steps and it calls again. This time, I know it's my name it's calling. My blood freezes in my veins. Eyes scanning the empty streets, I see no one but myself and a few stray leaves. Chalking up to an overactive imagination, I huddling in on myself and keep walking. As I pass a darkened alley, a sickly and half rotted face jumps out at me.

"Come home!" the corpse states.

I scream and scramble away, nearly getting hit by a small Volkswagen. The feeble horn blares in passing, drowning out my shriek. There's nothing in the alley now, just the silent dark. My heart races in my chest. It slams so hard against my ribcage, I fear it might break through. Giving the alley a wide berth as I pass, my feet quicken to get away. That place was supposed to stay put, not follow me home. Opening my curiosity to the dead, has only made them a permanent residence in my life. I pray this is only a one time thing, locking every bolt on my door when I pass through it.

Throughout my morning, I can't stop thinking about my night. With my head trapped in daydreams, my friends have gotten suspicious. I can't have them finding out what I've been doing, I'll never live it down. When a slumber party is suggested, I readily agree. Any distraction to keep me from that cursed place is welcome. Tonight, I need a normal night where 'supernatural' is just another term for 'ghost story'.

With plans for later, I continue through my day. It's going rather steady, the haunting of last night far from me now. Luck would have it, the spirits have fallen silent. I join my best friend in history class. Heather is a goodhearted person, the first to befriend me when I moved here. It hasn't been long, but I can't imagine being here without her. With a soft smile, I slide into my seat. She glances my way, leaning closer to whisper.

"What's going on with you today, Catori?"

"What do you mean?"

"You're acting really weird. Like all day you've been in la-la land. Is it because of the other night? Those guys were assholes, we never should've went there."

"They were being guys," I shrug off. "It's not that. I went to the library and heard about some weird lady. The story got me thinking."

"About what?"

"Don't tell anyone," I warn. "I swear, if you do, I'll never speak to you again."

"You know I can keep a secret," she hisses. "Why would you even have to say anything?"

"… The woman that died at the library worked at that old store. She was into black magic," I divulge excitedly. "What if she's the reason that store is cursed?"

"It's not cursed, it's haunted," she corrects.

"Do you know how many people 'just happened' to die there?" I frown. "I can honestly tell you, it's over twenty. I haven't found all of them yet, but I guarantee there's more off the records. I want to know what happened there."

"You're going down a really steep path," she comments. "You better hope you don't fall, those rabbit holes can be murder."

"Tell me about it," I murmur.

We turn our attention to the teacher, who's just entering the room. Mr. Abbott is a bookish type, with short black hair and light skin. I swear all he owns is sweater vests and suit jackets with patches on the elbows. I heard he was invited to teach at Yale, yet turned them down. *Yale*! Who the hell turns down *Yale*? As he writes the lesson upon the chalkboard, I open my notebook. Instead of the wars in the south, I see the names on my list. I only found a few when I got home, but it's still more than I had before. Glancing up, I'm surprised to see the lesson has changed. Mr. Abbott turns around with a large grin.

"Today, I thought it would be fun to be a little festive," he states. "Instead of reading about the wars, I thought we could talk about the ghost stories in this area. Maybe even a few derived from the southern wars. Anyone have one to start with?"

"The creepy old store no one goes near!" Eric, one of my guy friends, calls. "We went! I even went in."

"You liar, you did not! You dared *me* to go in," I shout. "You were too chickenshit!"

"Language," Mr. Abbott says. "But I like the idea. I'll tell you about the old store."

There's a cheer from the students, always ready for a good ghost story. I can't say I'm disappointed, this is way better than listening to a boring lecture. The teacher clears his throat and sits at his desk. With all eyes eagerly awaiting his story, he smiles and parts his lips to speak.

"Long ago, there was a woman keen on running her own business," he starts. "She wasn't well liked, but she had a solid idea for a store. She built it herself, though it took a long while. When she started getting a lot of business, she brought in more people to work for her. At night, she would find work at the library nearby. No one paid her much attention, but they probably should've."

"Why?" a girl, Melissa, questions from the front.

"He's getting to that, stop interrupting him," Brad, seated beside her, hisses.

"It was rumored that she was into witchcraft," Mr. Abbott answers, stopping their argument early. "Her workers started disappearing, one by one. Everyone thought they had just quit and moved. Then there were the deaths. When others noticed the disappearances, they stopped… but many of her workers were killed. Suicide, robberies, and even mysterious circumstances.

She just couldn't keep anyone, they all started leaving. No one stayed longer than a week or two, all afraid they would be next. Eventually, her store started losing business. The only thing she had left was the archives, where she killed herself. But the store's story didn't end with her death.

Another woman came to town, buying the building and the land it sits on. She hired in new faces, changed the venue with the times. Everything was going so well for her… until the first death.

After losing one of her workers, customers started seeing them walk the aisles. Things would move on their own, lights would flickers, and there was always a whisper in the background of the intercom. People were scared away, leaving the place empty once more.

Now, the only people that go missing are the ones that sneak in. A few have come back, but they would be found dead a week or two later. Some even commit suicide in the building itself. It doesn't matter now, though. Pretty soon, the building will be torn down and the story will finally end."

The conversation moves to another story, yet I don't hear it. Something within me is livid, though I can't explain why. It's not my emotion, I know that much, yet it hangs around me like a shroud. All I can think, is that the store knows. It's following me now, so it would've heard this as well. Cold washes through my veins at the realization. What if it takes this out on me? I need to figure this place out quickly, before it takes me down with it.

When I return from school, I head into the bathroom to shower. This is my last year. When I graduate, I'll be getting my first job. I haven't chosen a career yet, though private investigator strikes my interest. I like the puzzles more than I do the paper work. With a happy sigh, I step into the hot water. It beats down on sore muscles and cold skin. I didn't realize how stressed I had been today. It was likely near the beginning. A night of terrors, couple with nightmares and feared haunting, were enough to strike me weak. I relish in the heat of the steam, relaxing to a point I couldn't reach before. When I'm finished, I turn off the water and reach out for a towel. For a moment, I can't find it with my searching fingers. One digit finally touches the thick wool. I grab it and pull it into the shower with me.

I dry off quickly, pulling the curtain aside. On the wall beside the shower, around where I located my towel, there's a thick black hand print. I stare at it for a long while, trying to register where it came from. The lights begin to flicker, waking me from my stupor. I glance over to the mirror, gasping at the words drawn in the steam there… '*We're waiting*'. I almost slip back into the tub in my haste to get away. Grabbing my clothes, I hurry out of the small room and run for mine. It doesn't occur to me that I can't outrun, or even hide from it. I just need to put distance between myself and them. Within my room, all dressed and ready for bed, I hide beneath my covers. A child scared of the boogeyman. Glowing eyes stare at me through the pitch, I can feel them more than see them. They're grating on my every nerve. I know what they want. They want me to go back to that store. As much as I can't stand the idea, this won't stop until I give in.

Chapter 3

The wind is howling so loudly, a vicious beast looking for a meal. I'm here, though I don't want to be. Standing outside the building that's become my nightmare. My one regret. The lights flicker, sparks jumping from the sign. Laughter and voices sound from it. They grow louder even without me getting closer. Before I know it, I'm standing at the door. I take a deep breath and open the door. Although I saw nothing but ruin through the large glass windows, inside looks brand new. There are no faded signs or broken glass. No rusted registers and moldy clothes.

Inside this place is warmth and joy. People crowd the aisles, chatting with complete strangers as though they're family. It's such a welcoming place. Nervous, I step further in. A woman calls for me, waving her hand to grab my attention. She's the one I saw before, though the bullet hole is gone. I'm completely lost for what to do.

When I don't go to her, she heads over to me. The smile on her face is so deceptive, for I know what's happened here. Those perfect white teeth, grinning in such a childish happiness, insist nothing bad has gone down.

"*Hi, you must be Catori Hashna! The manager is waiting for you!*" she states. "*I'm so glad you'll be joining our family, you have no idea. I swear, this place has been so dead lately.*"

I don't miss the words used. She ushers me down the main aisle, all giddy and proud. We meet a woman halfway there, though I can't make her out. It would seem she were cut from shadows. Nothing but a silhouette.

Even that has me on guard, as I receive nothing but fear and anger when looking upon her. From her silhouette, I can tell she's short and plump. Her hair is curly and pulled back in a ponytail.

"*Welcome to the family*," she says, her tone raspy and echoic. "*They've all been waiting for you to arrive. They're so happy... my children. It's so rare they get new siblings these days.*"

"I'm not so sure..."

"*You'll, of course, need a uniform. We have to adhere to the dress code here. Before you join them, I'll have to make one final adjustment.*"

"Adjustment?"

She turns and a blade thrusts toward me. I manage to avoid it for the most part, instead taking damage to my side. The shock fills me like cold water, a scream leaving my parted lips.

I sit up in bed, cold beads of sweat covering my body. One hand touches my side on instinct. My fingertips touch warm liquid, so I pull my hand away to look. A dark red fluid covers them. I'm bleeding. With a gasp, I jump from bed and hurry to the bathroom. My tank top is stained red with blood, a shallow cut in the exact spot that woman hit.

"Oh my god," I whisper, stunned.

Trembling, I pull out some alcohol and band-aids. After applying it to a cotton-ball, I dab away at the blood. It stings, both my skin and my nose. I have no clue what to do with my dirtied tank-top, but I can't keep it. It also can't be seen by my parents, they would freak out. I quickly stuff it into the trash bag beneath my sink. As I clean up, I can hear a soft murmuring in the back of my mind. It's that woman and her 'children', I just know it is.

"So, you're stubborn," I comment, quiet and icy. "That's perfectly fine, so am I. You can bother me all you want, but I won't break. You hear me? This little game you play with your victims, I can play it, too. This time, *I'm* going to win."

"*We'll see about that*," a voice whispers near my ear.

I turn quickly, yet there's no one there. There are, however, blackened footprints on my floor. They're so close, almost touching the backs of my shoes. I shiver at the thought. Fear quickly turns to anger, though. I won't end up like those other victims, for that's all they really are. Unfortunate targets to a deranged store. I don't know what happened to them. I can guess from recent happenings, though. They probably went insane, unable to get away from their would be attacker. Too scared to admit what's going on, to seek help that might actually listen without skepticism. I feel so horrible for them, wish I were there to lend them a shoulder and an ear. If that's all it would've taken to save them, why wouldn't anyone give it to them? Hopefully, that's all that's needed at that cursed store. Hopefully, I can still save those lost within the aisles.

I check my bandage, satisfied with the work I've done. It's not a perfect patch job, but it'll hold. That's all that's needed. It'll be tough going through school with this injury, yet all I need is a viable excuse. That's shouldn't be difficult to think up. Especially since I'm a perfect klutz. I can cut myself on things one would never expect. After I'm dressed, I hurry downstairs to eat breakfast.

School is just as it was before, though I manage to keep my mind from drifting. I know Heather is worried, her eyes tell me that much, yet she doesn't attempt to stop me. We may not have been together long, but it was a 'friends at first sight' thing. When we met, it was like we've known each other through lifetimes. We just clicked.

At lunch, she gets her chance to speak with me. We sit off to the side, away from others. When I start eating, she starts prying. She's not the type to spread rumors, so I never have worries about telling her secrets. As I bite into my pizza, she sets down her milk.

"Okay, what's so interesting about that place?" she questions. "I mean… it's so *dangerous*! You shouldn't be going there without someone knowing."

"You know," I point out. "And it's not so much that it's interesting… I… I want to save them. The people trapped there."

"You'll end up trapped as well if you're not careful!"

"Trust me, I realized that. But it's too late now."

"What do you mean?" she asks, voice quiet with trepidation.

"It doesn't stay in the building," I offer in exasperation. "I think that's why those other people killed themselves. It followed me out when I went. I see them in the dark, find hand prints on my walls, and hear them whispering. No one was there to save those other people, but I'm going to fix that. I'm going to free them."

"You're just as crazy, you know that?" Heather frowns. "But… I'm here for you if you need me. Remember that, okay?"

"I will. Thank you."

My heart is warmed by her smile. This is what those others lacked, a friend that would believe them to the bitter end. One of my hands reaches over to hers, squeezing it in a thankful manner. Afterward, we both dig into our meal. The conversation is turned to mundane topics, mostly involving the upcoming sports season. With the end of lunch, that normal feeling begins to drain. I reluctantly let it go and head to my next class.

When the last bell rings, I sigh a breath of relief. As much as I like school, the days just seem to stretch on forever. Every last bell is like a ring of freedom. I walk out to get to my car, waiting for Heather there. The slumber party is tonight, so I'll be stopping by home just to grab my bag. We and three other girls will be staying at her home.

"Ready for a night of awesomeness?" she cheers.

"You know it," I laugh. "I just hope I don't ruin the night. What with all these damn spooks on me."

"You'll be fine," she waves off. "I have a full proof plan to keep your paranoia on the surface."

"… That doesn't sound like something I should be going for."

"Who's always got your back?" Heather asks with a smirk.

"You do," I smile.

"Too right! So, just trust your bestie. I got it all planned."

The doors close and I hit the gas. We don't live far from the school, but it's cold out. No one wants to walk in the cold more than they have to. Traffic is a little worse, considering everyone is driving now, but nothing we can't handle. When I park in my driveway, I hurry in to grab my bag. I leave the car running, so it's still warm when I get back. Afterward, I take us to Heather's house.

The girls are already there when I pull up, all chatting outside the car. Wendy, Melissa, and Brittany are part of the popular group… which means they're complete gossips most of the time. If they find out I'm seeing these ghosts, it'll be all over the school like a wildfire. The very thought makes me anxious. When they see me, they light up and wave. I'm not as close to them, however they're nice people and I don't mind them. We all go inside, leaving the cold behind with a slam of the front door…. At least…that's what I had hoped.

We're in our pajamas in no time. I'm waiting to hear what Heather's genius plan is, though I don't doubt she has my back. When she walks in with a heaping bowl of popcorn and a large bag full of horror movies… I thank the stars above she's my bestie. The first movie is pushed into the DVD player, and it's that moment when I feel the first shiver. Settled down on the plush carpet, wrapped in fuzzy blankets, it races down my spine. I ignore it, grabbing the popcorn bucket from Brittany. The movie overcomes the static on the television, opening to a creepy forest road. The scene flickers, a shadowy silhouette popping up on it.

"*Come home*," it calls out.

"I don't get why they decided to get out of the car and walk," Melissa comments. "That's like… the number one horror film 'don't'. You're just asking to be killed."

"They read the script," I comment.

"… That's such an unsatisfying comment."

"Shh, watch the movie."

We pass around the popcorn, criticizing the character's choices every now and then. The shadow doesn't come back. Instead, when I reach into the popcorn bowl, I touch something cold. I look down to see a rotted hand in the bowl. I scream, flipping the bowl out of my lap. At the laughter around me, I glare at the girls. Wendy picks up the hand, showing me it's fake.

"You should've seen your face!" my supposed best friend snorts in humor.

"I'll remember this," I point out. "Your punishment will be drawn out when you least expect it."

"I'm sorry, I couldn't help myself!" she chuckles. "You're not the only one I scared, you know."

"I almost had a fucking heart attack!" Melissa, beside me, comments.

"Movie!" Brittany huffs. "Childish pranks can be later, I want to see how this stupid bitch dies."

We all settle down once more, curling up beneath our blankets. I manage to shoulder Heather over, leaving her laughing on the floor. This normalcy is what I need after the nights I've had.

After about ten horror films, a pillow fight, and a couple snack runs, we all settled down to sleep. Heather is passed out on the blankets we were curled up on, so I jump in her bed. No sense letting it go to waste. Brittany and Melissa are in their sleeping bags, leaving Wendy to take the other side of the bed.

"Their loss," she snickers. "At least we won't have back problems tomorrow."

"No kidding," I laugh. "Goodnight."

"See you in the morning."

I turn out the lights and lay down, snuggling into the heavy blankets. When I close my eyes, all I see is darkness. At first, this is unnerving to me. When nothing jumps out at me, though, I let my mind fall into slumber.

Chapter 4

I find myself outside Heather's house, for some odd reason unknown to myself. I'm still in my pajamas, so the wind is cutting right through them. All the lights are out in the neighborhood, casting an evil shade upon the world. I shiver, wrapping my arms around me for warmth. I turn and head back to the front door. It's locked. When I knock upon the wood, I can't hear a sound. Yet another clue I should be fearing for my life. Instead of fear, however, I feel a large amount of anger. I'm never happy when my sleep is messed with.

With a quiet grumble, I walk over to a hollow rock. This is where Heather told me her spare key is. When I reach for it, a swarm of large tarantulas crawl from beneath it. I jerk my hand away from the hissing spiders, narrowly missing the one that jumped for me. With them on the spare key, there's no chance I'll be getting back in.

Admitting defeat, as far as though spiders are concerned, I back away. Instead of sleeping inside, I'll be staying in my car tonight. With a huff, I walk over to it. My feet are freezing upon the chilled concrete. I look up and freeze entirely. Laying upon the roof of my small Volkswagen… is a massive tarantula.

"*Hell* no," I mutter, backing away.

Little spiders are one thing. One the size of my car? I can't deal with that. It moves it's head to face me, the moonlight shimmering off it's many crimson eyes. One large hairy leg slides along the side of the car, tapping the driveway beneath, and I stop backing away. Long, thick, fangs click together. A bead of some fluid, whether saliva or venom I can't say, drips onto the light gray concrete. Although I want nothing more than to run, I know there won't be any escape. To my surprise, however, when my movement stops… so does the spider's.

"Okay… You stay there… and I'll just… run this way," I state, bolting down the street.

I look back a few times, screaming when the spider barrels after me. I can hear its feet clicking against the street, a quiet echo of death. My heart is hammering in my chest, the cold air painful on my lungs. A corner comes up, which I take without thinking. The concrete is a bit slick underfoot, so I slide as I take the turn. I pray I don't lose my footing. One hand touches the cold ground, keeping me upright through the turn.

When I attempt to take another, the gigantic spider leaps. I back pedal just in time to miss it. It watches as I take off once more, going in the opposite direction. The street sign comes up, alerting me to position. I'm only a block or two from the abandon store. As it looks now, that's my only other option for safety. So sad it's come down to this. Cursing under my breath, I race for that broken building.

A stream of white jets past me, slamming on the dirt to spread. I know it's webbing. Just a last minute attempt to catch its prey. I dive for the doorway, somersaulting through just as a web is spit. It clings to the doorway, blocking my only way out.

Triumphant, I turn to face the store. Like the other night, it seems new and welcoming. Customers are walking through the aisles, chatting with each other and the staff. I carefully walk in, eyes searching for the shadowy woman of before. Surprisingly, I can't even locate the gunshot victim.

"*Hello*," an elderly woman greets. "*Are you new here? I come in every day and I've never seen you before.*"

"I'm just… passing through."

"I hope you'll stay. You seem like a very nice girl."

She walks past me, humming to herself as she peruses the knick-knacks. I don't now her, nor have I seen anything about an elderly lady dying here. Perhaps she's a figment of this place… a memory. Or maybe the spirits like to shop as well, who knows? I sigh and head over to the right. The cash registers are there, cashiers behind them in the throws of a busy day.

Someone pushes past me, racing to put away clothing. They're of average height for a male and lanky. It seems like he's in his own world, focusing only only this single task. A couple customers quickly move for him. When the pile of clothes in his arms is put away, he heads back to the rack he started on.

I open my mouth to talk to him, yet his figure wavers. A reflection disturbed by a stone. When he's solid again, I try once more to speak. This time, he flickers between this lively form… and one of a corpse. His head lies upon his shoulder, barely connected to his neck. It's only a moment that I'm allowed to see it, but the sight will never leave me.

"This place is crazy," I mutter.

The floor warps around me, twisting and melting. It reminds me of an abstract painting. My stomach churns at the sight, nausea overwhelming me. I stagger to the side, leaning heavily on a clothing rack. The smooth metal rusts beneath my arm, creaking with the threat of breaking. Darkness trails from all over, gathering in the aisle before me. It forms the shadowy woman, a nasty grin on her face… the only feature I can see, aside from the glowing red eyes.

"*Welcome back,*" she says. "*You didn't finish your orientation last visit, so you'll have to finish it now. Hold still, it won't hurt for long.*"

She lifts her arm, gripping the blade from before. It's still stained with my blood. When she brings it down, I manage to leap away. My body hits the floor, turning to face her again. She's leaning over to strike my chest, so I kick upward into her stomach. At first, I don't expect to make contact. When I hear her gasp in pain, however, I kick again. She's thrown back into the rack. The rusted pole gives way. In a fit of anger, she stands and throws the knife. The blade cuts a shallow line across my cheek. Pain blossoms there, the warmth of blood trickling down to my chin.

I sit up quickly, nearly hitting Wendy with my flailing arm. Thankfully, she doesn't wake. The sting of cold metal has my cheek throbbing. I touch the cut, drawing my hand away… bloody. Any normal person would tremble and fear, but this only angers me more. With a huff, I slide out of bed and make my way around Melissa. No one stirs, leaving me to make an escape to the bathroom.

The house is so quiet and still. Each creak of time and clank of pipes has me nervous. I want to turn on the lights, yet I also don't want to see what might be waiting for that. In the bathroom, I close the door and look in the mirror. Blood has washed my cheek in red, dripping down onto my tank top as well. This will be a little harder to explain. With a resigned sigh, I grab a washcloth to dab it clean.

Heather is at the door when I open it. Her brow wrinkles in worry, eyes large at the sight of an injury.

Long slender fingers reach over, running along the length of the cut.

"Good lord, Catori," she whispers. "What happened?"

"I had a nightmare," I sigh, giving her a weak smile. "It would seem that damn store finds me even there."

"This is getting too dangerous," Heather bristles. "You need to leave it alone."

"No, it's a challenge now," I point out. "I'll win this game."

"This isn't a game, Catori, it's your life."

"I can't explain it, Heather. It's just... I feel as though I *need* to be there. Like... this is my purpose in life right now. I'll be careful, I swear it. But... I *need* to do this."

"... Don't do anything stupid, okay?" she comments, tone soft and quiet. "Nothing is worth losing your own life."

"Saving hundreds is... but I won't go that far. Whatever... demon... is there... I'll beat it. It's had its victims, but it's never met me. That bitch is toast."

Heather shakes her head, a minute smile on her lips. She pulls me into a hug, squeezing tightly before letting me go. That's all that's needed, I know she'll go as far as I will. Together, we walk back into the bedroom. As much as I want to go back to sleep, I know it won't come. The giant spider killed any wish of dreams.

Chapter 5

The slumber party wasn't a complete success, but at least I managed a little fun. The girls were worried about the random injury, yet I brushed it off rather well. Not many people can manage tripping in a kitchen while getting a late night snack, only to cut their cheek with a butter knife. Oh yeah, I'm just that good. They didn't even bat an eye at the explanation.

Now I sit in history class, doodling in the margins of my notebook. Still more ghost stories today, yet I can't focus on them. If I keep having nightmares like the last, I really might end up dead. However, I don't know how to keep them from torturing me. I wonder if it'll stop should I go back to the store. Either way, I need to return. I can't help those people without going back. There's just too much to learn.

"Catori, pay attention," Heather hisses. "You know he'll call on you if he thinks you're spacing."

"Sorry."

I force my attention back on the lesson. It seems to draw on forever, leaving me anxious in my seat. When the lunch bell rings, I bolt from the room to find my locker. It takes a moment, but I notice Heather on my heels. My speed falls just a bit, enough to let her catch up. Side by side, we put our books away.

In the cafeteria, the two of us grab a tray to fill. At our usual table, we take a seat and pick up our hamburgers. There's so much emotion in Heather's eyes, yet I know what's bothering her. Unfortunately, I won't back down and she knows that. With a soft sigh, she sets her food down and regards me.

"What have you learned so far?" she questions.

"Not much," I frown. "I learned some of the deaths, but that's about it."

"What about your nightmares?"

"I keep seeing some weird shadow woman," I divulge. "She tried to kill me twice, called it an 'adjustment'. I guess it was supposed to be like a uniform or something."

"Uniform?"

"I guess. That's what she said the first time I visited that place in my dreams."

Heather is quiet for a long while, and then hums to herself. I play with the green beans on my tray. Not sure why I got them… I don't even like green beans. Just when I think she's not about to say anything more, her lips part and she sighs.

"Do you really think she killed all those people?" she wonders. "Like… all her workers?"

"I have no doubt in my mind," I answer. "If it wasn't her, it was definitely something that possessed her."

That has her quiet, eyes distant with thought. She'll likely try again to dissuade me, yet it won't be successful. When I have my mind on something, I don't stop until it happens. It's a trait that's been passed through my family for centuries. I attempt to turn the chatter toward another topic. Heather takes the bait, if only to offer a sense of normalcy.

After school, I drop Heather off at home. She only lives down the street, so it's not out of the way. Like any good friend, she offered me to stay with her. I'm positive it's because she wants to monitor my sleep, but I have other plans tonight. If going to that damn place will keep me from nightmares, then that's what I'm going to do. I think she knows this, as she sends me that sisterly expression… the one that says 'I know what you're up to, but I'll pretend otherwise and bust you later'. I drive off when she gets inside.

At home, I send a passing greeting to my parents. They work so much, it's rare I see them. Normally, we would sit down and talk. Today, however, I want to do my homework and go. No luck, though, as mother dearest follows me to the stairs.

"Catori, I wanted to speak with you," she states. "It'll only take a moment."

"… Am I grounded?" I wonders warily.

"No."

"… Am I being suspended?"

"Why on earth would you be suspended?" she glares, tone carrying a warning to it.

"I didn't do anything," I immediately defend. "But how am I supposed to know someone isn't framing me?"

"… I really shouldn't have raised you on that damn crime channel," she murmurs. "Sit down."

With a huff, I walk into the living room and sit on the couch. She paces a few moments, only making me more anxious. My dad is in his armchair, pretending to browse the paper. He doesn't read the paper, I told him to stop buying it. His expression gives away nothing. I curse his poker face! Finally, mom stops and faces me.

"Honey, I heard you were interested in that abandoned building in town," she says. "The librarian told me you were doing a paper on it."

"Yeah," I nod. "I went to research it."

"… I know you too well, Catori. Don't go to that building. It's condemned for a reason."

"Because it's haunted," I smirk. "Didn't you hear that part, too? The old lady from the library cursed it."

"That's ridiculous. There's no such thing as ghosts," she points out. "And what the hell happened to your face? Not to mention the bloody shirt I found in your laundry. Are you doing drugs?"

"How does 'bloody shirt' and 'drugs' go together?"

"I don't know if you've killed someone or not!"

"*Now* who watches too much crime channel?" I snicker. "I'm not doing drugs, okay? I'm not doing anything illegal, just investigating. You know I want to be a private eye some day. Since I have to start somewhere, I figured an abandoned building, with a hundred mysterious deaths and no living suspects, would be a safe place to start."

"She's got a point, honey," dad smiles. "Much better than the drug filled streets, with gang members and guns."

"You're not helping."

"Sure I am, I'm helping Catori."

She rolls her eyes, throwing her hands up dramatically. It's no secret she likes those shows, nor is it that our family has a history. Our bloodline has bred a lot of investigators through the years. They're all on my dad's side. He's supportive of my decision, however mom doesn't like the idea. Dad is a retired cop, but was forced to do so. His health wasn't the best and he couldn't stand a desk job. He wants me to follow in his footsteps. Me being an only child and all.

"I wish you would find something else to be interested in," she whines. "Can't you be a fashion designer? Or a farmer? Even a model would be better than an investigator!"

"Sorry, mom. I didn't choose the path, it chose me," I smile. "I'll keep you posted on my progress, okay?"

"… Fine," she mutters. "Go do your homework."

I happily get up and race to my room. It's been a few months since my decision, but I think she's finally coming around. It won't be much longer and I'll have her asking for my services. Her cell phone and keys won't appear out of nowhere, after all.

When I get to my room, I shut the door and dump my bag out on the floor. I rummage through to get my notebook, flipping through the pages to find my work. I've already finished most of it. Having two study halls is a blessing. I sit at my desk, setting up my little workspace, and dive in.

Around six, I'm called down for dinner. Dad is already getting his coat on, looking for his keys so he can go. He hates the night-shift, but it pays very well. After his few years as a police officer, he got a security detail at a factory. It keeps him away at night. Both he and mom have two jobs to work. Not really for the money, but because inactivity drives them mad. I'm much the same, but school keeps me pretty busy.

I kiss him goodbye, grabbing my spaghetti off the counter. Mom has already left. She's a nurse and has a few patients she takes care of overnight. I don't mind being alone, especially when Heather is right down the street. She never seems to go anywhere, just as much a homebody as I am.

The second I'm finished eating, I clean my dishes and go upstairs. My bag is already empty, so I use that to my advantage. I pick up a flashlight and fill my bag with essentials… like a first aid kit, extra bandages, and a couple batons. I'm not much of a fighter, but dad insisted I go through training… just in case I'm a cop at heart. I took to the batons. He also put me through karate classes, so I'm deadly with a couple sticks.

Chapter 6

It's colder out tonight, so I dress for the weather. My heavy jacket and hood won't get in my way should I have to run. I pull up in front of the store, parking between faded yellow lines. The streetlights are out here, so the area is very dark. I carefully make my way up to the burnt out building.

A wrapper skitters along the ground in front of me, propelled by an eerie wind. The closer I get to the store, the heavier my feeling of anxiety is. One of the doors, already half off the hinges, creaks and falls inward. The glass shatters with a crystalline ring. I make sure to step through it with care.

Unlike my dreams, the store never changes. It's forever dead and decayed. There's no ghost by the register, not this time. I take that as a good sign and move forward. The intercom screeches like nails on a chalkboard, warming up for the swarm of voices that comes next.

"*Welcome home, Catori*," the mass comments. "*We've missed you so. We're so glad you've returned. Unfortunately, you're not in uniform. Don't worry, though, you'll receive it soon. For now, you'll be confined to the front of the store. At the time you feel you'd like to join us, you'll be allowed upstairs.*"

"Fat chance that's gonna happen," I mutter.

"Should you need anything at all, please address our friendly staff members. They'll be all too eager to help you."

Another screech, and then the intercom falls silent. The overhead lights flicker on, a couple sparking at the sudden use. No doubt the wires have been chewed through long ago. I'm glad they've been turned on, but I'll still keep my flashlight close.

Down the main aisle, I notice a slight glow. Uncertain how to approach it, I step closer slowly. My foot lands on a girl's tee shirt. With a slight frown, I turn my attention to the section. Kids clothes are everywhere, the racks nearly empty. Those that are still standing anyway. Closer to the glow, I notice a few onesies and tiny infant clothes.

Around the middle of a rather tall rack is that strange glow. A white chalk mark starts to travel, just as it had before, but this time it doesn't look like a body. I'm wary as I walk closer. A body comes into view. She's tall and built slender, her hair in tights braids along her scalp. A few onesies are tied together, laying about her neck as a noose. It would seem she just… sat down and waited for her end. I scoot closer, gasping when her eyes move in my direction.

"*You need to leave this place,*" she whispers, a rasp of death in her voice.

"I'm not leaving until I free you all."

"We'll never be free. This place… it's our grave. It's too late for us all, but not you. This place can't get you yet, you haven't

received your uniform. Run! Run while you still can!"

"It doesn't matter where I go," I point out. "It seems the only place I can get my uniform is in my dreams, so I have to come here. If I don't, I dream about this place. So, please, tell me what's going on."

"... This place is cursed. Within the walls are the souls of the dead. All those that were sacrificed are trapped within this building. With each passing, it grew stronger. By the time the witch knew what was really going on, it was too late. She tried to kill it with her, but didn't succeed. It just came back here and started killing more."

"What did? Some kind of demon?" I question.

"I guess you could call it that," she sighs. "It draws power from the dead... and it's gathered a *lot* of dead. It's never enough, though... never... it always wants more. You're next, you know. It wants your soul. You're stronger than the others... special... It'll draw more power from you. You need to run from here. It's reach ends outside this town, you can still get away."

"I'm not running from some unknown, power hungry jackass," I frown. "I'm going to free all of you..."

"If you free us... you free the demon," she states.

"Wait… what? What do you mean by that?"

"It draws it's power from us, but at a price. As it traps us here... we trap it. If you free us, it'll be powerless... but it'll have a whole town of vessels to choose from. We're happy to stay here and protect those outside. It's a burden, but it's all we have left to cling to. Please... let us protect you."

"… I'll keep your warning in mind," I offer. "But I'll still fight to free you. Knowing you and the others keep it here helps. I'll see if I can't find a way to destroy it for good."

She nods, eyes sad with understanding. I won't run, she knows that. Without another word, she disappears. I stay for a moment and stare upon the spot she died. What could've been so horrible that she would kill herself here? And in such an odd way. The noose of baby clothes remains on the bar, swaying ever so slightly with her disappearance. The intercom screeches to life, startling me from my thoughts. As irritated as the voice sounds, it tries hard to cloak it in a sickeningly sweet coating.

"I'm sure it hasn't escaped your notice that some of my children are rather rebellious. Please don't let them sway you,

they're just looking for attention. I'll be sure to keep them from bothering you again. Please, enjoy the remainder of your time here."

I frown and look away, hoping to see another 'rebellious child'. It doesn't escape my notice that I'm further in than before. The back of the store is just as disheveled, however it holds a more peaceful air. I wonder if the others here hold the same view as the last. If they've convinced themselves that their sacrifice wasn't in vain, then maybe they've come to terms with their ends. It just doesn't satisfy my own conscience. Perhaps it doesn't have to. The empty feeling resting in my chest, however, demands justice.

I trail over to some racks with moldy jackets. The sizes would fit smaller men. A heap of clothes lays on the floor with broken hangers, a discarded pair of shoes hidden in the midst of them. There's so much here that could've been salvaged. It suggests this place was too feared to chance theft. Once more, the thought gives me pause. I just keep coming across more clues, more reasons to leave this place be. It begs the question, why do I continue to return? I suppose it's just a driving force within me… the need to know. Curiosity can be a very deadly thing, after all.

And as any curious cat would do, I start wandering. Always on guard, waiting for the next scare, I walk over to a large area in the back. Furniture is set up nicely. Cloth is torn, chair legs gnawed through, and something moves inside a couch. I've no doubt it's a mouse, or even something bigger. That cushion, stuffed with foam, would be a wonderful place for a nest. With a disgusted shiver, I give it a wide berth.

One of the chairs managed to keep all four legs, though there's a hole in the seat. I keep it in mind should I need to get off the floor quickly. To get here, I had to pass shelves of toys. Rusted metal cars and broken plastic trucks are scattered everywhere. I can see a few more near the couch. A plastic bag, trapped beneath a fallen tile from the ceiling, flutters on an invisible wind. Near it are a few action figures.

Past the furniture section, I can see a wall of electronics. Some are hanging hap-hazardously from their bags, others have been left on the floor to decay. I kick one aside, stopping at the sound of scratching. My eyes trail to the suitcases. As I step closer, though I don't know what possesses me, my heart starts to hammer. A flap is knocked open, a black cat darting from the fabric. As glad as I am it isn't a rat, I can't help calling out in surprise.

The next surprise is my cell phone. It has me backing up into the couch, stirring the nest of mice inside it. As they pour from the fabric like water from a faucet, my hand makes a frantic search of my pockets. I reach the chair, stepping atop it as I answer my phone.

"Hello?" I question.

"Catori?" Heather inquires.

"The one and only," I smirk.

"Where are you?"

"I'm at the store."

"... The haunted one?"

"Yep."

"Can you come over?"

Her voice seems worried, though I can't tell from what. I know she's being hassled by a few guys at school, and one of them has a really nasty girlfriend. Her temper is a piece of work. She's not afraid to get her hands dirty either, so it's entirely plausible she's messing with my best friend. I glance down to see the last of the mice struggle from the couch. It's much smaller than the others, so I get down and scoop it up in my hand.

"Yeah, I'm on my way," I offer, setting the mouse on the floor. "It shouldn't take too long for me to reach you."

"Thank you so much," she says, breathing a sigh of relief. "I really appreciate it."

"Don't mention it," I smile. "You're my girl, you know that. I'd kick ass for you."

Heather laughs on the other end of the line, saying a fond 'later' before hanging up. I tuck my phone back in my pocket, watching the little mouse scamper off. Calling it a night, I head for the front door. The lights overhead flicker, sparks of electricity popping from the ends of the lights. As I leave, the lights behind me turn off one at a time.

I step outside and start walking. A loud clanking from the alley stops me. Alongside the building is a drive up area for trucks and customers, but I didn't think it very important. Now, I can't help wandering over that way. It won't take long to check it out, just a couple minutes. Heather will be okay until then.

A tire is resting against the rusted fence. I can see a tattered hole in the side. There's a long rope-like thing across the way, which I assume triggers a bell. An old trailer sits abandoned. As I walk around it, I can see where someone tried to break into it. I guess they never got it fixed afterward… though that amount of damage can't be fixed. The clank sounds again, drawing my attention to a large sliding door. There's a large dent in it, about the height of a human. It has my blood running cold.

"Hello?" I call out.

"*They were here, but I stopped them*," a soft voice calls out. "*They were here... but I stopped them... Didn't I?*"

I walk over to the door, realizing the dent isn't all that's there. My fingers run along a trail of bullet holes. They riddle the door, some stained with blood, and give off the impression of a war gone wrong. The sound of tires squealing has my turning around, eyes wide. There's no car, just the sound. I find myself looking through a haze of light, the image of another spirit. Before I have a chance to really take it in, I hear voices and the clacking of pallets hitting each other.

"*Hey! You can't take those!*" the spirit shouts. "*I'm calling the cops! You can't just come in here and steal...*"

Her words are cut off when the shooting starts. She's thrown back into the door… and through me. A wash of ice overtakes me, leaving me in shivers as I turn. She's small, but muscular. Years of sports, no doubt. Her hair is in braids tight to her head. Eyes wide in horror and shock, she's left to fall to the ground. Instead of the sound of more pallets, I can hear rushed voices eager to leave.

"*They were... here... but... I stopped them*," she whispers out again, eyes searching my own. "*Didn't I?*"

"Yes, you did," I offer her. "They ran and didn't get anything."

"You should run, too. Or this place will get you... just like it got us," she murmurs out. *"You should run... you should... run... Run!"*

As she fades away, I back up. I read about this death in the papers I studied. Some people were stealing pallets to resell, robbing this place blind at night. She was working late, walked out to see them moving pallets onto their truck. She fought bravely, injuring a couple of the men… but this was the end result. She was gunned down protecting her workplace… Loyal to the end.

I feel for her, but I can't help her right now. Soon, though. Soon I'll help them all. With the two women on my mind, I head to Heather's. At least I'll be able to help *her* tonight.

Chapter 7

Heather is waiting for me when I arrive. I managed to see a car parked outside, the blonde ringlets of the woman in the passenger side giving her away. Bridget is just bad news all together. At the sight of me, however, she and her friend drive off. She doesn't like fair fights. Heather thanks me again at the door, allowing me entrance. Her parents aren't home, but then… they rarely are. One of the reasons she and I are so close, is because of the similarities our families have.

"I can't believe she stayed out there that long," I comment. "Let me text my mom so she knows I'm staying here tonight."

"Okay."

I send the message as I take off my coat. She's in the kitchen, rummaging for pots and pans from the sound of it. When I walk in, after hanging my coat, she's pulling a pizza out of the oven. It smells delicious, already provoking saliva. I didn't realize how hungry I was. We sit at the small dining room table to eat.

"So? What happened tonight?" she wonders.

"You should've been there with me!" I grin. "There was a woman that hung herself in the kid's department, a nest of mice that filled a whole couch, and a woman that was gunned down outside!"

"… I'll take your word for it," she remarks. "I'm happy enough to extend support from right here."

"They kept telling me to run away," I sigh, pizza halfway to my mouth. "I don't understand it. Shouldn't they want help? Shouldn't they want to rest in peace?"

"Maybe they think there's a purpose for them there."

"Well… Baby did say they were keeping the demon trapped in the building. I guess they're a source of power for it, it feeds off them."

"That's likely why they don't mind lingering. Who's Baby?"

"The woman in the kid's section. I don't why, but I have a strange feeling she'll be a reoccurring visitor. Her name was lost to time, so… I'll name her Baby."

"Gotcha," she smirks. "So, regale me with your investigation thus far."

I explain to her everything I've learned, glad she's paying attention and not feigning it. Heather is a thinker more than a doer, which makes us a great duo. I jump before thinking. We balance each other out well. Right now, her mind is preoccupied with Bridget. I don't blame her. From what I've heard, the last girl she went after transferred.

"She won't bother you," I offer. "She's just trying to act big for her stupid boyfriend. How did you get on his bad side anyway?"

"He was picking on a little freshman, so I yelled at him. I told him that freshman will graduate before him, because he's as dim as a broken bulb. He tried to hit me… and I kicked his ass in front of his team."

"Heather!" I gasp. "How *dare* you beat someone up without me!"

"I couldn't help it! You weren't with me at the time," she says. "I'm sorry."

We laugh together, enjoying our time. Heather is a small girl, which makes it very difficult to catch her. She's more of a mouse, but has a strange Dr. Jekyll/Mr. Hyde thing going on. The second she's attacked or pushed into a corner, she goes from mouse to wildcat. I like it… everyone that presses her doesn't.

"So now his stupid girlfriend is bugging me!" Heather huffs. "Can't even fight his battles himself, the coward."

"I'll threaten him tomorrow," I wave off. "Now… which movie will we be eating popcorn to?"

She brightens immediately, a grin breaking out on her face. If anything can get her happy, it's a good movie night. We're barely done with dinner, but she's on her feet and running for her collection. Shaking my head, I go back to my pizza.

After we eat, I pop the popcorn and Heather grabs the movies she picked out. Because every good movie night has more than one pic. Gathering up fuzzy blankets and pillows, we settle down in front of her television.

"Okay, prepare to be horrified!" she announces.

"Have you forgotten where I was before coming here?" I laugh.

"Oh right… nest of mice… Prepare to be semi-horrified!"

She hits the play button and the movie comes to life. It opens up on a forest trail, a man with a bloody knife, and a woman's corpse. Heather likes a good scare, so most of her collection is horror movies. I can never understand why, but I don't mind them. Sometimes a good scare is all you need to jump start your day.

As another woman wanders the forest, searching for her friend, the lights flicker. I look to her, however she's just as surprised as I am. This time, it's not her doing. One of the bulbs gives a loud pop and Heather screams. We're in each others arms, hearts hammering against ribcages. The broken glass showers down onto the floor, leaving us in the dark. The only source of light is the television.

On the screen, the woman starts to scream. The pitch grows higher, a shrill whistle. To protect our hearing, we cover each others ears. The character on screen flickers, changing between forms, and then it goes out. Before we can relax, the television turns back on… but it's not our movie. Glowing red eyes stare back at us. They disappear, giving way to a long chain of tormented souls. The run down the screen like the credits, faces twisted in agony as they scream. They cry for help, beg to be set free.

Heather is gritting her teeth, huddled against me as she watches. I don't blame her, it's impossible to look away. It doesn't last long, but long enough to seem as eternity. When it all stops, we're left in the dark with only each other. Heather takes a deep, soothing breath.

"Now I understand why you want to help them," she whispers.

"I'll set them free," I state, confident.

"… If you can't… no one can," she murmurs quietly. "I think I've had enough scare for one night, how about we skip the movies?"

"How about we watch an animated? I am *not* letting this popcorn go to waste."

She laughs and nods her agreement, the recent spook nearly gone. We put in the far less graphic and bloody cartoon, relaxing to the antics of a talking dog and his gang. That's how we fall asleep, wrapped up in blankets and curled around one another.

Chapter 8

The next morning, I wake to Heather drooling on my pillow. Shaking my head, I sit up and stretch. It's still early, but I decide to get ready anyway. When I wake, it's very hard for me to get back to sleep.

I decide to take a shower, eager to relax beneath hot spray. I keep clothes at Heather's, as we spend more time together than apart. She also has some at my house. I honestly wouldn't be surprised if those at school think we're an item. I've thought about it before, I won't lie. I swing both ways, but I've had trouble fingering Heather's tastes. I think it's that Dr. Jekyll/Mr. Hyde thing.

Before I head to the bathroom, I tuck her in and gather some clothes. After shutting the door, I search the room in case a spook has lingered. Thankfully, there doesn't seem to be any issues. The hot water flows from the shower head, pounding down on the tub's floor. I get undressed and hop in. It feels wonderful. As I sigh in content, I realize the water isn't going down the drain. I pull at the sliding glass door, however it doesn't budge.

"Great," I mutter.

I put a little more force behind it, yet I almost slip on the gathering water. When the faucet is turned off, the water keeps flowing. A little more worried, I try calling for Heather. She's a deep sleeper, so I don't expect an answer. It's more to soothe my frustration before I shatter the door. By now, liquid is nearly to my knee. Nothing leaks through the edges of the shower door, giving it more climb.

A sinister laugh sounds in the room, echoing off the walls. It doesn't scare me, it pisses me off. I bang my fists onto the glass, an act of rage more than escape. The water has reached mid-thigh, crawling faster than I had anticipated. It occurs to me that others have died this way… those that visited but came back out. The deaths were ruled suicide, but I'm beginning to question the judgment.

"Catori?" Heather calls. "Are you okay?"

"I'm drowning!" I answer.

"You're what?" she exclaims. "I'm coming in."

"Please do. I think I might need some help."

"I'm not helping you drown yourself," she states, opening the door. "I'll do just about anything for you, but I will not be an accessory to murder… unless we're killing someone else together."

"Open the door for me."

"… Why can't you?"

I growl and start yanking at the glass door. Heather gasps and her hands grab the other side, throwing all her weight on the handle. It's just not enough to force it. I hear her leaving, her footsteps beating against the floor as she runs. When she comes back, she gives a hefty grunt and slams a crowbar into the door. The glass shatters, neck high water washing me out of the tub. We're both on the floor, panting in exhaustion and fear. I wrap a towel around me and Heather pulls me into a hug.

"Are you okay?" she cries. "Did you get hurt? I'll kill that fucking demon! How dare she hurt you!"

"Calm down, Heather, I'm fine," I say, giving her a weak smile. "We had it perfectly under control."

"She's dead!"

Her eyes seem to turn red in her rage, catching me off guard. It's happened before, but it's so rare I haven't gotten used to it. Once I've calmed her down, we finish getting ready for school. It's tense all the way there, but mostly because of the scare. I can only think of those that have already died from that, how terrified they must've been. Heather… can only think about the near loss.

"This is getting out of hand," she remarks in the silence.

"Even if I stopped looking into it, it would still try to kill me," I reason. "The only chance I have, is to get to the bottom of store 1084. If I can free the other spirits, that demon has no power to kill me."

"Then we better find it soon."

"We?" I question. "Uh… no. *You're* not going anywhere near that place! I appreciate the help from *outside*, but you're not setting foot *inside*! I don't need to worry about them killing you, too."

"I'll be fine," she assures.

"I know you will, because you're not going into that store. End of story. If I find out you did, I'll never speak to you again!"

"You will too," she scoffs, skeptical. "But if it means that much to you… I'll stay out of the store, okay? But you better keep me informed!"

"You know I will."

We fall into silence once more, pulling into the school's parking lot. My parking spot is still open, so I pull in and turn off the car. We get out and head to the front doors. Bridget is there with her boyfriend, sending a mean smirk at Heather. She walks to meet us, Heather just behind me. When she tries to push past me, I lift my fist and plant it right in her face. There's a crunch of cartilage when her nose breaks, blood gushing from it, and she falls to the ground sobbing.

"Don't touch my friend again," I remark. "And *you*! You cowardly little speck of shit! If you don't leave Heather alone, I'll kick your ass *myself*! But it won't be in front of your friends. I'll record it and share it on every social media site I know of!"

"I'll have you expelled for this, you bitch!" he shouts, crouching down with his girlfriend.

"Go ahead, that doesn't mean I won't find you," I spit back. "If anything happens to Heather, I'll blame you *instantly*! You better pray she doesn't get so much as a *paper-cut* for the remainder of the year!"

I grab Heather's hand and pull her through the front doors, not even glancing back at the two. Her echoed sobs don't phase me. Everyone is staring at us in the hallway, the clank of lockers silenced in our wake. They can hear her crying, too. The whispers are a river that proceeds us, forewarning others before we reach them. One of the teachers hears them, stopping us in the hall and leading us to the office.

The principal never bothers me, he's pretty easy-going. I've been called to his office more than once. Fighting isn't new to me, I have quite the temper, but Heather is rarely caught. She's too meek, no one is willing to admit they lost to her. She seems defeated beside me, so I reach over to hold her hand. That's when the door opens and Mr. Kaiser peeks out.

"Catori?" he sighs in exasperation. "Okay, come on in."

I get up, sending Heather an assuring smile, and head over. He's at his desk by the time I step in. The door closes behind me, and I make myself comfortable in the chair across from him. For a long moment, all he can do is watch me in disappointment. I've become immune to that look. Finally, he sighs.

"What did you do this time?" he asks.

"I punched Bridget in the face," I offer with a shrug.

"… Fighting… why am I not surprised," he comments. "I hope you have a very good reason."

"Stalking is a crime, Mr. Kaiser," I frown, tone harsh and serious. "And although bullying isn't, it's certainly not acceptable."

"And someone was stalking you?"

"No, sir. Bridget was stalking Heather," I explain. "Just because she embarrassed her boyfriend in front of his teammates. She was waiting outside her house just last night. I can tell you right now, it wasn't because she wanted a slice of pizza."

"Be that as it may, there's no reason to assault her at school."

"Yeah? Were you going to stop her?" I wonder. "What if I hadn't showed up last night? She could've hurt Heather badly! Or worse! I'm not standing for it, so I nipped it in the bud. If you want to expel me for that, go right ahead. I know I was in the right. I'll see you next year."

"I'm not going to expel you," he sighs out. "But you're definitely getting detention! And I'm going to look into this complaint of stalking. If I find you're not making it up, I'll adjust your punishment to something more lenient."

"And I thank you for that," I remark. "I am in the middle of an investigation, detention would make it difficult to continue."

"… I'm not even going to ask. Go to class, please. Send Heather in, I want her account of things."

I walk out and send Heather a satisfied smirk. As she stands on shaky legs, I give her an account of the discussion. She's much calmer by the time she walks in. With a little bounce in my step, I head toward an all too familiar room.

Detention is no longer served after hours, but during. A cold, empty room with the bare necessities is where it's held. The dry erase board is empty, papers stacked in neat piles on the desk, and four people are sharing the room with me. Mrs. Caldwell clears her throat, waving a hand for me to sit. I go to my usual desk, in the back and away from the others.

She walks up and sets some books and papers in front of me. I waste no time getting started. Classes aren't particularly hard, so the homework should be easy.

I pick up my pencil and start on class one. This is actually a great opportunity for me. If I finish all my class work, which I likely will, I'll have more time to investigate the store.

Around lunch, the third one, we're let go. Although we'll have to go back, everyone needs to eat. It's my usual lunch, so I'm not worried about missing Heather. She waves me down as I step away from the line with my tray. I sit down across from her.

"He told me you were in detention," she frowns. "I'm sorry I got you in trouble."

"You didn't get me in trouble," I wave off. "My fist did, when it connected with Bridget's face."

"She's so pissed at you," Heather whispers, almost giddy. "I heard her talking about jumping you after school."

"Perfect," I grin meanly. "I can't wait to break something else. Is she leaving you alone?"

"Her and Travis won't even look at me, you scared the shit out of them. They won't admit it, but it's easy to see when someone says your name."

I laugh, picking up a french fry. Bridget is near the top of my 'never like' list, so her discomfort amuses me. I'm glad I still get to have lunch with Heather, she's a ray of sunshine. Before we can get into our food, I can't help asking about her own visit to the principal.

"I told him exactly what was going on," she answers. "He's not happy with her. I don't think you'll be going to detention again tomorrow. He said something about calling their parents, maybe the police… If it gets bad enough. He's not taking this lightly at all."

"And he shouldn't," I frown. "She's borderline stalker, Heather. That leads down a dangerous road. One that might have left you injured or dead."

"I could've taken her."

"Maybe her, but not her and three friends," I point out. "And we both know she would've had them lined up to kick your ass."

"… Yeah, you're probably right," she pouts. "So, any plans for tonight?"

"I think I'm gonna head to the library again. I want to learn more about the origins of that store. Maybe there's something deeper about it, something that manifested when it was first opened."

"Can I at least help you look into it there?"

"… I don't see how it can hurt. Just… stay out of the building."

She squeals happily, clapping her hands and kicking her feet. I can't help the small smile pulling at my lips. Although I still worry about the store targeting her, I also know that Heather won't just leave me go. It's better I can watch her… make sure she doesn't get in too deep.

Chapter 9

After school, Heather and I drive to my house. When I pull in, I can see my father's car already parked in the garage. Unfortunately, when I walk into the house… I know he's sleeping. Quietly, the two of us go upstairs. In truth, I had hoped to catch my father before he went to bed. Now I have to leave a note for my mother, who'll call me the second she gets home… no matter the timing.

"I'm gonna write a note for mom," I explain. "I'll just have to turn my ringer to vibrate. I don't want the store hearing it if she calls then."

"You're visiting the store, too?"

"I hadn't planned on it, but… I might have to. Every time I don't, I nearly die in my sleep. And now I'm getting attacked while I'm awake, too. If going slows the process, I'm more than willing to pay a visit."

"… Still..."

"I'll be fine, Heather. Come on, let's leave this note on the fridge. Right now, we just have to worry about reaching the library. A perfectly sane and safe plan of direction."

"… Okay."

I drop the note on the kitchen counter, picking up the keys I left by the door. After we're outside, I lock up the house and head to the car. My mom probably won't be back for a few hours, she normally works late, so we should still be at the library. We pull out and head back toward the eerie building.

In the daylight, it doesn't look as imposing. The stone lions still stare, following you with their gaze. The building itself looming. Other than that, it seems rather ordinary. Heather and I wander in. Sadie, the librarian I first met here, is still behind the desk. She flips through a cosmetic magazine, enjoying some free-time. At the sight of me, she grins and sets the magazine aside.

"Back again, I see," she smiles. "Come to meet the witch?"

"I wish," I scoff. "We are here to do a little more research, though. Last time I barely scratched the surface. There are so many deaths and disappearances, it's no wonder the place is called 'haunted'."

"Too true! Right this way, ladies."

Once more, I follow her to the forgotten archives. Heather is close to my side, giving off a rather anxious air. When we reach the old door, Sadie opens it. Again, she refuses to go in. I bid her a good night and step in, pulling my best friend with me.

The room still smells of old parchment and must. Dust is kicked up when we walk across the floor. Heather sneezes, trying to wave the dust from her face.

"Geez," she mutters. "Have they ever heard of maid service? This place needs a thorough cleaning."

"Yeah, the librarians don't like coming in here," I explain. "They said no one does, not since they found the body."

"… You're lucky I like you so much," she hisses. "I thought they found that body at the store!"

"No, it was here," I wave off. "Surrounded by occult symbols and hanging from the rafter."

"Catori!"

"Don't worry, nothing was left over. And no one reported seeing her here. It was just a superstition… I think. Come on, the computer had a lot of the information on it. Some didn't get there, though, so I'll search the files if you search the computer."

"… Okay."

We split up, Heather looking around for the dead witch. Shaking my head, I disappear into the stacks of shelves, searching for anything in the year of the store. Deeper in, a few moths fly about listlessly. There's a scratching, and then a mouse bolts from beneath a shelf.

The years are all etched in fancy writing, each box holding a good amount of history.

Nothing on the store is there. With a huff, I try the next row of boxes. That's when I notice a rather darkened area. The light above blinks in and out, drained of life and so close to its end. I walk over, hesitant at the deep darkness that lies ahead. With a glance behind me, a quick check that Heather is busy, I take the plunge. Just as I'm covered in the dark, the light blinks to life. A half decayed face is right in front of mine. One eye is falling out of the socket, the teeth on the opposite side shown through the ragged hole in her cheek. Scraggly gray hair hangs around pale skin. It takes all I have not to run. I go to step back, but a cold and bony hand grips my upper arm.

"*You walk a fine line*," the woman states. "*The witch walked that line as well. I'll tell you what I told her. The demon that walks this world is not Death, but a shadow of the cruelest dark. It creates death to feed off the innocent souls, no one is safe. Let it into your life and it will overtake it. You will not be you anymore, it will be you. It will destroy those you love, those you hate, and those you have never met. Walk away from that demon, leave this place. You will not win.*"

"Obviously, you've never met me," I bite out. "Let that demon come. Let it promise gold and jewels, power and eternity. I know what I want, I know how to get it, and I'll be damned if I accept help from that evil little troll! I can get it *myself*, on my *own* just like everything else I've fought for!"

"... *Perhaps your spirit is stronger than hers*," the old corpse murmurs. "*But mark my word, one misstep... and everything you love will be lost*."

"Let's hope it's not that stupid then, shall we?"

She releases me, leaving a bruise the shape of her fingers. The cold that surrounds her is stifling, chilling me to my bones. The light finally gives in to the inevitable, dying with a final flicker. Now that she's stepped back, I can see she's wearing a dark cloak. Although it's tattered and worn, I can still make out the bloodstains it holds. Bone is showing on her arms and legs, a hole torn into her throat. This isn't the witch of before, it feels like something... more important.

"Who are you?" I ask. "You weren't in the store, nor are you dressed like a recent death. I can only imagine you know all about what's going on."

"*I am a harbinger of Death*," she rasps out. "*I was sent by my master to warn you. Should you fail, it will not only be your life taken... but thousands. The residents of this town will be first. And then it will spread its influence*."

"... No pressure or anything," I mutter.

She vanishes, leaving me alone in the dust. I cough at the cloud, waving it away, and look to my left. A small metal label catches my eye. It says 'Store 1084'. The store was so dangerous and thick with history, it was given an entire section. I step back, lifting my cell phone for the flashlight. It shines on the many boxes. As I reach for one, something slithers beside my hand. I jerk it away, watching a snake fall apart on the air. It floats down to the floor, just another pile of dust.

Shaking my head, dispelling the image completely, I grab that box. It's heavy with paper, but I manage to set it on a nearby table. Upon opening it, I find a leather bound book. It's old, the leather red with gold trim, and it glows with an eerie light. Easily explained by the poor lighting. When my fingertips lay upon it, I can feel a slight heartbeat. If that's not enough to warn me away, it's warm to the touch. Disregarding any and all survival instincts, I lift the strange book from it's prison.

"What the hell is this?" I murmur.

"Find anything?"

I jump, nearly throwing the book at Heather. When I spin around to face her, eyes wide in shock, she sends me a sheepish look. Now standing beside me, she reaches for the weird book. Without thinking, I pull it away from her. If this thing is cursed, I'm not about to let her touch it.

"What's that?" she asks curiously.

"A book."

"Well, duh. I mean, what's it about? Where did you find it?"

"It was in this box, although… I don't know why," I frown. "I think this is the witch's box. Maybe this is the book she used to try and kill the demon."

Heather takes it from me, moving too fast for me to stop. In seconds, it's open on the table and we're perusing the pages. The ink is faded with age, written by hand with a quill. Symbols are strewn about, clicking something within my mind. They look familiar, though I can't remember ever seeing them.

"This is crazy!" Heather states. "These spells have been lost for ages! I wonder how she got them."

"Wait… you know what those are?"

"Of course I do, my mother was a Wiccan. She taught me some stuff. I don't use it, but at least I know it. You know… just in case."

"In case of what?" I exclaim.

"I don't know… something. In any case, this isn't the type of book you want for light reading. Or any kind of reading. It has a prison sigil on it. Something nasty was sealed in here long ago."

I know without a doubt it's the demon. It makes sense now. The witch must've come across the book, opened it with the desire to learn more spells, and released the demon that possessed her. It's the easiest course I can pull together. Heather hums to herself and puts the book back in the box. Before she's about to put it back, she stops and looks it over.

"We really need to put it somewhere no one will come across it," she says.

"Can't we use it to trap that demon again?" I wonder.

"I don't know enough to do that," she admits, brow wrinkled in worry. "Besides, with all those spirits… there's no way it'll be caught so easily. It's destruction or nothing, I'm afraid."

I frown, nodding in understanding. I don't have much knowledge of vanquishing demons, but I'm really good at avoiding death. I'm sure I'll be able to stay alive long enough to learn a new trade. We set the box back on the shelf, lifting a heavier one to set atop it. When that deed is done, a small box with a 'de-classified' stamp on it catches my eye.

Eager to search it, I walk over and pull it off the shelf. It's a bit heavier than I thought it would be. Before I can dump it all over the floor, Heather is on the other side to help hold the weight. With the small table nearby cleared, we deposit it there. The top is just as dusty as the last, if not more-so. We turn away as it's disturbed, floating into the stale air around us. I pull out a file, flipping through it curiously.

"Oh my god! Heather, these are autopsy reports!" I gasp.

"What? Seriously? What are they doing in the library?"

"I suppose they were marked declassified and transferred to archive. The library is a good place to put these things. No one ever comes here," I shrug. "We're probably the first people to see these since they were put down here!"

"Hey, I know that name!" she exclaims. "When I was searching the newspaper articles. He was one of the victims in the store!"

"It says he died of a drowning," I read. "They marked it 'undetermined' at first. Further investigation left them lost, so it was marked 'suicide'. There weren't any markings on him except… a bruise on his upper arm, shaped like a skeletal hand print."

"Uh… like that one?" Heather whispers, pointing to my arm.

"… I think we should look through these and find similarities."

We split the files in the box, relocating them to the table up front. There's more light there, making it easier to read. Silence reigns as we sit across from one another. The bruise on my arm is beginning to throb, though I think it's only because of the files. One after another, death after death, I read they held that same mark. Chills are running the length of my spine, leaving my blood cold. Heather looks up at me curiously.

"Do you know how you got it?" she asks.

"Yeah, an old woman's corpse," I answer. "She said she was a harbinger of Death, come to warn me about the demon that'll soon kill me."

"… You saw her?"

"And spoke to her," I nod. "Why?"

"Catori… only those with wiccan blood can see her," she explains quietly. "And not just any wiccan blood… they need to be a descendant of the first clans. My mother was one, which makes me one. But… where did you get that blood from?"

"Beats the hell out of me. Mom and Dad never said anything about being witches. Do you think they know?"

She shrugs her shoulders, going back to the papers in front of her. I can see the worry lines around her eyes, though. Something about this revelation has stirred her curiosity… has stirred mine. Hopefully, I'll live long enough to start that investigation as well.

Chapter 10

Night has come far too quickly. Though we haven't left the library, I can feel the store breathing down my neck. Heather and I managed to clear a good amount of the reports, finding some interesting clippings I hadn't gotten to. All in all, I call it a success. Now, however, it's time to take her home… and return to that forsaken place.

As I pull into her driveway, Heather gives me a pleading look. She knows exactly what I'm planning. I can't take her with me, I refuse to. The stubborn expression I give her is enough to convey that. With a weary sigh, she opens the door and gets out. I wait until she's inside to pull away.

I have a lot of time to think on my way to the store. So much has happened since my move here… since I first visited that place. Wicca bloodlines? Spell book prisons? I feel as though I've stepped into a hole I can't climb out of. A feeling of utter dread is starting to bubble up within me. Although I don't know where this journey will lead me, I can't help but think I know where it'll end.

The store stands just as stubbornly as it always has, waiting for my arrival. My engine turns off and I exit the car, just in time for the lights to turn on. I open the door, stepping through to the nightmare yet again. A cash register rings nearby, drawing my attention there. I can see a cart moving on its own, filled with bags and tattered clothing. It rolls over to the exit, one wheel creaking ever so slightly, and stops with a squeak. Curious, I wander over to take a look. One piece of cloth is pulled away and a baby doll stares back at me. It's eyes are so empty.

"Welcome home. Please stay with us," it chimes. "Welcome home. Please stay… stay with us… please… stay… stay."

I shiver and cover it back up, walking away from the cart. Another squeaky wheel draws my gaze. There are more carts roaming about the aisles. No one is pushing them, but they move never the less. As I walk toward the back, I'm forced to dodge them. They obviously haven't developed eyes along with their movement.

With a sigh, I dodge another. In hopes of seeing the woman in the baby section, I force my way up the aisle that leads there. When I finally get past the barrage of free-moving carts, I find I'm left disappointed. Hoping perhaps the spirit from outside is still there, I try to backtrack. That's when everything falls silent. It's not just quiet, the type that hovers when there's nothing to say… but absolute silence. I search for the carts, watching one roll by. It was squeaking not too long ago. Just a breath was all it took to snuff out the sound. The electricity sparks above, yet there's not the typical snap and pop accompanying it. All the noise was drowned out by absolute nothingness.

"*Isn't it beautiful*," a woman says behind me. "*The sound of a grave… so quiet. It's utter peace. Just ask any of those before you. They've never been happier.*"

"I'm sure you'll excuse my disbelief," I spit out, turning to see the demon shadow. "What do you want?"

"*I've come to offer you a deal, Catori. A six day trial period of sorts.*"

"Trial period?"

"*You'll be allowed access to the entire store, as any employee would. Should this store fail in turning you, I'll let you leave. No tricks. However, should you happen to have an accident... You'll belong to this family like all the rest.*"

The deal is shady, the person proposing it… even more-so. After everything I've learned, only an idiot wouldn't see through this last ditch effort. In this creature's opinion, I'm dead no matter what. However, this could give me more insight to this place. Clues on how to kill this plague of evil. That's how I know it's too good to be true. There's no way in hell it would allow me to get near a clue like that. I set my gaze in a determined expression, sizing up the shadowy entity.

"… So… either I drag my feet and you kill me, or… I get full access and you kill me," I wonder out loud. "That sounds extremely shady, especially coming from a demon. How do I know you'll hold to this agreement?"

"*This isn't the first time I've made it, you know. Unfortunately for the others, this place can be extremely hazardous. You're no different from them. Once you get rattled enough, when you learn there's no escape, you'll come to the same end as they did.*"

"I'm nothing like them, I'm still alive," I point out. "And that's how I'm going to stay. What I'm asking is, how do I know you won't go back on your word, when I'm on that last day and I'm still alive?"

"*I'm nothing if not a demon of my word.*"

"I'm sure you are," I frown. "But I'm gonna need a little incentive to trust you. Tell me something I can prove, about yourself. I'm sure you weren't always a lying demon bent on destroying lives."

"... *Aren't you a smart little one*," the demon hisses. "*Very well. There's little you can do to stop me. I wasn't always a demon... I used to be a witch. Dark magic was my forte, something that leaked into the very soul of my being. When I was caught and killed, my soul lived on as a demon... trapped in a wretched spell book... The very book that I used. Is that enough for you?*"

"... I'll check the validity and get back to you tomorrow. Sound good?" I wonder.

"... *Fine, but my offer has an expiration date*."

"I expected nothing less."

The carts stop abruptly. I only take a moment to look between them and the demon. When I look back, however, the creature of darkness is gone. Taking that as a signal to leave, I hurry out of the building. I can't wait to talk to Heather about all this. Now that she's taken a more active role, we'll be able to save these souls all the faster.

Chapter 11

My mother is home when I arrive, her posture irritated. I've never really been given a curfew, but I always call when I'll be late. This time, she knows why I was late. Although my father indulges my chosen profession, she doesn't. She wants me to live without conflict and near death experiences. What parent doesn't want that for their children? I understand completely, though I wish she were more supportive.

"Any ghosts tonight?" she frowns.

"I guess you can call them that," I comment. "Some carts were moving on their own, and then a nasty demon popped up to make a deal with me."

"Your imagination isn't going to get you in trouble some day," she points out. "Keep talking like that and you'll wind up in the loony bin."

"How do you know I'm not telling the truth?"

"There's no such thing as ghosts. I left your dinner in the microwave. Eat up and head to bed, you have a long day tomorrow."

I nod and head into the kitchen. She means well, I'm sure, but it always comes off as sarcasm. As I sit and eat, I wonder what my best friend is doing. She won't be a target anymore, I made sure of that. My stomach, however, churns with an ill feeling. Something is wrong and I need to talk to her.

I pull out my phone between bites, dialing her number and listening to the ringer. She doesn't answer. I hit the dial button again, and two more times after. Still no answer. By now, my meal is forgotten and I'm pacing the tiled floor. My mother must've heard the tapping of my feet, as she's standing in the doorway.

"What's wrong?" she asks.

"Heather isn't answering her phone."

"She's probably asleep, Catori, it's late."

"She *always* answers. No matter what time it is!" I stress, panic setting in. "Something is wrong, I need to go see her."

"Catori!"

I'm out the door, keys in my hand. I don't look back to see her in the doorway, too busy backing up onto the road. My tires squeal on the asphalt as I hit the gas. she's not too far away, but that doesn't make me go any slower. It takes every bit of self control not to speed.

When Heather's house comes up, I can see a light flickering in the living room. No one is in the drive, as always, so I pull in. I almost leave the car in drive in my haste. Taking the time to remedy the mistake, I turn it off and run to the front door. Heather is still in the process of getting my key made, but she told me where to find the hidden one. I unscrew in the top of a lantern shaped light, picking it out of the bottom.

The door is unlocked and I hurry inside, not bothering to shut it behind me. I search the house, struggling not to scream out her name. Eventually, I notice her basement door is cracked open. Heather doesn't like leaving that door open. It's always locked tight. She once told me she had discovered a dark presence down there. I thought she was joking at the time, but she was quite adamant it was a poltergeist. After all I've learned and experienced this week, I simply can't play ignorant anymore.

"Heather?" I call quietly. "Are you down there?"

There's no answer, so I push the door open a little more. It's pitch black. With a glance to the side, I realize the switch is turned on. The bulb must've blown. I rummage through a cabinet, pulling out a new bulb. Taking a deep breath, I turn on the flashlight on my cell and start down the steps. The wood creaks beneath my sneakers.

I find the light, so I grab a chair nearby to stand on. It doesn't take long to change the bulb. When the light flares to life, as I hadn't turned off the switch upstairs, I shield my eyes. Through the spots I see before me, I manage to take in my surroundings. The shelves are all filled by jars, a mortar and pestle on the counter with some empty jars. Heather is lying on the floor by the counter, a broomstick at her feet and a cut on her head.

I gasp and hurry over to her, lifting her into my arms. The cut isn't a bad one, but head wounds always bleed profusely. It was enough to knock her out, that's for sure. I carefully shift her, slapping her cheek gently to rouse her. She groans, eyes opening slowly. Blurry and unfocused, Heather sits up and holds her head.

"Are you okay?" I ask. "What happened?"

"I… Catori? What are you doing here?"

"You didn't answer your phone. You *always* answer your phone," I point out. "What happened?"

"I was reading and… I heard something thump down here. I figured it was the ghost. I just wanted to make it feel better. When I got down here, though, the lights went out and I tripped. I guess I hit my head on the way down."

"I thought you hated it down here," I frown. "Why would you want to calm down a ghost you fear?"

"I don't fear her," Heather states. "I mean… Well… I guess I don't have to sugarcoat it for you anymore. Just… Let's go upstairs so I can heal my headache."

I nod and help her to her feet. Curiosity, the bane of my existence, is creeping up again. As we go upstairs, I catch sight of a blurry figure across the room. It's an older woman, carrying a basket of herbs to the counter. She doesn't look very dangerous. With a quiet hum, I shut the door and lock it tight. Heather pulls out some rubbing alcohol from beneath the sink. As she wets a cotton ball with it, I take it from her. I dab her wound, cleaning it as best I can.

"I told you my family is descended from witches, right?" she wonders.

"From one of the original bloodlines. I remember," I point out. "Bandages?"

"Well," she sighs, handing them to me. "The ghost downstairs is my grandmother, only… there's a *lot* of greats before that word. I asked her once why she didn't move on. She told me it's because there's something very important she's supposed to be guarding."

"What is it?"

"I honestly don't know, but… I'll bet just about anything it's that demon's prison. All the family's were supposed to protect it from falling into another's hands."

"They did a superb job," I mutter. "The witch was probably a member of the last family to carry it. Which brings me to the reason I was calling. I mean… aside from the unnerving feeling I was getting."

Heather pokes at my bandage job, eyes trailing over to me. I've peaked her interest. Although that was my intention, now I'm having second thoughts. I've never been as close to anyone as I am with Heather. If I tell her about the proposition and she takes it badly, she might march into the store herself. She can sense my doubts, nailing me with a glare I never thought her capable of.

"Tell me," she demands.

"… The demon wants to make a deal with me," I sigh.

"And you said no, right? Please tell me you're not stupid enough to agree to a demon's terms."

"I didn't!" I frown. "But the terms don't leave much room for me. That place is going to kill me no matter what I do, but at least with the agreement I'll have a slim chance."

"It won't hold to the deal!"

"I know that, Heather, but… I'll have full access to the store," I explain. "And, I made sure it told me something completely true."

"… How is that supposed to help you?"

"I learned it wasn't always a demon."

She stops there, a light going off in her eyes. I don't know what switch I hit, but it seems to be the right one. Much like myself when I'm deep in thought, Heather begins to pace. It doesn't take long before she comes to a halt, facing me with a renewed eagerness.

"Tell me everything."

"There isn't much to say," I shrug. "The demon said it used to be a witch. She used dark magic and when she was caught, the villagers killed her. It didn't have the affect they wanted, though. Instead of dying, her soul lived on as a demon… trapped in the spell book she, herself, used all her life."

"Irony," Heather smirks. "If she was a witch, she was likely one of the ancient clans. I can find out who she was, how she died… and that will tell us how to stop her."

"How?" I question.

"Basically, the death is the only way to kill it. I mean… when a soul becomes a demon, only the way the human died will kill it. That death anchors them to the world," she tries to explain. "The witch that opened the store had the right idea, but she got the wrong death. She hung herself, thinking the demon got the gallows. There weren't many ways to kill witches back then."

"But it didn't," I realize. "She must've gotten the identity wrong."

My cell phone rings, reminding me I left my mother standing outside. Palming my face, I pull the phone out of my back pocket. Heather is ready to continue with our conversation, but I know this is a discussion I can't put off.

"Hello?" I answers.

"Is everything okay?"

"I found her in the basement," I inform. "She fell and hit her head. I bandaged it up, but I want to stay over and make sure she doesn't have a concussion."

"Oh my god! Is she okay?" she asks. "Is she having issues speaking? Trouble remembering?"

"No," I sigh. "No nausea, but she has a headache. Her balance seems fine… are you dizzy or anything?"

"No."

"She not dizzy, looks tired, her emotions are all over the board… That's about it."

"I'll be right over to take her to the hospital."

"It's okay, mom. I got this. I'll keep watch and make sure she's okay. If her headache gets worse, or she starts stumbling, any seizures at all, I'll take her straight to the hospital and call you."

"… Okay, but..."

"I got this, mom. Goodnight."

"… Goodnight, Catori."

I hang up before she can say anything more. I know there's a whole rant she was waiting to give me, she *is* a nurse after all. When I hang up, Heather takes that as a signal to move. She grips my wrist and pulls me toward the basement door. When we reach it, she hesitates a moment… and then pushes the door open. Downstairs, right where we left her, is the old woman. She's like a ball of floating light, so unlike the demonic spirit I saw at the store.

"Drink the tea," she comments, one hand waving toward the counter.

On top of the counter, surrounded by crushed herbs, is a piping hot cup of tea. Heather takes it and downs it with one gulp, grimacing afterward. When she's finished, the old woman starts to pick up her mess.

Heather clears her throat, likely trying to banish the awful taste of the herbs.

"Nana, I have to ask you a question," she says.

"*Speak, child. I have all the time in the world to listen.*"

"Nana, Catori and I met an awful demon. She was a follower of the dark arts, killed by witch hunters."

"*Ah, I have known the like. Stay clear of that unholy creature, they desire naught but souls for feeding.*"

"I know, Nana, but its already gotten a hold of Catori. She has to defeat it, or she'll be killed. It said its prison was the book it used in life. I think I took a picture. If I show you the cover, will you know which clan it is? Maybe even the witch that last used it?"

"*I know all the clans and the members within. Show me this picture and I will reveal its secrets.*"

Heather pulls her phone out and searches the photos, humming to herself. When she locates it, she turns the phone around. The old woman squints her eyes, searching for anything she recognizes. I notice her eyes keep trailing to me, curious and filled with the desire to say something. Finally, she moves away from the phone and points with a bony finger.

"*This book... we used it long ago. How did you come to be in possession of it?*"

"We found it in the library's archives," Heather offers. "They say a witch hung herself there, that book was in her possession."

"Then she released the soul we trapped within it. Sylvian was a powerful coven leader, she was difficult to capture. If she has been released, I fear for the world outside these walls. You must stop her before she continues the work we stopped long ago."

"How do I do that?" I ask.

"You are the head of the parent clan, you should have the power to stop anything."

"Parent clan? What the hell?" I gape. "I'm a high schooler on my last year, I haven't even graduated and I'm in a coven!"

"The blood of the Brassblade clan is strong in you, surely you've been taught."

We both stare at her, expression mirrors of disbelief. The old woman shakes her head, 'tsk'ing in pity before she disappears. Heather is the first to recover, bustling about to pull books off the shelves. When she locates what she's looking for, she hurries back to me. The two of us return to the kitchen.

"Okay, so now we just have to find out what Sylvian died from."

"I have to let that thing possess me," I comment. "That's how you trap it, isn't it?"

"Well, you can do that, or you can use a devil's trap," she shrugs. "Don't worry, we'll figure it out. You need to keep that thing busy while I look, though. I think… you should take the deal. I'll make sure you know everything you need to keep yourself safe. We'll defeat this thing together!"

She seems so determined, it's almost cute… if I weren't playing the bait. It's getting very late, though, and we have school in the morning. With a little shove from me, we head to the bedroom to get ready. She takes the bathroom first, so I get dressed in the bedroom.

Together, we crawl into bed and I stay awake. I need to watch Heather, make sure she doesn't have a concussion. She's under in a short while, leaving me alone in the dark. Before I close my eyes, a shimmering light appears in the room. It's Heather's Nana, a kindly smile assuring me she'll keep watch. I fall asleep.

Chapter 12

The next day, I wake to Heather laying on my chest. She's drooling in her sleep, drawing a snigger from me. I shake her awake, getting out of bed to stretch. When she stands, I watch closely for any imbalance. When nothing is there, I'm satisfied she's better. Heather drags her feet to the bathroom, grumbling to herself, and I head to the kitchen to make breakfast. Nana is back in the basement, so I don't get the chance to thank her for last night.

As I scrap scrambled eggs onto two plates, already holding toast and bacon, Heather joins me. We both eat in silence. I don't think she should go to school today, just in case, but she'll argue with me. She does the dishes while I get dressed. When we're both done, we head to my car.

The second we walk into school, I'm met by Bridget. She's glaring daggers at Heather, a splint on her nose. I smirk at the sight. Keeping myself between Heather and her tormenter, I help her reach the door without confrontation.

"That's it, protect your girlfriend," Bridget bites out. "She can't hide behind you forever, you know."

"You touch my girlfriend again and I'll break more than your fucking nose!" I bite back.

Bridget and I both stop, realizing just what I've said. Trying to save as much face as possible, I turn around and start walking. Heather is right beside me, her fingers entwining with mine. That's all I need to relax. We leave Bridget outside, heading to our first class.

At lunch, I find myself at our usual table. Heather is late, though, and it's worrying me. Just when I'm regretting earlier, she sits down. A thick book is plopped onto the tabletop. I'm curious about the book, however she seems to have something she needs to get off her chest. She clears her throat.

"Catori… I really like you," she says awkwardly. "I mean, I *really* like you. It's just… my life is really complicated. Plus… you might be dead in six days. I would much rather we get all this behind us before pursuing something more permanent."

"… We're not a business deal Heather," I snort in humor. "We're best friends. I'm going to try really hard to stay alive after night six, so… we can see what happens after that. Now… what the hell is that massive book?"

"It's an old history book I found in the library," she blushes. "I thought maybe it would have more information on the witch hunts. It is a big part of history, after all."

"Find anything?" I wonder, taking a bite out of my pizza.

"I found Sylvian, but it says she was hung," she states. "I'm thinking her body was mixed up with someone else. I'll have to ask Nana what happened."

"What if she can't remember?" I wonder.

"Nana remembers everything… Mostly… I'll think of a backup plan."

With a short sigh, I look down on my lunch once more. Tonight, I go back to accept the demon's offer. Deep down, though, I feel a certain amount of trepidation. Six days is all I have, then I might be dead. I've no doubt the store will attempt to kill me at every turn. Although I've tried thinking up any possible way the demon can twist the offer, any way at all they can go back on their word, I know they'll find a way.

"Catori… maybe you should rethink this," Heather says quietly. "I mean, demons are really crafty. There's no guarantee you'll be coming out of that place again. Tonight might be the end of your life and… I don't want that. We can go away… move out of town together..."

"Then who will stop that demon?" I counter. "This isn't about me. That store will continue to stand, to take victims. I know Mr. Abbott said they were tearing it down, but… I don't think that's gonna happen. Those people will go in there and never come out."

"They don't have to go in to tear it down."

"But they won't do their job without making sure no one is in there. The store is good at messing with your mind, trust me on that. It'll lure them in."

"… You won't change your mind about this, will you?"

"No. I'm sorry, Heather. As awesome as running away with you sounds, I can't do it knowing more people will die."

The guilt would kill me, I have to admit. At the forefront are all those who might go, but deep down… I'm terrified my parents would go there looking for me. If anything happened to them, it would kill me. Heather's gaze drops, a sadness there I never see. I can't apologize enough to her, but this is something I have to do.

Lunch is silent after that. Back in classes, I'm too distracted to pay attention. Thankfully, it doesn't land me in detention. I can barely contain myself when the last bell rings. It's not that I'm eager to reach the store, but because I'm eager to get moving. Stepping outside, the world just seems different. I can smell the rain upon the air, feel the heat of the sun, and hear the laughter of those leaving. I've never appreciated it as much as I do now.

When I reach my car, I see that Heather isn't there. My cell is in my hand, fingers dancing across the keys. I text her, waiting for a reply. It comes, but not the one I thought. She's walking home, ready to start on her studies. It's a change, but at least we can skip the impending argument. I really did want to tell her 'goodbye', though… just in case.

At home, my parents are gone. Another blade I wish I didn't feel. It's for the best, I'm sure. If I said 'goodbye' to them, I'd be locked up in my room for the rest of my life. Climbing to my room, I pull out a notebook and pen. With a few quick scrawls, I write a short note. Again, it's just a precaution. I don't plan on meeting my maker anytime soon, but demons really are crafty things.

Downstairs, I grab something to eat. It feels so strange, glancing around a room I'm in every day. Studying it in case this is the last time I see it. Thoughts like that leave such a nostalgic feeling. When my sandwich is gone, I take one more look around the house. The door slamming shut sounds so final, sending shivers down my spine.

"I'm coming back," I assure myself.

The ride there is so quiet, like a grave waiting for its next inhabitant. When the store comes into view, I can't help imagining it's broken sign as a tombstone. The tires screech to a halt, the engine shutting off. I sit within the safety of my car for a few more minutes. The walk up may be the last walk I take. Steeling my nerve, I open the door and glare at the beaten structure.

Lights flicker to life, revealing the bleakness within… and a shadowy figure waiting. Taking a calming breath, I begin the long walk to the front doors. Crinkling paper from a torn sign is carried on the wind. Glass cracks beneath my sneaker, signaling my entrance. When I'm standing in front of the demon, a sickly white smile breaks out on an expanse of black.

"I've decided to take your offer," I comment. "But should I manage to beat the store, I want to add a clause of my own making."

"*Interesting, do tell.*"

"Should I survive six nights, and this store… or you…tries or succeeds in killing me... *You* will cease to exist."

"*Well, aren't you a smart little thing,*" she hisses. "*I suppose I'll have to add your clause, just to be fair. Be grateful, this isn't something I would normally allow.*"

"Then why do it now?" I needle. "I heard you were particularly interested in me, though I can't imagine why. Could that be the reason you'd go off script?"

"*You have an abnormally high sixth sense, along with a gracious amount of energy. The more energy and purity a soul has, the more power I get from them. You'll be a five star meal compared to the others.*"

"Wow… that's rude," I mutter. "So, do we sign a contract in blood or something?"

"*There is a contract, but we don't need blood to sign it... just a pen.*"

She holds out her hand, palm up, and the shadows from her body collect there. A scroll rests there, one she lets fall open. A pen floats in the air, waiting for my touch. I take it, carefully reading over the long contract. It seems to irritate the demon, however contracts are no joke. I need to make sure my clause was added… and there are no loopholes. Well… none I can't use for my own benefit. Slowly, I listen to the pen scratch against the paper. I sign my name and the deal has been sealed.

"*Pleasure doing business with you,*" the demon chuckles. "*Or it will be, anyway. Take your time looking around, you have six days you know.*"

"Thanks for the reminder," I mutter.

The demon laughs, dispersing into the air before vanishing. With a sigh, I turn to face the store. It's as desolate as it's always been. A creak echos within the silent grave, the carts leaving their coral to wander. I dodge them, focused on reaching the back. Just as I'm about to push through the double doors, they slam back toward me. With a gasp of surprise, I dive out of the way.

A rack rolls out, my eyes traveling up from the wheels. Horror fills me at the sight. Five children dangle from nooses, blood dripping from their clothes. Its origin is the slice across each their necks, the ropes only pulling the wound wider. Their sightless eyes blink, trailing down to me. As I slowly get to my feet, the rack stops and the children stare.

"*Are you here to play with us?*" they ask in tandem. "*Play with us... Play... Won't you play? Please... play with us.*"

Pale faces gaze upon me pleadingly, my mind racing through the many articles I found. There were a few children that came up missing, more than these five. As I make that connection, though, the rack begins to move once more. Another comes out after it, also holding hanging children. Each that comes out join in the first's plea, a symphony of tiny voices calling for a friend. I cover my ears, but it seems they echo in my mind.

As I watch them move, they seem to float off the rack and onto the bars. One of the racks starts back, a figure shimmering to existence beside it. He's average in height, built slim with dark hair. A pair of shattered glasses sit on the bridge of his nose. He moves without concern for the carts, ignoring all those around him. Some of the carts veer off path, some hitting clothing racks or shelves. As he gets closer, he looks up. There are no eyes within his sockets. Claw marks are scored across eyelids, blood drenching his face like tear tracks.

"*Sorry*," he murmurs. "*Sorry… so sorry… I'm sorry… Sorry…*"

One rack of children, on their to the floor, giggles in passing. Shaking my head, I wonder if I really do what to go through those doors. Collecting my inner strength, I push passed the swinging doors. The back is far less impressive than the front. Water drips from the ceiling, trailing past a few electrical wires. The floor is dirty, small holes and cracks scattered about the concrete. Past some strips of plastic is another room, the sound of a machine filling the air.

As I walk forward, mindful of the rushing man, I can see piles of dust in the corners. There's a table on both sides of the room, one much longer than the other. The longer one has more tables coming off it. Two are piled high with tattered rags, a mouse squeaking as it wiggles from them. A pot falls from the table off on its own, hitting the floor with a loud clang. I turn just in time to see a stray cat scamper away. Steadying my racing heart, I wander closer there.

"*You took the deal.*"

I turn to see the woman from the baby section, throat bruised from her noose. Her eyes are pitying, lips turned in a frown. It's obvious she isn't happy. I don't move, but she steps closer.

"*Why couldn't you let us protect you?*"

"No one is safe as long as that demon lives," I answer. "You may be containing it, but I want it gone for good."

"*It's impossible. Even the witch couldn't destroy it, so how will you?*"

"Don't worry, I have a plan," I wave off. "Right now, though, I'm more interested in this building. It reeks of death and decay."

"*This place was built on the bodies of employees and customers… literally. We're standing on some now. I think mine was placed over there,*" Baby says, pointing to the back of the room where hangers are splayed about.

"Your body was taken to the coroner," I correct. "It was cremated."

"*No it wasn't, it was stolen from the morgue and laid to rest over there. It makes the demon stronger to have the bodies near.*"

As disgusting as that is, I say nothing more. Instead, I look down at my feet. The concrete beneath my sneakers seems to breathe, twisting my gut in nervous sickness. This whole place is a cemetery for the damned. Worried about standing on a body, I take a step back. The concrete cracks, opening a cut wide enough to see an eye. Goosebumps spread all over at the sight. When it moves to gaze at me, I squeak in fright.

Behind me, a metal door with a broken hinge rattles. With a gasp, I redirect my movement to the side. Eyes darting over to the rattling door. It starts opening and closing, the loud bang echoing through the empty place. Garnering a bit of courage, I make my way over. A cold breeze rushes through the opening, blowing back my hair. With a frown, I reach for the door and grip it. It was moving harshly enough to harm me, yet stills immediately at my touch.

I look in to see… nothing. Confused and slightly curious, I try to look deeper into it. There's some garbage and a couple small plastic bags, ripped and filled with broken knickknacks. There's a singed coloring within it, a few holes in the metal, and smoke rises from the soot.

"How odd."

"*Don't crawl in, that thing is dangerous*," Baby comments, beginning to vanish. "*People die in there.*"

When she's completely gone, I turn my attention back to the machine. There's no way I'm crawling in. To the side is a control pad, a key switch at the bottom. It doesn't take much to guess it crushes things. Just when I'm about to move away, something glows on the sides of the machine. The clumps of luminescent liquid rises up, flowing through the air to land behind me. Slowly, it piles up. When it's a little taller than I am, it begins to take shape. A woman, slender and beautiful, levels me with a curious gaze.

"*So you're the new victim*?" she wonders.

"Uh… I guess so. I'm Catori," I answer. "What were you doing in there? Is that where you died?"

"*Sure is. I was looking for my cell phone. You wouldn't believe how much coincidence led to my end. I mean, how* often does a cell phone fall into a compactor with an aerosol can and a mirror?"

"… How do those things kill a person?" I wonder in confusion.

"Sunshine on a mirror, flammable aerosol can… you do the math. I guess I can be happy it was fast and painless."

"Is there anyone this place *hasn't* killed?" I huff.

"You… for now, anyway," she answers. "Wouldn't hold onto that one, though. It's only a matter of time."

"… Gee, thanks."

She shrugs, the only answer she can give. Obviously, these spirits have little to no faith in newcomers. I guess they just don't last long here. With yet another nameless spirit breaking the demon's rules, I have one more to name. Carrie will be her name… mainly because she seems like she can turn very evil, very fast. As she shimmers out of view, I turn my attention back to the room.

Mold clings to the walls like a coat of paint, leaving the air musty and stale. I hope it isn't black mold as I wander toward the back. Broken glass is scattered along the floor, some covered in dried blood. A few large carts sit in the back, filled with trash bags and boxes. One of the bags is ripped open, spilling cloth onto the floor like life's blood.

More of the floor crumbles, eyes gazing up from beneath it. At one point, a few fingers managed to wiggle up. They were rotted down to the bone. In the back is a wall of long bars, laying horizontal to hold unused hangers. To the left and on the same wall is a massive hole. Cautiously, I move toward it. Just as I'm about to peer inside, a hand shoots out and grasps my throat. It's thin and boney, though flesh still covers it.

I fight to get away, yet they keep an iron grip. When it starts to tighten, my eyes narrow in a glare. I grip their wrist in one hand, working my own fingers beneath one of theirs… and then I bend it back until it snaps. A cry of pain swells from the hole, yanking back its injured finger. I know I'll have bruises after that, I'll figure out a way to explain them later.

"This store won't take me," I growl out. "So you keep trying, and I'll keep fighting. But in the end, I'll come out on top."

"*We'll see about that*," the demon says through the intercom. "*Be patient, my children, she'll join us soon enough*."

The building creaks in answer, groaning through the walls as though its stomach is rumbling. It's an unnerving thought. Finished for the night, I start back the way I came. As I pass through the double doors, I can swear someone is watching me. In this place, they very well may have been.

Dodging more carts in the aisles, I dance my way to the front of the store. There's no need to look back, I'll be there again tomorrow. Holding my breath in case there's no escape, my hand pushes against the door. A breath of relief leaves my lips when it opens. I did what I came to do, there's no reason to torture myself anymore than I have to. As I walk away from the store, a growing feeling of dread rests upon my shoulders.

Chapter 13

Heather is waiting for me when I get home, a solemn look on her face. My parents are home this time, oblivious to the danger I just faced. We go to my room so I can destroy the note I left. No sense in getting them worried over nothing. When that's finished, I sit on my bed to talk with Heather.

"You can't stay here, Catori," she states. "Not until all this is over. Your parents might get hurt… or think you're completely insane. They can't protect you in a state of ignorance."

"I know, but… what can I do?"

"Stay with me," she offers. "I know what's going on, I have the power to help protect you. Even Nana has enough power to ward off the demon's minions."

"What am I supposed to say to my parents?" I ask. "Mom already accused me of doing drugs."

"… Seriously?"

"Yes, seriously."

Heather shakes her head. The two of us try to think up some excuse, yet fall short. There isn't much we can use, and the truth will get me locked up. I can't help anyone from a padded cell. Finally, I admit defeat. Heather, on the other hand, seems to have gotten an idea. She grips my wrist and drags me down to the living room. Surprisingly, even my father is awake.

"Where's the fire?" my father wonders.

"I… um… my parents are going on vacation," Heather states. "I'll be all alone in the house… I was hoping Catori could stay over with me for the next couple weeks."

"Why aren't you going with them?" my mother inquires.

"School. It's almost finished. I told them I wanted to finish my education, but it's a business trip for my dad. They couldn't postpone it."

"Sure," my father says. "You girls stay out of trouble and call if you need anything."

Although my mother's expression is suspicious, she doesn't challenge my dad. I suppose it *is* odd they would go on vacation after Heather's accident. But then, it wasn't serious. I breathe a sigh of relief as we head upstairs. After I pack a small bag, we leave the house and start the journey to hers.

The car is quiet the whole way there, making the trip seem all the longer. It's as though we're strangers. The feeling is so alien to me, as we didn't even feel that way when we *were*. I clear my throat, preparing to talk about tonight's experience, when Heather bursts.

"I can't believe you made that deal!" she grumbles.

"Heather, we agreed it would be..."

"*We* didn't agree! This part of 'we' definitely did *not* agree! *This* part of 'we' said to wait until we had a solid plan!"

I can't help the groan that sounds. These are the types of arguments I don't like having with her. Heather shares the wonderful trait of 'stubbornness' with me. We can butt heads all day and get nowhere. Eager to end the conversation before it evolves into tongue lashing, I say the first thing that comes to mind. Not always the right thing, but it works about ten percent of the time. Thankfully, I hit that percentage this time.

"You knew I was going to make the deal when I left."

"And I'm still pissed about it!" she bites. "I just needed to get it out. Now… What the fuck are we going to do!"

"That part of 'we' said to leave it to her," I point out. "This part of 'we' is going to continue investigating the building. There has to be something in there to help."

"The building isn't going to tell you anything," Heather mumbles.

"Maybe not the building, but the spirits *inside* it are rather chatty. One of them has to know how to take her out."

"… I suppose it wouldn't hurt to hear their stories," she comments, tone a bit lighter. "Did you meet any good ones yet?"

"I met a few," I inform. "A couple have held lengthy conversations."

"Ask them if the demon acts strangely around anything," she says. "Like, something she's afraid of. Maybe something she avoids completely. That's usually a good indicator of a death. Spirits avoid the very thing that killed them in life."

I nod my head, making a mental note for tomorrow. Tonight, I'm ready to go to sleep. The two of us enter Heather's house, weary and beat. We drag our feet to her room, kicking off our shoes on the way. Just like any other night we're together, we change into our pajamas and pass out on the bed.

I wake a couple hours later to whispers in the dark. They sound familiar, the voices. Rubbing sleep from my eyes, I carefully slide away from Heather and get out of bed. The night seems darker than usual, the sound of rain pattering against the window all that there is. One glance outside and I know it'll be flooded tomorrow. I sigh in annoyance, caught once more by the voices. Curious, I make my way to the hallway. Nothing is there. My eyes cut to the side, checking on Heather, and then I'm walking to the living room.

A crack races along the wall from behind me, my heart leaping into my throat at the sound. Eyes are everywhere, bloodshot and glazed over in death. I'm not in Heather's safe home anymore, I'm lost in a sea of pitch eager to swallow me.

"*Isn't it lovely? Forever black... forever bleak. You can make it go away, make everything go away.*"

There's a small spotlight in the dark, shining down on a counter top. Sitting upon it is a knife. I reach for it cautiously, afraid it might attack. Instead of the knife, a bloody hand grabs me from the other side of the counter. It reaches up from below. I walk around to see my attacker, gasping when I see a boy around nineteen. His wrists are sliced through to the bone. Dark bags are beneath his bloodshot eyes, the red a dead giveaway to tears.

"*It only hurts a few seconds,*" he states, a hysterical laugh in his voice. "*Just a few seconds. Then you close your eyes and it all goes away. You just go to sleep, and then you wake up. Easy... just like she said... so easy.*"

"I'll pass, thanks," I frown.

He lets go of my wrist, slowly fading back into the forever sleep he was lost to. I read about him, he was a victim a few months ago… the most recent. Star athlete, straight 'A' student, real people person. They were all shocked when they found him bled out in his kitchen. Sighing, I catch sight of a familiar marking on his arm… the same I was given by the harbinger of Death. She really did try to warn them all. It's a shame they couldn't see her like I could.

"Catori?" a faraway voice says. "Catori, are you all right? Hey, wake up. Catori, wake up!"

I'm startled awake by Heather shaking me. Thunder claps outside, helping the process a bit more. Fully awake, I take in the room around me. Heather's expression is one of worry. I run a hand through my hair and frown.

"They're back to nightmares again," I mutter.

"I'm going to ask Nana about a tea that might help," Heather comments. "I'm sure there's something."

"I saw another victim… the teen that committed suicide in his kitchen," I inform through a yawn. "He seemed so restless, bags under his eyes and all. Maybe he was trapped in nightmares, too."

"Don't worry, I'll think of something," Heather states quietly. "I won't let that happen to you."

"I appreciate that," I smirk. "But I won't let it happen either. I need my beauty sleep after all. This much awesome doesn't manifest itself, you know."

With a quiet chuckle, Heather lays back down. She holds my hand as she falls asleep this time, an anchor for my mind. Listening to the rain, I slip under as well. There isn't another nightmare.

In the morning, I'm second to wake. Heather is already making breakfast, so I head for the shower. There's a curtain now, the door still busted from our last accident here. I wonder how her parents took it. Although I'm still wary, I need to bathe. I jump in the shower and turn on the hot water. Uncertain how far this demon will go, my shower doesn't last long. The second I'm clean, I jump out again to get dressed.

Distracted by my socks, I don't notice the shadow reaching from my own. A hand grips my ankle, cold and clammy, and gives it a yank. I'm off balance, falling to the floor. This time I see it moving, heading for the sink's counter. I try to remember what was placed up there.

Sharp scissors come tumbling down. I dodge them, though barely, and quickly get to my feet.

"Uncalled for!" I hiss.

"Catori? Are you okay?" Heather asks from the bedroom. "I heard a thud."

"I fell," I comment. "I think I might need stitches."

"What? From a fall?" she gasps, bursting in. "What happened?"

"The scissors fell after me," I shrug. "I guess that demon can reach through my shadow now. I should've seen it coming, considering all I see of her is a shadow."

She grumbles to herself, rummaging around the bathroom to find the first aid kit. Granted it doesn't have stitches in it, but I'm sure we can wrap it until later. I sit to eat in the kitchen while Heather mends my arm. We don't have school today, so no one will be asking questions. Unfortunately, my mom is working at the hospital today. They'll know me just by look, so there's no way I'm going there. Heather pulls out some dental floss and a sewing needle, disinfecting them and the wound.

"You're so lucky I took up cross stitch," she mumbles. "Now hold still."

Pain shoots up my arm when she puts the needle through my skin. It takes all I am to keep still. Slowly, she stitches up the cut in my arm. I thank every religion I know of that it wasn't a long cut. When she's finished, I let out the breath I had been holding.

"Did it hurt?" she asks.

"Of course it hurt!"

"Good, then don't let it happen again."

I roll my eyes, yet say nothing. I probably would've done the same to her. It's the little things that let people know you care. Today we don't have much of a plan. I don't visit the store until after dark, so I'll likely end up helping Heather study. The only question left is, in the library or here?

"Nana and I are going to look for spells to protect you in sleep today," Heather offers. "If you want, you can look in Nana's old books to find how Sylvian died."

"Sounds like a plan," I smirk. "To the basement!"

I know Heather is shaking her head behind me. Heather leads the way to the basement. Down within the dull light, Nana floats about her counter. She doesn't still when Heather calls her name. Although she continues to rummage about, it's easy to tell she's listening.

"Nana, the demon attacked Catori in her sleep again," she frowns. "Is there any warding symbols or spells we can use to protect her?"

"*There is always a symbol or spell*," she chuckles. "*You just have to know where to look*."

"I would very much like to know where to look," Heather comments, taking a seat on an old bar stool.

Nana waves her hand, a book sliding a bit off the shelf. I pull it down completely, handing it over to Heather. Clearing her throat, she begins to flip through the pages. I'm curious, as always, and try to look over her shoulder. There are spells scrawled on some pages, others hold symbols, and still others have recipes.

"What is this?" I wonder.

"My family's grimoire," Heather offers. "There's one for the coven, but this one is strictly our family's."

"Is there a difference?"

"Sometimes the family has special recipes or spells that only they know. The coven's is a collection of all the family's spells. Though they're all known, not all are at their fingertips."

"And this is supposed to help me?"

"Yep! I found the symbol we need!" she grins. "How do you feel about getting a tattoo?"

I can only stare at her in shock. The thought had honestly never crossed my mind. Nana goes back to her rummaging, pulling out a small inkwell and a needle. Heather picks them up and smiles at me.

"*You're* going to give it to me?" I ask, skeptical.

"I know how to draw," she answers.

"This isn't drawing, Heather, it's jabbing my skin with a needle!"

"I just sewed your arm shut! Sit down and shut the hell up! You're not leaving this place without it!"

Groaning in irritation, I close my eyes and hold out my arm. It's the uninjured one, which probably wasn't the best choice. I hiss when the needle goes in my wrist, opening one eye to watch her work. Thankfully, it isn't as painful as I thought it would be. The method she's using is a hand-poking method, once used by Native Americans. I remember doing a report on it. This is probably the most gentle way to do it.

When she's finished, I chance a look. It's a circle with a triangle in the center. Inside the triangle is a sun with a face, below is a Victorian cross. On the two bottom points of the pyramid are stars, and on top is three teardrops. This is the Wiccan symbol for protection from evil. That demon is most definitely evil.

"There we go!" Heather grins, pride radiating from her. "All finished. What do you think?"

"I think I'm going to have to start wearing thick bracelets," I sigh. "My mom is going to kill me for this."

"Speaking of your mom," Heather offers. "Do you think your witch blood comes from her side?"

"… I can't answer that without being bias."

"Catori, this is important. You're not just a descendant of a witch, you're the new head of the parent coven. If anyone has complete records of all witches, past and present, it would be your family."

"You're going to make me ask, aren't you?"

"Yes I am."

Hanging my head, I start for the stairs. Heather is right behind me, but I motion for her to stay. There's no point in the two of us getting trapped in a scolding. She goes back to her grimoire, searching for anything that may help. In the kitchen, I stop long enough to grab an apple. Afterward, I leave the house and jump in my car.

Chapter 14

The drive home feels longer than it is. I'm almost praying my parents aren't there, so it's no surprise when both their cars are in the driveway. Feet dragging the whole way, I go inside. My mother is in the kitchen, but it seems my father is sleeping. When I walk in, mom stops and looks my way.

"Oh, I wasn't expecting you home," she frowns. "Is everything okay, honey?"

"Yeah, fine," I comment. "I was just wondering… about my heritage."

"… That's a pretty random thing to be thinking about. Is there a reason?"

"All this digging into the store's history, I was just curious about mine. I came across some papers that had our last name… it talked about witches."

"Why on earth would our family be connected to witches?"

I sit down at the table, already picking out her blocks. This isn't a subject she wants to talk about. Unfortunately, it has to come out. If I want to survive these next six days, I have to know what I'm capable of. I motion for her to sit across from me, which she does hesitantly.

"Catori, can't you find normal interests?" she huffs.

"Normal is last week," I shrug. "I want to know if it's true. Was it on your side or dad's? Why wasn't I told before? Do you practice?"

"Absolutely not!" she says, affronted. "And your father wasn't into that either! This isn't the past, magic doesn't exist! Ghosts don't exist!"

"… I didn't say they did," I comment. "I just want to know..."

"Ignorance is bliss, dear," she bites. "Stop digging into the past and start living in the present."

"… I knew I shouldn't have talked to you," I mutter, disappointment soaking every word. "You never give me the answers I want, I knew you were blocking the second you opened your mouth. And what's worse, you didn't confirm nor deny if it was your side of the family. Why can't you just tell me the complete truth for once? I deserve to know where I came from, who I'm descended from! The past creates the present and future! Without it, none of us would be here!"

"That doesn't mean you need to look to it! Now, go find something productive to do. It's the weekend, you should be out watching movies or shopping."

I glare at her, yet say nothing. She knows I'm gritting my teeth, fighting to keep quiet. I hate when she does this, acts like I'm supposed to be this completely normal child. I refuse to conform to society's idea of 'normal'. It takes far more courage to be yourself nowadays, and I take pride in being different. How I wish I had grandparents to talk to, perhaps they would be more open about our heritage.

Speaking of grandparents, I think my father inherited everything from his parents. He wouldn't let mom go through any of it, yet wouldn't sell anything either. At least, that's what I was told. Humming to myself, I get up. I get a pop from the fridge, glancing at my father's schedule in the process. He'll be free to talk tomorrow night, home just in time for me to catch.

"I'm helping Heather with her family tree," I comment. "Probably one of the reasons I'm interested in mine. She's descended from witch blood, too. Strange connection to have, but I don't mind."

"She's into witchcraft?" my mom says, face paling.

"Is that what I said?" I glare. "Because I'm pretty sure I just said she was 'descended from witch blood'. It's not the same thing, you know. *I'm* descended from witch blood and *I* don't do witchcraft."

"You're not descended from..."

"Yes, I am," I say, tone firm with each syllable. "I have to go, I don't want to find her on the floor again."

I don't say 'goodbye', I'm too angry for that. The door slamming between us is the final sound between us. Had I not been fuming, I probably would've apologized. As it is, she's only making me angrier. I jump in my car and drive over to Heather's.

When I open the front door, I hear her voice from the living room. Heather is curled up on the couch with a fuzzy blanket and a laptop. She grins at the sight of me, lifting one side of her massive blanket. I kick off my shoes and join her, glancing at the pile of musty books on the coffee table.

"Any luck?" I wonder.

"No, not really," she sighs. "I found her, but… information on her is vague. I mean, there's enough during her early lifetime. When it gets to the point there's a dark witch among them… well… they sort of stopped recording things on her."

"Did Nana tell you why?"

"She said the investigation was done by the parent clan, so they were the ones that recorded the majority of it. I don't have that book. How did things go with your parents?"

"Mother," I correct. "And they went just as well as they ever do. She flat out denied my heritage, basically building a wall between the subject and herself."

"… I wonder why. I mean, I know *why*. I just… that's so wrong. I'm proud of my family's past. They endured so much for what they believed in. How could anyone just sweep them under the rug like that?"

"Beats me," I shrug. "Let's go back to the library and check out the rest of those files. I met a new spirit I can't remember from the news articles. Maybe we'll even find something that'll help me connect to them."

"You can go, I'll stay here in my warm blanket and read moldy old tomes. Those archives scares the hell out of me."

Rolling my eyes, I get up to leave. I don't blame her, the archives are a little eerie. However, she isn't the one getting attacked by corpses in the dark. With a sigh, I get to my feet. After sliding into my sneakers, I grab my keys and exit the house.

The library isn't as quiet as it usually is, filled to the brim with people. Teens have planted themselves at the computers, children are listening to an attendant read to them, and a few are running through the tall shelves. There's a different librarian today, my brow wrinkling in confusion. A bad feeling is settling in my gut. Slowly, I walk over to the counter.

"Hey, is Sadie on vacation or something?"

"Sadie?" she frowns. "I haven't seen her today. In fact, I was called in this morning. The manager said he couldn't get a hold of her. Not surprising, she left all her stuff here last night."

"… She just left it?" I frown.

"Sure did. What can I help you with?"

"… I was hoping to go into the archives again," I comment.

"I heard Sadie was visiting those archives frequently… I was hoping that was just a rumor," she frowns. "I, unlike Sadie, don't mess with that area. It's cursed. I'll give you the keys, though. Be careful, the curse calls to even those that stand outside the door."

My nerves are so rattled I think my teeth are chattering. I take the keys from her, turning to take the path I've memorized. Sadie's disappearance weighs heavily upon my mind. She was so sure that curse was just superstition… maybe it can even get to nonbelievers. A couple teens are roughhousing, slamming into me on my way by. The keys fall from my hands, sliding along the floor.

With snickered apologies, they run off. Footsteps on the wooden floor thud, echoing in the building. The change in sound startles me. Everything else has been drowned out by it. It's a vacuum of nothingness. Then I hear an evil cackle. Shivers race along my spine. The second the keys are located, they're scooped up. It takes so much not to run to the archives.

The hallway seems to stretch on forever, dark and foreboding. One of the lights flicker, weak against the pitch trying to swallow it. The second I step beneath it, those behind me turn off. At first, it's slow. The progress, however, quickens with my footsteps. I can't unlock the door fast enough. It's swung open and I back in, staring upon the fading lights. The last one blows. I'm safe within the archives.

A sigh of relief rises from my lungs as I shut the door. When I turn around, however, I'm struck with horror. Hanging from a noose just inside the room is Sadie. Her messy bun is hanging loose, stray strands tangled in the rope. Both her wrists are cut, the ruby fluid dripping down onto the floor. She's been this way for a while, if the puddle is anything to go by. The horror subsides to sadness… and guilt. Had I not visited so frequently, perhaps she would still be alive.

"Oh, Sadie, I'm so sorry," I whisper.

I back up to leave, yet hesitate. I need some of those files, but Sadie needs to be put to rest. If anything, I wanted to reclaim the grimoire left here. Putting it on the back burner, I open the door and leave. My heart is heavy with loss. Not only for Sadie, but for myself. I've lost a day of my own life, and any potential leads I can find there.

After reporting back to the librarian, the place is thrown into chaos. Sirens wail outside, a warning of greater pandemonium to come. Teenagers linger, trying hard to find out what's happening. The children have been taken out. As they carry Sadie out in a body bag, a lieutenant steps up to me. I know him, he used to work alongside my father. Ray Hagan was his partner. Just like then, he's all business until he gets the answers he needs.

"You were the one to find her?" he asks.

"Yes," I answer quietly. "I can't believe she's gone, I was just here yesterday with my friend."

"I was told you've been spending a lot of time here. Any reason why?"

"I've been investigating the old store," I inform. "I figured, it couldn't hurt any. I want to be an investigator and starting on something that has no living connections… it seemed like a good idea at the time."

"Mrs. Tucker took you to the archives each time?"

"Yes, sir."

"Did she seem stressed? Upset, or..."

"She didn't commit suicide!" I say firmly. "She was very happy each time I spoke with her. There's no reason for her to have done that! It's that damn store! The curse is *real*! That's what killed her."

"… We'll chase every lead we can, but I think it's quite obvious what the cause of death is."

"Did she… did she have a bruise on her upper arm?" I question, lifting my sleeve. "Like this one?"

"She did… How would you know that? Do you know if she was being stalked? How did you get a matching mark? If someone is hurting you, I need to know. They could be a serial killer."

"I wasn't attacked by anyone," I sigh. "I told you what happened. The best advice I can give you, is to not be so narrow minded. If you need me, I'm sure you know where I live."

"Tell Frank I said hello," he smirks, tipping his hat. "And I know about that curse, Catori. You need to step lightly, it's no joke."

"Tell me about it," I sigh. "See you around."

He waves, moving to question the librarian. All this ruckus has gone on long enough, my stomach is rumbling. Tail tucked in disappointment, I drive back to Heather's house. When I walk in, I find her sleeping on the couch. The fuzzy blanket was just too much for her. With a chuckle, I leave her be. The fridge is cold, the air spilling out upon opening, and it leaves me with a strange feeling.

"Catori?" Heather calls, still half asleep. "Is that you?"

"No, I'm robbing the house," I call. "Do you have anything good to eat?"

"Very funny," she responds. "I thought you would take longer at the library. What happened?"

"… Sadie is dead."

"The librarian?" she gasps. "Oh my god, what happened?"

"She hung herself in the archives," I sigh, tone filled with guilt. "She even had the mark of Death's harbinger. I called the cops, so the archives were off limits."

Heather is beside me now, pulling me into a hug. Together, we sit at the small dining room table. I hang my head, guilt weighing heavily upon my shoulders. She deserved so much better than that. My best friend reaches over to me, holding my hand. It's an attempt to reassure me, but I'm beyond that point.

"This wasn't your fault, Catori," Heather remarks firmly. "I know you think it is, but it isn't."

"She never would've went down there had I left that store alone."

"A curse doesn't just stay still because no one is paying attention," she argues. "It *calls* to victims. The need to go there would've eventually gotten the better of her. You needing access only sped it up."

"… That doesn't make me feel better."

She gives up, sighing miserably before laying her head down. Unable to think of anything else to say, I stand to make us lunch. The silence is heavy around us, something we don't normally experience. I wasn't close to Sadie, not like I am with Heather, but her death is on my conscience. I look down and gasp, yanking my hands away from the bread. I hold them up in front of me, eyes wide and horrified. They're covered in blood. It stains them crimson, running down my palms and dripping onto the floor.

"Catori? Are you okay?"

Her voice sounds so far away. I see her, face drawn in worry, yet everything is so muffled. I feel weightless, the world spinning around me. Then I hit the floor. It should hurt, however I feel nothing. Even as my vision blackens around the edges, Heather rushing to my side, I feel nothing. The last thing I recall is Heather pulling me into her arms. After that… the world goes dark.

Chapter 15

I wake, finding myself laying on the couch. Heather is in the armchair near me, browsing her laptop. When she notices the eyes on her, so much relief floods her I can feel it from where I lay. There's a soft patter from rain outside, the air cooler with the loss of sun. I can almost hear the spirits wailing in the gloom.

"What happened?" I murmur.

"You passed out," Heather comments. "Almost nailed your head on the counter corner. You have *got* to stop scaring me like this, Catori. My heart just can't take it."

"I saw blood," I say quietly. "It was all over my hands… dripping onto the floor..."

"It wasn't your fault," she states, more bristled. "That damn demon is using this to get to you! Don't let that fucker win! Dig in like you always do, weather the storm, and shove it down that bitch's throat!"

"… Wow… I forget you can be violent sometimes," I say, wide-eyed. "Nice pep-talk, by the way."

She shrugs it off, yet I catch a slight smirk on her lips. With the weather turning for the worse, a trip to the store seems unlikely. Unfortunately, I haven't much choice. No longer will the library be open. With that path of study gone, there's no other place to learn of the demon. Resigned to going out in the storm, I send Heather an apologetic glance.

"What?" she frowns.

"How long have I been out?"

"A few hours. I was beginning to worry. Why?"

"… I can't go research at the library anymore. I have no choice but to go to the store."

"It's pouring outside!"

"I can't help it Heather. The countdown started last night, I only have six nights to go. If I can't figure out the cause of death for Sylvian by then, those poor spirits will never be free."

"… Why is it so important to you?" she asks quietly.

"I… I don't know," I admit, tone sheepish. "I just have to do this. I feel like… like this is my purpose in life. Do you understand?"

"I do," she nods. "I understand completely. Be careful on the road, don't what you dying before the store gets the chance to try."

With a grateful smile, I head for the door. It might be early, but there isn't much more for me to do. Before leaving, I grab an extra jacket and pull on my sneakers. Outside, I immediately step into a puddle. The day just keeps getting better. With a sigh, I follow the walkway to my car. The engine purrs to life when I turn the key, cold air blasting from the vents. Already wet, it does me no favors.

Driving down the empty street, I'm tormented by the suspense. This would be the perfect time for the demon to attempt my end. With each pothole, puddle, and slide of the tires, my heart skips. I'm so nerved I want to puke. Just as I'm beginning to relax, the car's headlights shine on something in the road. The woman is in a gray ragged dress, her hair a mess of long tangles. There are no eyes, her skin is ashen, and she's reaching for the car. She opens her mouth, jaw unhinging, and a black fog pours out. Gasping is surprise, I jerk the wheel to avoid her. Thankfully, I also avoid the light post.

"What the fuck!" I yell, hitting the steering wheel after coming to a halt.

Enraged at the near miss, I throw open my door and get out. Rain pounds down on me, my eyes cutting daggers into the zombie woman. She pivots slowly, dragging one foot as she approaches. I wait, rainwater soaking through my jacket. There's no way I'm stepping into that street. I may be crazy, but I'm not that crazy. The second she's close enough, I swing. Instead of the satisfying impact of my fist to her face, I punch through a cloud of green.

"You're lucky my car wasn't dented!" I shout to the sky. "Try it again! I dare you! I'm saving the next punch for your curse ridden ass!"

Still fuming, I get back in the car and start it up. It isn't much further to the store. By now, I'm more interested in going back to Heather's. When I pull into the parking lot, one of the light posts flickers in the night. It's a lonely walk, reminding me of just how hopeless those trapped feel.

Like the first time I stepped through the doorway, I can feel myself being drained of any happiness. The aisles are just as empty as that day as well. Walking through the main aisle, I'm ready for anything. A quiet giggle catches my attention. Eyes searching the hanging rags, I spy a moving figure. They're small and fast. Another follows, a few more behind me, and a couple to my left. It's the children from before. Bloody footprints are smeared in trails of crimson, painting the floor in a macabre scene.

One of the little boys peeks through the rags, one eye blind and loose in the socket. He reaches up, a wide grin on his face, and pulls that eye out. I almost puke at the squelching sound it makes. Like a child sharing candy, he holds it out to me. I know my face pulls in disgust, yet it seems to be exactly what he's looking for. With a joyous laugh, he stuffs his eye back in the socket and runs off.

As I continue to the back, I can hear them circling. As much as I try to ignore it, their distance is cutting closer. Praying they don't touch me, I slip through the doors as fast as possible. Thankfully, they don't come back here. For a few minutes, my thoughts attempt to figure out why.

"They're customers," Baby comments. *"Customers aren't allowed back here."*

She's standing over by the compactor, the spirits from there appearing beside her. Had their bodies not wavered with see-through sections, they could be mistaken as coworkers taking a break. One sits atop an upturned tote, the other leaning against the wall.

"You're a stubborn one," Carrie remarks. *"Just can't seem to learn your lesson, or what?"*

"I have issues with authority," I smirk.

"Welcome to the club, we're thinking of making shirts," the other snorts in dry humor.

"You really shouldn't be here, though. Tonight is a sort of anniversary."

"Anniversary?"

"Yep. Our resident wraith died on this date, so many years ago. I figured he should've forgotten by now. We all do... Forget, that is. Memories become fuzzy after the first hundred years or so."

"He hasn't, just like us. We're strong souls, so we last forever. Every year, on this

day, he wakes up and throws a hell of a tantrum."

"Why?"

"*No clue. Probably not happy about being dead, or something.*"

I roll my eyes. Before I can ask anything further, they vanish. I'm left with the silence of night and the eerie pitch. Sighing out, steadying my heartbeat, I turn to take in the room. It's long, but the ceiling isn't very high. Something rattles over by the lone table. Slowly, I move over there. Next to a tall cart is a pile of debris. Just looking at it reveals boxes, glass, kitchenware, and stone from the ceiling overhead. The cart itself is singed, along with the table and the floor.

"How odd," I murmur. "The rest of the building isn't singed like this."

Just as I'm about to pick up a blackened pot, a spark jumps from the rock. It doesn't take a genius to step back as fast as possible. No sooner am I out of range, a fire flares to life. It grows larger, the heat unbelievable. From beneath the pile, the floor changes. No longer is the room broken and dark. It's as though I've traveled back through time.

Debris is gone, the picture is whole… and the fire rages on around me. A beam groans and creaks, giving way and blocking the door to the store. Smoke is rising, filling my lungs and burning my eyes. The rubble before me rises off the ground, moving back onto the cart. A skeleton lies beneath it, the bones rattling as they stand up. Flames lick along the bones, gathering there until they're completely gone.

"They left me! They left me! They... they left me... left me to... left me to die... they left me!"

The tone is deep and filled with anger tinted with sorrow. In his rage, the wraith flings items cloaked in fire. I'm forced to dodge both; flames and debris. My body scoots back toward the emergency exit, yet when I lean against it… I find it locked. Go figure. The burning skeleton turns to face me, teeth scrapping together. The skull tilts a little to the side in thought.

As though a target has been placed over my head, he pinpoints me. A box filled with fire is thrown my way. I dive out of the way, almost slamming right into a burning cart. It occurs to me that the demon hasn't even spoken tonight. Usually so chatty, I had expected something more. Then again… I certainly didn't expect this. Perhaps this wraith's rage is too much for even her.

With the acrid smoke and fire working against me, it's becoming difficult to keep up. If I don't figure out how to stop this soon, I'll be yet another lost soul. From the corner of my eye, I see a fire extinguisher. It isn't wise to put much hope on it working, yet it never hurts to try… or rather… it hasn't *yet.* Sprinting with my life on the line, I leap to dodge a burning crate. The heat leaves traces of a scalding feel upon my cheek. After a somersault, rather poorly executed to keep from catching aflame, I grab it up off the floor. The only way to end this, is to end the wraith's suffering.

It won't be easy, there's no obvious trail to reach it. More fearful of smoke inhalation than fire, I charge the wraith. Thankfully, the move stuns him just long enough. I pull the pin inches from reaching him, whipping the hose around and pressing down the trigger. White foam blasts him in the face, the grinning skull lost in it. As it falls back to the floor, I empty the can on it. It doesn't take long to notice the room has returned to its former shambles.

"*But... they left me*," the wraith states quietly, its sobs causing bubbles in the foam. "*They left... They left me... to die... all alone*."

"I'm not them," I point out, triumphant. "I will *never* leave you."

"*You can't save me anymore*," he says, tone soaked in a sad tone of loss.

"And yet, I'm going to."

I kneel down beside the pile of junk, all returned after the wraith's defeat. Carefully, I start to pull it away. Broken glass is set aside, concrete brushed off, until I finally see the skull. Digging around a bit more, I uncover the rest of it. One of the smaller neck bones is loose, so I pick it up. I hold it close to me, standing back up.

"I'll *always* carry you with me," I state softly. "You'll never have to be alone again. I promise."

Already having wasted time playing 'catch', I head back to the front of the store. Tomorrow, I'll search the upstairs. As I pass the compactor, though I can't see them, I bid goodnight to the girls there. It strikes me that, of all the spirits trapped here, only a few have appeared. They're likely some of the few that kept their wits about them. They're strong, it's easy enough to see. If that's the case... how did they come to die?

Outside, the rain still pouring unchecked, I rush to my car. The bone is tucked safely inside my pocket. After shutting my door and pulling out my keys, I notice a small spark in my mirror. It's a tiny orb of light, lingering in the backseat. It makes me nervous, especially with the incident earlier.

"Okay, stop and go. If you're friendly, I don't mind you staying," I comment. "But I would appreciate knowing either way."

The light lists a moment, and then turns green. It's only a moment, but it's enough for me. Putting the car in gear, I head out for the street. My seat belt is tight, eyes squinting against the downpour. I see no zombies or ghosts.

Another car comes zooming from the opposite direction. They're not paying attention, drifting over to my side of the street. Heart stopping in my chest, my foot slams on the brake. They see me at the last moment, doing the same. We're going to collide, I know we are. I close my eyes, waiting for the crunching metal and broken bones. It never comes. Chancing a glance, I peek an eye open. Everything has stopped. The light in the backseat is glowing brighter, growing larger, and both cars are lifted off the pavement.

"… Whoa," I murmur. "Thanks for that."

"You're welcome," it answers.

The voice is that of the burning spirit. The other car is set down first, speeding away. Mine is next, yet I don't hurry. Unlike my other encounters, I feel perfectly safe with this one. The wraith and the girls of before are the only ghosts I felt safe with. They're good people with bad endings, nothing more. I'm going to change those endings, though. I'm going to save them. Spirits lifted, I focus on the road before me. The light floats to the passenger seat, resting in the middle of it.

Chapter 16

Heather is still awake when I reach her house. I can see the light in the living room. After turning off the car, I wait a few minutes. It's still raining pretty hard and I just dried out, I don't want to get wet again so soon. Inhaling to ready myself, I throw open the door. It doesn't matter how fast it's executed, the rain will always win. By the time I reach the door, I'm soaked again.

"Honey, I'm home," I call out. "And I need like five towels."

"I have one," she smirks, walking into view.

"Thanks," I sigh, grateful, as I take the offered towel. "The store was crazy today. I almost burned to death!"

"I really don't like you going there, Catori. I mean, I understand why you have to, but that doesn't mean I have to like it. This is seriously dangerous."

"I know, I'm being as careful as possible," I frown. "I even made a friend tonight."

"Oh? That light that followed you in?"

"That's the one."

I take the bone from my pocket and show it to her. It doesn't take much to explain it, leaving her wary of our visitor. I'm in the kitchen, trying to pull together dinner, when she finally comes to terms with it. She asks for the bone and, though I'm nervous giving it up, I allow her to take it. The light doesn't follow her. I regard him a moment. He needs a name, much like the others, but this one is special. He'll be with me a long time.

"You need a name," I remark. "Do you remember yours?"

"*No*," he admits.

"Then I'll have to choose one for you," I hum in thought. "How about Shadow?"

"*Better than nothing, I suppose,*" he answers.

Now that that's out of the way, I concentrate on dinner. With the manner of his death, I'm uncertain about using a flame to cook. Shadow doesn't seem to mind it, though. He just stays a good distance from it. The best I can pull together is spaghetti. Master chef, I'm not. When the pasta is finished, I start on the sauce. It's just the kind in the jar. By the time I have everything on the table, Heather is coming back. She holds out her hand to give me something. When I set mine beneath hers, she drops a smooth stone.

"What's this?" I ask.

"Nana was in the jewelry trade when she was alive," she explains. "She used that bone to make this ring for you. That way you don't lose it on accident. I'm sure you wouldn't, but… better safe than sorry."

"Thanks, Heather," I smile. "This is great! It's beautiful, it really is. See, Shadow? Isn't it awesome?"

"… Shadow?" Heather frowns.

"It's his name," I inform. "He has to have a name."

The light turns green, circling the new ring. It just fits when I slide it on. On the bottom, stretching around half the band is the infinity sign. It means 'immortality' in the Wicca symbol book. On the top, where gemstones are normally set, is a triangle. That one means 'fire'.

"Any special reason for the symbols?"

"Your family's element is fire. You'll be stronger with the symbol on your person," Heather offers, sitting down to eat. "The other was Nana's idea. It was probably wishful thinking."

"Well, I love it. I'll thank her before bed tonight."

We sit down to eat. The silence is companionable interrupted only by a quiet hum from the spectral light. I had set a place for Shadow as well, but I'll take Nana's down to her. She rarely leaves the basement, after all. I know they won't eat it, but the offering is polite either way. Heather sends a few glances toward the ball of light. Her expression is curious just as much as it is mistrustful. I don't know what to say about it.

"Where did it come from?" she frowns.

"The store," I shrug.

"I thought they were all tied down to the store," she comments. "Are you sure this one is friendly?"

"He saved me from dying in a car crash."

"… I'll thank him for that. But… that doesn't ease my mind any. Why did it follow you? The others haven't stayed around like this."

"I don't know, but… I think some of the spirits there are fighting the demon's hold. I mean, there are many souls trapped and only a few have shown themselves. I don't think they're capable of being overpowered, their wills are very strong."

"So… is this one attached to the store?"

"I don't know. Are you controlled by the demon?" I ask, getting a red light in response. "I guess that's a 'no'."

"Of course the ghost is going to say 'no', it's going to kill you for that demon."

The table rattles at that moment, plates lifting off the top. Heather sucks in a sharp breath, leaning back in her chair. As I grab my plate from the air, drawing it closer to get the last of my food, the ball of light flickers. Tiny flames dance along it. Heather's spaghetti starts to burn, my friend crying out in surprise.

"She's only joking," I wave off. "I know you aren't going to kill me."

"*She didn't leave me,*" the spirit states firmly. "*She didn't... she didn't leave me. I won't leave her.*"

"Okay, okay," Heather says. "I'm sorry! Stop burning my food!"

The fires stop, disappearing in a poof. As the table sets back on the floor, Heather glares in my direction. With a shrug, I offer her the rest of mine. An exasperated sigh is my answer, yet she still takes my food. It doesn't matter, I'm full anyway. As I lean back in my chair, my eyes drift to our new house guest. It *is* odd he's following me, yet I'm sure he has an easy explanation.

"How is it possible?" I question aloud. "How are you able to follow me like this?"

"*I wanted to,*" he answers. "*I died in the store, so I was trapped there. You came and took me with you. You won't leave me, so I won't leave you.*"

"The demon really doesn't have her claws in you?" Heather gapes. "Seriously? Why would she overlook you? You seem to be a strong spirit, the perfect feed for her… uh… so to speak."

"*She feeds off me, but she doesn't control me. I died there, that's all. She never deals with me and I only showed up this night every year. I sleep for the rest. Now that I'm not anchored to the store, she can't even feed off me.*"

"You're not anchored there?" Heather frowns. "Where are you anchored?"

"To her… and her ring. It's a piece of me, that's all that's needed. I may not have passed over, but I can. I choose not to. She didn't leave me, so I'll never leave her."

It warms the heart, the loyalty this one specter shows. When dinner is over, I help Heather clean off the table. The plates shiver before floating into the air, dancing over to the trash. Afterward, they're flowing to the sink. It might not be much, however the offer warms Heather to our new guest. We wash dishes together, as we normally do, and then retire to the living room. Before I sit down, I pick up a plate I had made and placed in the microwave.

"Going to see Nana?"

"Yeah. I want to thank her for the ring."

"Okay. I'm going to put in a movie."

"Not another horror story," I frown. "The last one was active enough."

"Comedy it is."

At the basement stairs, I turn on the light and start down. Nana is drifting around the counter, reading a book set atop it. When I step off the last step, she turns to send me a questioning gaze. With a smile, I hold up the plate and walk over. It's set upon the counter, just far enough away from the book it won't spill.

"I brought you dinner," I say.

"I do not eat."

"I know, but I thought it would be nice anyway. Thank you for the ring, it's so beautiful. I really appreciate it."

"You have a ghost of your element following you. It will strengthen you all the more. Be careful, though. As beautiful as fire can be, it can also be just as dangerous. You need to learn to sway it. Though… I feel you already know how."

"He's not bad," I offer. "He's a good person with a bad ending. The demon, though… it doesn't control him."

"Fire cannot be controlled, child. It can merely be directed."

"She doesn't direct him."

"Then you are stronger than her."

"Thanks, Nana. I'll see you tomorrow."

"I have no doubt of that."

I return to Heather upstairs. She's already passed out on the couch, drooling a bit on her pillow. The ball of light is drawing a blanket over her. I'll wake her in a little while. Calm from the talk with Nana, I walk to the back of the house. Her bedroom hasn't been touched since this morning, as per usual. It won't take long to get ready for bed, I'll wake her after.

When I'm comfortable in my pajamas, I get ready to return to the living room… and I'm stopped. Unable to move my own body, fear starts to bubble up in my chest. Blackness leaks from the walls like blood, covering them completely. Slowly, it starts moving toward me. It's so agonizing, the wait. I almost wish it would hurry up and finish me. Breathing is becoming harder, my lungs aching in my chest. The panic is just so surreal.

When the darkness touches my shoe, I'm consumed by it. My head spins, stomach lurching, and I find myself in a strange room. A woman is sitting at a table, lunch spread before her, murmuring to herself. Now fully in control of my body, I make my way to her. Every step seems harder than the next. Halfway there, I can hear what she's saying.

"*I'm such a pretty girl*," she mumbles, tone soaked in hysteria. "*Such a pretty girl. So pretty... so pretty... I know I am... I am... Don't you think?*"

She turns and my stomach drops like a stone. It's not her lunch before her, as I first thought… It's her face. Bleeding muscle and tendon faces me. Her lips are torn off, eyes ripped out. Small veins once connected to them hang loose from her eye sockets. Her face, skin porcelain and perfect, is stretched out on the table. A scalpel is beside it, stained with her blood. I'm paralyzed once more.

"*I can make you pretty, too, you know. It won't hurt long. The bleeding stops... eventually.*"

She feels around for one of her eyes, lifting it up and shoving it back in place. Afterward, she grabs her knife. Her progression is slow, killing me on the inside, but it gives me time to think. I glance around and notice there are no mirrors here. She did all that without seeing the end result. I wonder, for only a second, if it would change her mind. Before she can touch me with that blade, I open my mouth in an attempt to talk my way free.

"Do you have a mirror?"

“A… mirror? No, I don’t. Why?”

“Well, I would like to see what you do.”

“I’m going to take your eyes first, that way you can see.”

“It’s just not the same,” I argue. “How can I truly appreciate your work if I can’t see it? Looking from a mirror is like looking from another person’s eyes, I’ll see what they see. I want to know how beautiful they’ll think I am.”

“… I think there’s one in the bathroom. I’ll go get it. It’s not like you’re going anywhere.”

I wait with bated breath as her footsteps walk away. The click of her heels echos down the hall. After a few minutes, a door creaks open and slams shut. It only takes a few moments, and then the scream sounds. It’s bloodcurdling, a shriek fit for a banshee. Had we been in the same room, I’ve no doubt I would’ve gone deaf. The sobs come after, confirming my suspicions. The room rattles, walls falling away. The floor disappears from beneath me, by body plummeting into the dark.

I hit the carpet with a thud. Back in Heather’s room, I breathe a sigh of relief. This is the best pain I’ve ever felt in my life. The bedroom door opens and I tilt my head back to see Heather, the wisp floating behind her.

“What are you doing lying on my floor?” she questions.

“I love your floor,” I comment. “It’s so soft and fluffy… and safe.”

“I missed something, didn’t I,” she frowns.

"I'm not even going to tell you, I don't want you throwing up. I almost did… It took a lot not to," I admit. "Let's just go to sleep, I'm exhausted."

"*You must have met the 'pretty girl',*" Shadow comments. "*I know her, but not in life. She really was a pretty girl, an aspiring model, but the store got to her.*"

"I so don't want to know," Heather groans. "My stomach is too weak for this."

Getting to my feet, I follow her to bed. I send an uncertain look toward my wisp, yet brush it off. If Nana thought he was dangerous, she would never have allowed him in the house. When Heather turns out the light, I stay awake a while longer. I'm afraid to go to sleep, I don't want to have that dream again.

"*I won't let them hurt you,*" the wisp assures.

"Thanks."

There's no answer, but I can feel a warmth upon the air. Spending so many centuries a vengeful wraith, I can't see him having made many friends in death. Right now, though, I know he had hundreds in life.

Chapter 17

In the morning, I'm woken by a crackling sound. The smell of smoke is light, yet I can still smell it. Panic shoots through me, my body sitting up in seconds. The house isn't on fire, though. It's just the wraith. He's turned into a small flame, sitting high enough off the ground he won't catch anything aflame. Heather is already awake and out of the room.

"Thanks," I smile. "I slept like a rock."

"*You're welcome.*"

"Let's go pester Heather."

I climb out of bed and walk out the door, Shadow floating over my head. Heather is at the table with a cup of coffee. She only uses it when she's cramming, so I'm rather surprised. When I sit across from her, she pushes a bowl over to me. It's filled with cereal and milk. I eat quietly, watching her read on her laptop. Finally, she leans back and looks over to me.

"I couldn't wake you to save your soul," she says. "If it weren't for your heartbeat, I would've sworn you were dead."

"I had a little help with the nightmares," I smirk. "What has you cramming?"

"I'm looking up the history of your family's clan. I figured I could track the book's movement from it. Maybe even find it, or a copy of it. If we're going to find out what killed that demon, your family's book is a must. That's they only place that we'll find the cause."

"Wouldn't it be in my attic?"

"Not necessarily. If your mother was the next in line, I have a feeling she would've sold it or something. Maybe even burnt it. I'm not sure if you have a family member that was labeled the 'black sheep' either. If you did, they likely practiced and would've taken the book in order to protect it. You probably wouldn't have known them growing up or anything."

I frown and tap my chin in thought. I know there are a few members of my family we don't talk much about. My father's parents are on that list, along with my mother's half-sister and a couple uncles. I know their stories, though, and none included witchcraft. Then again, how much was true?

"I'll try and talk to my dad today," I sigh. "But no promises. He's had a pretty hectic schedule lately. Short of showing up at his job, I don't think I'll get a chance to talk to him alone."

"It can wait for now, you've been strong against Sylvian," Heather sighs. "I'll keep tracking it through the net, just in case. What are you going to do today?"

"I'm not sure," I admit. "I would like to gather that book from the archives, but I'm not positive it's been cleared. I'll go find out, I've nothing better to do until tonight."

"Okay, but be careful. Just because the sun is up, that doesn't mean you're safe."

I nod in understanding, finishing up my breakfast. When I leave the house, Heather is still glued to her screen. Shadow comes with me, though I had no doubt he would. My new ring is warm around my finger, reminding me of our unconventional bond. Climbing into my car, I turn it on and pull out of the driveway. The drive is quiet and peaceful. My guard is up the whole while, but I wish it didn't have to be. The day is so beautiful and nice out, I would like to enjoy it on some level.

At the library, I can see a few officers around. There's no yellow tape outside. I'm not sure what the protocol for a suicide is, yet I'm praying they don't ban me. Taking a calming breath, I step inside. There's a morbid air here, a reminder of the victim lost to us.

Teenagers, more excited to be questioned than they should be, linger about. There are no children here today. I don't even bother asking, as I catch sight of the tape. It's over the doorway in a large 'X'.

"Back again?" the new librarian asks.

"Uh… yeah, but… I guess it's for nothing," I sigh. "I'll have to look elsewhere for my investigation."

"On that cursed store?" she hums to herself. "You could ask some of the older people around town. A lot of them know about it. The curse isn't taken seriously by the youth, but we're still wary of it."

"Is there anyone that might know about the witch?" I question. "Uh… I mean… the woman that hung herself in that ritual?"

"No, I'm afraid not. She was long before even my time," she admits. "All I have are stories passed down over a hundred years. You know how those go, changing all the time."

"… I'm not saying you're into it, but… well, I'd think you know a lot about this place and it's history… I was just wondering if… maybe you..."

"Spit it out, honey," she chuckles. "I'm an old bat, I've heard just about everything in my years."

"… Do you know anything about the witch clans?" I ask hurriedly.

"Surprisingly, I *have* heard that," she smirks. "I know much about them, my grandmother was a white witch. She used to tell me stories when I was little. What would you like to know about?"

Relief washes over me in a waterfall, my breath leaving in a grateful sigh. Together, we walk over to the counter. Another woman is there, younger though not by much. I pull up a chair and sit at the table nearby, the elderly woman doing the same. I can see her name tag today, not blinded by death. Her name is Rowan. No last name.

"My family is descended from one of the first clans," she offers, voice clear and proud. "I used to practice when I was younger, at my grandmother's side. My mother never really cared to take it up. She taught me of all the clans."

"Did you hear about the witch Sylvian?"

"I did, but no one liked to speak of her," she frowns. "From what I heard, she turned dark and practiced black magic. She was caught during a witch hunt."

"She was hung."

"No, she wasn't," Rowan corrects. "I don't know how she met her end, but I know it wasn't that. My grandmother told me she was mistaken for another. She learned this from her friend, who was the head of the parent clan."

My heart skips a beat, opportunity singing like a choir of angels. If I can learn about the most recent clan head, maybe I can learn what happened to the book! Almost too eager, I jump on the chance. The question falls from my lips before I can stop it, stopping Rowan's train of thought.

"Do you know what happened to her? The head of the parent clan, I mean."

"I do. She grew old and her children placed her in a home," she explains. "When she died, they were given what she wished them to have… and then I suppose they sold the rest."

"And the grimoire?"

"It was given to the child she chose," she smiles. "The one she felt could best carry on her legacy. Unfortunately, I never met them. They decided against meeting with the rest of us, but still contact us about current events."

"So… they're still practicing?" I wonder. "But… why not meet?"

"I don't know. Maybe they're just honoring their mother's last wish. I'm afraid that's all I know, dear."

"... What clan are you from?" I try, praying she's not from Sylvian's.

"I hail from the Western Winds," she smiles. "The element of water. Now... why are you so interested in the clans? Are you looking to join one?"

"No, not really," I smile softly. "I'm working on the theory that the curse was placed by a witch. I think the grimoire the witch was found with, held the spirit of Sylvian. She was sealed inside that book. When the witch opened it, she was possessed by the demon version of Sylvian. Now that demon lingers in the store, feeding off its many kills."

"Demons are no laughing matter, child. I suggest you give up on this endeavor."

"I... I can't," I frown. "The demon has targeted me. My only chance is to defeat it. I thank you for the information, I really appreciate it. I'll try back again for the archives."

I get up and turn to leave. Rowan doesn't stop me, though I hear her defeated sigh. That really was more than I was learning in the archives, but I still want that book. There's this feeling in the back of my mind, that it can help more. Hoping I can defeat this evil without it, I step out of the library.

There isn't really much for me to do right now. The sun is still high in the sky, and Heather is taking care of everything on her end. Which is more than my end. I only have to worry about investigating the store... and surviving. I'm doing well on both for now.

To waste a bit of time, I drive close to my house. Neither parent is home. Determined to enjoy my day, I park back at Heather's and walk inside. Some down time will be good for the both of us. I say nothing as I walk in, gripping her wrist when I find her in the living room. Together, we walk out the door.

"Where are we going?" she wonders in the car.

"The mall," I state. "We need to relax a bit."

"... You're kidding, right?"

"Nope. We need a break, and I'm bored. I heard a new movie came out yesterday, it's supposed to be awesome. And then we can grab a bite to eat after."

"Well... I guess that'll be okay."

On Sundays, we usually go out for lunch. It's been a tradition since I arrived a few months ago. Today, however, feels different. Her mind is far away and my guard is on high alert. It's not the relaxing time I was hoping for. After parking in the vast parking lot, we get out and start walking. I like walking, it gives me time to clear my head.

A car flies by in front of me, and Shadow bumps into the back of my head when I stop. Glaring in the direction they went, I finish the trek to the front doors. Heather seems more relaxed, her eyes taking in the entrance. The clothing store is here, so we'll have to walk through it to reach the theater. Heather loves clothes. We're not there three minutes and she's dancing in excitement. There's a new black dress that just screams her name.

"After the movie," I comment, pulling her along.

"*You'd look the bomb in that*," the wisp says excitedly. "*Especially with a gold chain belt and some high heels. Ooh, girl, we could deck you out!*"

"I like him more and more," Heather grins.

I laugh at them, shaking my head. Heather just may have found a soul-mate. The mall is busy today, hundreds of people crowding the walkways. So many are chatting on the side, running about to view new product, and sitting around the food court. Surrounded by so much life, I sigh in relief. There's no way this moment can be destroyed.

Together, we walk over to the movie theater. It's on the second floor of the mall, so we have to take an escalator to reach it. Stepping in, my eyes immediately turn to the large screens. They're set over the registers, displaying movies and their times. Usually, Heather picks the spookiest movie there. This time, however, we decide an action movie is a better choice. The last thing we need is for the ghosts to start crawling out of the screen. I think we would both piss ourselves.

After getting the tickets, popcorn, and Icees we walk in to our theater. We're lucky enough to get first pic of chairs, seating ourselves in the center of the stadium seats. More people pile in soon after. Heather is to my right, already munching on popcorn. When the light go dim, I get comfortable in my seat. The screen flickers to life, entering the beginning of the film. The person on my left, one seat between us, turns to look at me. Out of the side of my view, I can see their face. Their head jerks about like a video game glitch.

"What the..?"

"What's wrong?" Heather whispers.

"N-nothing," I return. "Let's just watch the movie."

Although I can feel her gaze upon me, heavy with suspicion, she returns her attention to the screen. A few viewers in front turn to look at me, once more a glitch centers on their heads. The theater goes completely dark, leaving me wary of what comes next. The screen lights up, but the movie isn't where I am. I'm seated in a chair, surrounded by the dead. My heartbeat picks up, the scene changing between the theater and the store. It happens so quickly, as though I just blink and it's wrong.

My hand seeks out Heather's, squeezing it firmly. By now, I know she's aware I'm panicking. Although she goes to stand, I pull her back into her seat. This demon won't beat me, I won't let it. A spark glows faintly near my head, reminding me of my new friend. He seems to understand what's going on. Without any warning at all, a fire ignites deep inside me. My skin is too warm, practically melting on my skeleton. When I open my eyes, there's a tunnel of fire around my vision. Everything on the outside is warped and dreary, a film between the living and the dead. Through the middle of it, all that melts away and I'm seeing the movie. At first, I try to fight it. My eyes glance over at a skeletal hand, the boney fingers reaching to grip my wrist.

"*It can't hurt you, or I'll hurt it,*" Shadow states, a vicious tone beneath the assurance. "*I'm blocking it. The same thing that keeps me from the demon's control, will protect you here. But you can't fight me.*"

I inhale, slow and deep, and then exhale. Every muscle in my body relaxes. The fire starts to lessen, left in a comfortable coat within my veins. It's more bearable. My hand loosens on Heathers, her gaze checking in on me. When it's obvious I'm better, she turns to the hero on the screen. The corpses leave me, moving on all fours toward her. Like parasites, they gather around her and reach out.

"Don't even," I hiss quietly.

As though testing me, they hover their hands over my oblivious friend. Heather continues munching her snacks, eyes now glued to the fight scene. One of them ruffles her hair, which she swats at as though it's a fly. The second time it happens, she's a little more aware. Before she can question the glare I'm giving her, my hand darts out and grabs the nearest wrist.

"I said… don't... even," I growl out.

All eyes are on us. What they see, is my hand behind Heather's head. I'm too busy glaring at the unseen specters to be embarrassed. Heather looks between them and me, giving a sheepish chuckle.

"Sorry," she offers. "I almost ruined the ending. She *really* loves the surprise."

Raising confused brows, they all turn back to the screen. Heather gives a relieved sigh, slouching in her seat a bit. When she's positive they're all preoccupied, she whispers over to me.

"What's the matter?" she whispers. "Should we leave?"

"No," I comment. "I just… they're *everywhere*! They keep trying to touch you."

"… Like… creeper touching?" she shivers.

"No, like annoying little brother 'I'm not touching you' touching. It's driving me crazy!"

"… Seriously?" she frowns. "Just watch the movie, don't worry about them. I'm not a part of your curse, so they can't hurt me. They want your attention, so don't give it to them."

As hard as it is, I force my attention away from her. My ire burns as hot as the wraith's flames. It makes it hard to enjoy the movie. Although I keep glancing over, I don't say anything more. After a short while, they get bored and start to vanish altogether. When they're gone, Shadow separates from me. The rest of the movie goes without interruption.

"That was so cool!" Heather cheers upon exit. "We should go see it again!"

"Maybe tomorrow," I chuckle. "Right now, I'm starving."

"You should've ate more popcorn."

We take the escalator down to the food court. There are still a lot of people around, mostly grouped at tables with their phones. We're lucky enough to find a small table empty. Heather stays there to save it and I go to get our food. Tacos and pops are on the menu today. As we sit in companionable silence, we people watch and eat our food. There's a fountain nearby, the water feature spouting crystalline waters. It sputters and stills. Black goo pours from it, filling the fountain and spilling over. It bleeds up from the tile cracks, covering the floor. I pull my feet on my chair, careful not to allow another incident like the last.

"What's wrong?" Heather wonders, setting a taco in front of the empty chair.

"The floor is bleeding," I answer.

"… That's a new one. Isn't it usually 'the walls are bleeding'?"

"But it's the floor this time. Black goo. It's all over the floor and in the fountain, and… Good lord! There's an eyeball by my chair!"

I stare down at it, almost gagging as it rolls back to show off veins. Next to it, fingers reach and a hand follows. It tries to touch the seat of my chair. With a gasp, I relocate to the table. Heather is quick to move our food. Once again, all eyes are on us.

"Don't worry, she's just really dedicated to the upcoming play," Heather calls out. "Isn't her acting marvelous? So real. She'll be a hit on Broadway someday!"

She claps her hands with a sincere smile, getting the others to join in. While they enjoy my 'acting', I'm trying to get away from the rotted hand searching for my foot. A light passes my head, dropping down to sink into the black goo. I gasp and reach for it, ignoring the boney fingers on my wrist. In a flash, the light reminding me of a flare, all the black goo is gone.

Afterward, he floats back up and to his seat. I thank him quietly and return to mine as well. My audience turns their attention now that I'm finished. Now, completely flustered with my supernatural stalker, I down my food.

"I'm ready to leave," I say in defeat.

"You and me both," Heather smirks. "I don't have many more excuses for your insanity."

"Funny," I chuckle. "Ready to go, buddy?"

"... *I wish I could eat my taco*," he says forlorn. "*I really like tacos*."

"Sorry," Heather frowns. "I wish you could eat it, too."

I stand up and he slowly floats away from his taco, ending to hover over my head. I'm beginning to feel like a computer game character. Heather is at my side when we walk out, dodging cars and rude visitors to get to the car. Inside it, I lay my head back on the headrest and sigh. It's getting late and I have to get back to that damn store.

"Heather..."

"I know, I know," she murmurs. "You have to go there tonight. Please, don't remind me."

"... They're using you to get to me."

"They can't hurt me..."

"They hurt Sadie."

"I'm not Sadie. Trust me, Catori, they can't hurt me," she insists. "No matter what you do, never let them use that. I *swear* to you, they can't touch me. *Never* give up because they threaten my life. Do you understand?"

"... You better be right."

"I am."

Her tone is convincing and fearless, easing my mind. She knows me so well. She could probably hear my thoughts, see the plan starting to form. As much as I don't want to, I trust her. If she says they can't harm her, I'll trust that. If I don't and she finds out, I'll be better off dead. I put the car in gear and head to Heather's. The drive is so quiet. It's filled with unspoken words and heavy hearts.

Chapter 18

After I drop of Heather, I take the drive to the store. I can drive it in my sleep by now, I think. Speaking of sleep, my eyelids are heavy with the lack of it. My body feels weary and drained, a weight on all my limbs from fatigue. Although I've been sleeping, I haven't been getting any rest. It's going to take more of a toll on me than the store's guest list of specters. The only thing that keeps my eyes open, is my passenger. His light is so bright, it's impossible to block it out.

I'm uncertain about taking him with me. He may not have been bound to the store, but I have no doubt the demon might try when he returns. My eyes leave the road for only a second, trailing to look at him through my peripheral vision. At a red light, I take the opportunity to speak to him.

"Are you sure about going back?" I ask. "I don't want that demon to get to you. You were lucky enough to get out of that damn place, I might not be able to pull it off twice."

"*I don't fear the demon there,*" he offers.

"I just don't want you trapped like the rest."

"*We're all trapped. Maybe not in the store, but on this plain. That's what a ghost is; a trapped spirit. There or here, it's all the same to me.*"

His words don't inspire much hope in me, yet I leave him to his decision. In the end, he's the only one that holds sway over his actions. When I park, I wait a few more moments. He's already floating out of the car. With a soft sigh, I follow him. At the door, the small spark of a wraith bursts into a tower of flames. Through the door, he takes a more human shape. He's a big guy, with dreadlocks and bright eyes. A teddy bear is the first thing that comes to mind. To think that this man was the wailing spirit seeking vengeance… it just doesn't click in my mind. He looks back to me and smiles. Such a bright action in this dreary place, it seems to light it up in a way his fires can't.

"*I worked up here for a short time,*" he remarks. "*The girls I worked with were really nice. I went before them, but I couldn't save them... I couldn't save any of them.*"

"It's not your fault," I offer. "There was a woman that tried to warn everyone, but they couldn't see her like I could. The others probably couldn't see you either. At least you tried."

"*I wanted to scare them all away, so they wouldn't get hurt, too. I wish I could've. I was one of the first, you know. The building burned the very day it was erected, the day I died.*"

"We're going to save them, I promise," I state.

"*You shouldn't make promises you can't keep,*" a woman says.

I already know the voice, so it isn't a surprise when I turn toward them. The woman from the baby department is sitting on a counter, the register behind her opened. The wraith hurries over to her, lifting her into a big hug.

"I thought you done lost your damn mind," the woman huffs. "Every year you went crazy. We couldn't even go near you! I'm so glad you're back to your old self."

"Me, too."

"Where the hell have you been?"

"I'm staying with Catori and her girlfriend."

"Heather's not my girlfriend," I respond moving toward a ragged display of shoes. "She's my best friend."

"Mm-hmm. That's why you two look at each other with those goo-goo eyes all the time. Don't think I haven't seen it, it's only every other second."

I roll my eyes at him, going back to the display. The two catch up while I wander, eager to face the demon that's plagued me. One of the shelves is broken, an assortment of shoes spilled along the floor. Many are brand names. Glancing back, I shrug and head toward the kid's department. Along that wall is the door to the break rooms upstairs. The intercoms have yet to speak, but the offices should be up there as well.

At the door, I realize there's a keypad. Thankfully, the door's been broken for far too long. I push it open without issues. Along the stairs is a strange goo. It looks like spit turned to slime. The stuff coats the steps on the edges. Time has torn up the walls, the drywall cracking in places. The long metal railing has been pulled clean off the wall in a couple spots. It certainly won't be any help clearing the slime. With a huff, I steal my resolve and go to step up.

With a gasp, I move away. The slime is glowing and moving listlessly. I only just now notice it on the ceiling as well. It slides to the middle and gathers like a raindrop. A face looks at me curiously, long hair falling to hang beneath her.

"*Hi*," she grins.

"Uh… hi," I answer, fingers in an unmoving wave.

"*If you don't mind, can you wait for me to pull myself together? I'd rather you didn't step on me. I mean, I'm dead… yeah, I get that… but it's still rude.*"

"Sorry, I… didn't know it was… uh… you."

"*You must be the new recruit! Welcome to the family! I hope you're as interesting as you seem. It's been pretty dead around here, maybe you can liven it up.*"

I watch as all the slime is pulled together. Her head slides along the wall, across a step, and onto her body. When it reaches her shoulders, it stops and she's no longer slime. She's small, short and muscular, with long brown hair. Her features are petite and cute, her attitude rather peppy. It's obvious she enjoys having fun.

"What… pray-tell… happened here?" I ask.

"*Isn't it obvious? We all died.*"

"No, I mean… here. In this stairwell. The cause of your death."

"*Oh! Why didn't you just say so? Someone sent in a grenade. I thought it was a dud and slipped it into my pocket, but I forgot about it. When I was coming up for some paperwork, it fell out of my pocket and... well... BOOM! No more me,*" she comments. "*It was a real blast! Get it?*"

She laughs at her joke, reaching over to grip my wrist. It's a gentle grip, so I allow it. She leads me upstairs. At the top and to the right is another doorway. It leads into lockers, that immediately start slamming. I cover my ears against the noise, grimacing in their direction. The small woman reaches over and pats the large collection on the side, silencing them for now.

"*That's the time clock,*" she explains. "*Not that we need it anymore. To the left is a hall that will take you to the break rooms, straight ahead will take you to the restrooms and offices. Have fun, but not too much fun. Too much fun can kill you here.*"

She poofs away, leaving the wet footprints of her sneakers behind. I take the hall in front of me, eager to reach the office. On the right are hangers filled with coats, most of which are barely recognizable. On the left are the bathrooms, a door to a small office, and another at the end of the hall for the larger office. That door is locked, the lights out, and I hear no sound. Grumbling to myself, I turn toward the smaller office. When I step in, the computer flickers to life with static on the screen.

There's another door open to a supply area. From what I can remember, this area has a spot with a hinged gate. I'd rather stay away from potentially fatal areas like that.

Upset I don't get to pester the one irritating me, I walk over to the break rooms. The first is the small one, with a fridge, sink, table, and snack machines. The sink is clogged, the murky water home to some manner of fish. It circles the drain quietly. One of the snack machines has broken glass, the food moldy and disgusting. Out of the pop machines pours an endless supply of blood.

"… Wow… gross," I mutter.

A glance into the microwave and I nearly puke. Tiny little arms reach from the caked on food. I back away slowly, never removing my eyes from them. Taking the small room as a lost cause, I walk over to the larger one. In a far corner is another door, a large cocoon of spider silk set just in front of it. A woman sits at a table, staring at the wall. There's a television that doesn't work, a couple more microwaves, and two more tables.

"*I thought I was pretty*," the woman mutters, tone lost. "*I was pretty… so pretty… now? I… I thought I was… I thought…*"

"Excuse me, but… should I be worried about a giant spider?" I ask timidly.

"*Spider? No. That is another death, but they're sleeping. They only come out in the morning hours.*"

"Morning? Really?"

"*They love the sunlight. I did, too. I wish I could feel it on my skin again. Just… just one more time… just once…*"

She's getting more depressed the longer she talks, so I keep the conversation short. I've already upset her, I don't want to make things worse. Without the ability to break into the large office, there isn't really much I can do. With a frown on my face, I leave the tortured soul alone. The hallway groans, black sludge dripping from the walls and ceiling. I dodge a couple drops, passing the time clock and turning toward the office.

I'm determined to find a way into those offices. There has to be something there to help. With a small sigh, I walk in and sit at the computer. The swivel seat is barely comfortable, one wheel squeaking and a spring in the seat sticking out. For a moment, I try to imagine myself as one of them. I turn in the chair, eyes circling the walls. Where would I place a clue? Where would I hide something important?

With nothing standing out, I tap a couple keys on the computer. A yellowed piece of paper, protected by the tape over it, tells me the password. Once it's entered, the home page comes up. There are a few files on it, their titles rather vague. I click on the one that says 'store 1084'.

"Welcome to… *your grave*... store 1084," a happy voice says, an underlying whisper divulging the truth. "This is a wonderful store devoted to our customers. Our small family… *victims*... are expected to work… *suffer*... hard to make them happy. Our history is a rich one, starting with our founding lady… *demon*. For more information on our store, please click the link."

With nothing better to do, I shrug and click the link. A video appears, automatically playing. It's a scene of the first store. As it gets closer, fire blasts from the windows. I can hear the screaming, taste the acrid smoke on my tongue. The video changes to a thousand different deaths, a thousand different victims all crying out for mercy. My hands cover my ears, yet my eyes are glued to the screen.

It seems like everything is getting hotter, the heat prickling along my skin. I finally manage to tear my gaze away. Flames lick along the walls, the thick smoke gathering at the ceiling. With a gasp, I rush from the office, nearly slipping in the hall. The stairs are taken two at a time. When I break free from the doorway, I can see fire singing the whole store. My wraith friend and the baby section lady are waving their hands. They frantically attempt to lead me to safety.

I dodge a falling beam, heart pounding in my throat. When the door comes up, I don't even open it. Instead, I jump through a broken window and roll out on the concrete. Stepping away from the building ablaze, I realize… it's not showing out here. I can hear the flames crackling and I can hear the phantom screams, but there's no evidence outside.

"What the..?" I murmur.

"She's good, isn't she?" the wraith comments. "She has to be, to fool so many people."

"Fool?"

"Yep. That fire isn't real, it's a trick on your mind. If your mind thinks it's real, than it'll hurt you. It's really hard not to believe it, though. That's how so many people die here. Stress and tricks on the mind."

"Well… she's had long enough to perfect it, I guess. Come on, let's get out of here. I don't think I can take the screaming anymore tonight."

“*Screaming*?”

I stop there, turning to study him. He can’t hear it like I can. It’s odd, considering he’s on the same plain as them. My brain is tired, though, and the screaming sounds like nails on a chalkboard. With a tired sigh, I continue on to the car. Turning back into a small flicker, the wraith joins me. The drive back to Heather’s is long, taking me past my own house. Surprisingly, I see my father’s car in the driveway. I park and head inside, the spirit following over my head. My mother isn’t in the house when I enter, but my father is in the kitchen.

“Hey, dad!” I state. “How was your night?”

“It wasn’t so… bad,” he says after a moment of hesitation, eyes glancing over my head. “I was just getting something for dinner, want to join me?”

“Sure!” I smile. “I wanted to talk to you anyway, about grandma.”

“What do you want to know about your grandma for?” he frowns, making a couple sandwiches.

“Well, I didn’t really know her,” I comment. “But this investigation into the store, has lead me down some interesting paths. One of which being the new librarian. Apparently, she knew my grandma… who was a Wiccan of the parent clan. I need her book, her grimoire, to study the demon that placed a curse on the store.”

“… Have you been smoking something?” he wonders. “If the answer is yes, we won’t tell your mother as long as you stop tonight.”

“Dad, I already had this talk with mom,” I frown. “Heather’s family is part of another Wiccan clan, so I know it’s true. Don’t lie to me, okay? I wouldn’t be asking if it weren’t detrimental. Please tell me which side of the family it is, I need that book.”

“… Are you in trouble, Catori?”

“Yes, but I can’t explain it all right...”

"You went into that store and are now part of the curse," he states, eyes half-mast and tone monotonous.

"… Okay, so… no explanation needed," I comment, sheepishly.

He sighs and takes a seat, sliding a plate over to me. Together, we sit down to eat. This is a place I find myself more often than not. I'm more like him than my mother, so he understands me better. It's easier to talk to him. Unfortunately, it's also something I don't get to do. It's always late night chats after a stressful day, and before a good night's sleep.

"Dad, I asked mom about it and she blocked me," I state. "This isn't something I have the luxury of ignoring right now. That store is lethal, and it's not staying where the foundation is."

"I can see that," he frowns, pointing his fork at my new friend. "Is that the demon from the store?"

"Him? No, he's a victim of the store," I remark. "He was one of the first. I'm guessing the fact you can see him answers my question."

"My mom was a Wiccan," he sighs. "I'm her youngest, so I was always with her. I can see the spirits and I know some spells, but… when I met your mother, I promised I would never deal with it again."

"And you lied," I point out. "The woman at the library, she said you're still involved. Just not physically."

"I am. I promised my mother, I was the only one that could see what she saw… I never thought it would pass to you, though. Had I known, I would've involved you more. Demons and spirits can be very dangerous, you needed to be prepared for all this."

"It's not your fault," I assure him. "But there is something you can do to help. I need to find the parent clan's grimoire. That's the only record of Sylvian's true death."

He stills a moment, setting his fork back down. His expression is thoughtful, a soft hum leaving him. I've seen this look before, the look reserved for puzzles. I have the same look, learned from him. Something must've risen in his memories. Patience isn't a strong point for me, yet I manage to stay quiet long enough for him to continue.

"Sylvian… my mother told me of her. She practiced the dark arts, was extremely powerful. They sealed her soul inside her own grimoire after her death. Is that the demon in the store? How did she get loose?"

"Long story," I wave off. "I'll tell you all of it when I get the chance, but right now… I only have four days left to live. I need that book, that way I know how to kill the demon Sylvian's become. Where is it?"

"When your grandmother passed, everything from her Wiccan life was willed to me. Your mother, however, refused to let it passed the doorway. All her things are stored in a unit in town. The book might be there as well."

"Is there a key?"

"There is, but your mother keeps it with her. You know… just to be safe. I don't understand why she's so against a little ghost now and then. It would make things so much more interesting. I'll try to get it from her when she gets home. Now… what's this about having only four days to live?"

"Nice talk, dad!" I cheer from the doorway. "We should do this again sometime! Bye!"

I shut the door between us and book it for the car. My poor friend didn't even realize I was sneaking for the door, passing through the door to hurry after me. My father isn't even opening the door before I'm peeling out of the driveway. I needed the information, but I'll never get that key from my mom. This might end in possible jail time, because there's only one way I can think of to get to that book. And it might not even be there. What if she burned it? Would she do something like that?

When I reach Heather's house, my mind is so distracted I almost pass it. In the passenger seat, the wraith takes control of the car. When the wheel fights my hold, I'm snapped from my musings. We're parked without problem and I murmur a 'thank you'. Inside the house, the lights are flickering. It's strange enough when it happens at the store, so this is starting to unnerve me. My new friend seems to read that. He flits over to float before my face, keeping me in the car.

"*You fear for your girlfriend, but you don't have to. She's a special person, the spirits of the world can't harm her.*"

"So what's going on there?"

"*They're just trying to scare her. The demon knows she's trying to help you, so she's trying to force her away from you. It won't work, though. She really loves you.*"

"... You think?" I ask, a little blush on the bridge of my nose. "I mean, we're really good friends, but..."

"*She does. I'm happy for her. People like her don't typically find love.*"

"People like her?" I frown. "What's that supposed to mean? You mean, those labeled witches for their beliefs?"

He's already floating over to the house, though. With a questioning gaze, I decide to store it away for another long drive. Opening the front door seems to be a cue of some sort, as the lights completely blow. I can hear the shattered glass on the floor. Heather doesn't say a word. For only a moment, I fear she may have been harmed. When I walk into the living room, however, I'm stunned at what I see. With all the furniture floating about, screams and howling from disembodied voices, and blood dripping down the walls of the room… Heather is completely unfazed. She sits on the couch, wrapped in a blanket with a book. Next to her is a flashlight, which she's turned on to see the print. She looks like she's weathering a storm instead of a supernatural haunting. As I watch, she reaches toward the coffee table and picks up a mug. The table floats away, yet hesitantly returns when she clears her throat in warning.

"That's what I thought," she states, setting the cup back on the glass top.

"This is what you do in your free time?" I chuckle. "Pester the spirits that are supposed to be scaring you?"

"My forte is dealing with spirits," she grins. "One of the perks of having one in your basement. How was the store? I see you're still alive, so it probably wasn't all that great."

"It was interesting," I shrug off. "Apparently, one of them was killed by a giant spider. I learned a bit from the small office, but I can't get into the larger one. I think that's where Sylvian is hiding out. When did the party start?"

"Not long after you left," she says. "It wasn't all that bad, once they learn their place."

"I'm sure you have your mysterious ways," I smirk, sitting beside her. "I talked to my dad while I was out. Seems he's the secret Wiccan in the family. He told me where to find the book, but… mom has the only key. He's going to try and get it from her, but I wouldn't hold my breath. Hopefully it's in the unit."

"I'll think of something," she assures. "Right now, however, I'd like to think about sleep. Which probably isn't going to happen if your uninvited guests don't leave."

"Uh… right," I blush. "Hey, buddy, can you help us out, please?"

"*Of course,*" the wraith comments.

His fire gathers around him, pulsing outward to wash the room in warmth. The furniture drops to the floor, some of the chairs toppling over in the process. I know a few scratches are on the wooden floor now. With a sigh, I stand to correct the positioning. Heather waits a moment, making sure they're all gone, and then stands to help. It doesn't take long, and then we're heading back to get ready for bed. Dressed in pajamas and raiding the kitchen for a snack, I leave Heather to fall asleep first.

I throw in a bag of popcorn, pushing the button the microwave. With all that happened in the theater, I didn't get the chance to enjoy it there. When it's finished, I pour the fresh popcorn in a big bowl and toss out the package. I eat as I walk back to the bedroom. Heather isn't asleep yet, skimming through her book.

"Ooh! Popcorn!" she grins.

"Didn't you have enough at the theater?"

"I can never have enough popcorn."

I laugh and sit beside her, my eyes sweeping the pages of her book. There's a lot of handwritten notes scribbled down, a bunch of symbols I'm only just learning, and a few highlighted spaces. She closes the book and digs into my snack.

"I didn't find much on your demon," she says. "I looked through as much history as I could, even looked through the grimoire again, but there's just nothing. On a brighter note, I learned more on containing and destroying demons. Especially containing them. We need to figure out how to trap the demon until we can destroy it."

"Don't worry, four days is plenty of time," I wave off. "Let's get some sleep, okay?"

"… If you say so."

I set aside the bowl, now empty, and she moves her book to the bedside table. The second we turn out the lights, our heads hit the pillows and we're out. Sleep is a welcome visitor after all the stress today.

Chapter 19

The next morning, I'm tempted to stay home. I need to find that book and I can't do that from school. Pushing myself forward, I crawl out of bed and wake up Heather. She's less than eager as well. While brushing my teeth, she enters the bathroom and sits on the side of the tub.

"We can't go to school," she says. "You have three days left, Catori. We don't have time to waste there."

"I know," I sigh, spitting out the toothpaste. "But we can't stay home, either. My mom will flip if she finds out. She'll never let me around you again."

"I'm sure she'll understand if we just..."

"Explain it to her?" I laugh, humorless. "A demon could be strangling me right in front of her, but she'll deny it unless it's an actual person. She doesn't believe in demons and ghosts and magic, that's why my dad has to send messages behind her back."

"That's ridiculous, she's your mom," Heather frowns. "Your life is in danger, we need to be spending this time on saving it. School can wait."

"I'm going," I sigh. "I know you don't want to, but… I have to. If you want to stay here, I'll understand. But don't you *dare* go to that damn store!"

"I won't go, I promise," she assures. "But I'd really like you to stay with me. I want to keep an eye on you. Unlike me, the rest of the school won't be so easy with a haunting. I have a feeling that's reason enough for them to pay you a visit there."

I know she's right, yet I don't readily agree. Perhaps it's just wishful thinking, or the desire to have a 'normal' life until the end. I finish getting ready and head out to the car. As always, my wraith is above my head. When I pull out of the driveway, I can't help looking to

Heather. She's standing in the doorway, waving to me. My heart swells at the sight.

School starts the same as always, however I can sense something lurking in the shadows. Near lunch is when the bomb finally goes off. The bells suddenly go off along with the sirens, lights flashing and popping, papers caught in phantom winds. If I weren't the one being haunted, this would've been the highlight of my senior year.

Students are screaming, running about with no particular destination in mind. The windows all shatter, shards of glass raining down on everyone. There is no order, not anymore. The teachers try so hard to calm the masses. Hands reach from the dry-erase boards, gripping shirts and faces. The lab teacher has bloody scratches across his cheeks.

"Everyone head outside," he calls. "Walk in an orderly fash… No, don't run! You'll trample..! Someone get that kid before he kills someone!"

"Don't be so dramatic," I comment, rolling my eyes. "They're all scared, orderly fashion doesn't exist right now. Just let them get to the doors and they'll be fine."

"… Why aren't you panicking?"

"You have no idea the shit I've seen this past week," I comment. "This is a poorly conceived prank in comparison."

With that, I wander over to the felled student. With one good jerk, he's back on his feet. I monitor their movement, making my way to the front doors. A wailing woman flies past, head barely hanging onto her neck. She passes through a few students, cackling at their renewed screams. Out on the lawn, the principal is trying to count heads. It seems everyone is here, huddled into a large mass like scared sheep.

"What was that?" someone asks.

"It's the store's curse! It's coming for us!" Eric panics. "I told you guys that was a bad idea!"

"Eric, you're so full of yourself," I comment. "You probably set all that shit up to get out of class early."

"I did not!"

"Enough!" the principal huffs. "At any rate, we're not having class inside today. We'll just have to have it out here."

There's a moment of hesitation, yet the students are happy with the decision. Well… they're happy until hands reach up from the ground. The screaming starts up again, everyone struggling to get away from the reaching arms. I kick an arm and step on a hand.

"Okay, everyone go home," the principal tries. "I'm canceling classes today!"

Everyone bolts to the cars. I take my time, unwilling to get run over because of a stupid haunting. No doubt, this was an attempt at killing me. The trampling could've done me in easily had I gone with the rest. Thankfully, I'm stronger than a few upset spirits. As I slide into the driver's seat, my wraith appears in the passenger side.

"So, where were you?" I smirk.

"*I don't like school,*" he answers. "*But I didn't want you to go either. Heather was right, you need to focus on surviving.*"

"Traitor," I comment, smirk only growing. "Let's go home."

"*Home… I like that,*" he says, glowing brighter in happiness.

When the last of the cars leave, I put the car in drive and pull out. I never expected my new friend to team up with Heather, but it's not unwelcome. At least I have a good excuse for missing school today. The drive back is slow and careful, my mind focused on nothing but the road ahead.

When I reach Heather's house, I park the car and head inside. She's not in the living room, nor is she in the kitchen. I find her out in the backyard, tending to a small herb garden. She normally doesn't go there unless she's upset about something. The foliage calms her.

"Hey, honey, I'm home," I call out. "How's the garden coming along?"

"What happened to school?" she frowns.

"When you're right, you're right," I shrug. "Major haunting, no casualties. Principal canceled school for the day. Then again, with the way his face looked, it might be longer."

"At least we have a little more time today. We should attempt getting that key from your mom, or at least look into the storage unit."

"There's no way we'll get that key," I frown. "Thankfully, we can check on the unit. We might not be able to get in, but at least our spectral friend can sneak in. He'll be able to survey what's in there, save us the trouble of jail time if it's not in there."

"The more you say 'jail time', the more I feel like a criminal," she sighs. "It's only one lock, it's not like we make a habit of breaking into places."

"Let's go," I chuckle. "Maybe we can sneak in a good lunch or something. It won't take us too long to peek in."

The roads are still as we head to our destination, yet my guard is ever strong. There's no telling when another attempt on my life will happen. The next intersection is a dangerous one. There has been countless accidents there in the past, so one more won't alarm anyone. It's to be expected by now. When I pull up to it, I take a deep breath to calm myself and look both ways.

No one is coming from what I can see. I pull out carefully, eyes wide and searching.

There's a blaring horn to my left, a speeding mustang slams on their brakes just as I do. The tires squeal against the asphalt, leaving black marks and the smell of burning rubber. I can't breath, my eyes focused on Heather's face. It's twisted in shock, her eyes closed tight as she leans away from the door. For a moment, there's a sense of utter relief. I just breath out and close my eyes. My body relaxes and I can't help thinking this absurd haunting is finally over… but the twisting metal never comes. No impact at all… just silence.

"What the hell?" Heather questions. "I thought dying would hurt more than that."

"*You really think I'd let my favorite living people die? I'm insulted,*" the wraith comments from the backseat.

"… You can freeze time?" she gapes.

"*No, but I can levitate stuff like nobody's business. I also know how to start fires, leave writing on walls, make the ceiling bleed, rearrange furniture, turn water to mud… that's great in washers. It really freaks people out.*"

"You're just a textbook on haunting, aren't you?" she frowns.

"*The majority of that is basic. It's the fires that are rare. Shit like that is connected to the spirit itself. Depending on what kills them, it gives them power over that element.*"

"And fire is a very difficult element for the dead to control," Heather points out. "Even for those that died in it. The stronger the spirit, the better the chance of connecting. Catori was lucky to come across you."

"*I was luckier. Without her, my mind would still be lost to torment.*"

I step on the gas and the car pulls forward slowly. The other car is at the stoplight, its driver dazed and confused. That's all I take the time to see, my eyes back on the road ahead of me. That wasn't the demon trying to kill me, just coincidence. Unfortunately, those keep popping up now that I'm expecting foul play.

The rest of the ride is uneventful. When I park in the lot outside the main office, we take a moment to gather our thoughts. This unit belongs to my father, so I have no legal right to raid it. I shouldn't even be allowed near the units behind the chain-link fence.

"What are we supposed to tell him?" I wonder.

"I don't know," Heather shrugs. "Let's just tell him the censored truth."

"… Censored truth?"

"Yeah, like… Hey, my dad owns a unit here and left a book in it I need," she comments. "He might say no, but it's better than asking for 'a magic book, that might hold the key to defeating a demon in a haunted store'."

"… Good point. Let's just play it by ear."

She nods and opens her door. As we walk up to the store, we catch sight of an older man inside. He's fumbling with a ring of keys. Just by the uniform, I know he's a security guard here. Hopefully, he'll know my dad and make this a little easier for us. A bell chimes when I open the door, drawing attention to us. Although the guard says nothing, he's very sharp. I can tell by his eyes. Another man stands behind a desk, arms crossed over his chest defensively.

"May I help you?" he wonders.

"Hi, my name is Catori Hashna," I respond. "My father owns a unit here. I was looking for a book yesterday, and he told me it might be in his unit. Is there a chance I might be able to retrieve it?"

"… Hashna… Hashna," he murmurs, skimming a book in front of him. "Ah, here it is. Unit number one thirty-two."

"Excellent," I grin. "So, do you have an extra key..?"

"If you don't have a key, I can't let you in," he comments. "You're not on the list, so you can't access it without the key. It says here, only Miriam and Henry Hashna are allowed in."

I groan and turn my face to the heavens. Why can't anything go easy for me? This is inhumane! No one should have to suffer this much in one day! Heather pats me on the shoulder, drawing me from my misery. The security guard is still watching us, but I'm positive it's because he's pegged us as 'problem children'. There's no way he doesn't know my father with that look.

"Okay," I sigh. "I'll see if I can get the key from my mom."

We walk outside and to the car, yet don't get in it. I pull myself up onto the hood, leaning back to sun my face. It's warm out today considering the weather. Heather sits beside me, yet she leans forward to rest her arms on her thighs.

"Am I gonna be a spy?" the wraith wonders, tone crackling with excitement.

"Unit one thirty-two," Heather smiles. "Can you find it?"

"I sure can. What does the book look like?"

"Leather bound," she answers. "There should be metal locks around it, probably no title."

He doesn't say anything more. The ball of light floats through the fence, bobbing around as he sings his own theme song. We have nothing to do aside from wait, yet the security guard isn't giving us much choice. He's already outside, pacing near the door. Thankfully, there's a small diner next to this place. Hoping he'll think to look there, we walk over that way. There's no reason to take the car, it's only a short distance.

Upon entry, another bell rings. There are a couple waitresses and cooks on the clock, a few customers scattered about, and the smell of fresh pie in the air. My stomach rumbles in answer. There's no seating, so we just pick a booth. It doesn't take long for the waitress to wander over. She sets down a couple menus and takes our drink orders. Everything looks so good, it's hard to choose just one thing. Plus, I'm starving. Debating what to get, I decide on a burger and fries. It's always a good time to have a burger and fries. When the waitress returns with our drinks, we tell her we're ready to order. Notepad in hand, she jots them down and walks off once more.

"Do you think he'll look here for us?" I wonder.

"He'll know where we are, he's connected to you," Heather assures. "I'm just hoping that book is in the unit. Without it, we're running blind."

The two of us keep quiet as our food is set before us. The second our waitress is out of earshot, we continue the conversation as we eat. The food smells delicious and tastes just as good. I forgo the ketchup on my fries, the seasoning all I need.

"If the book isn't there, what then? How will we find out what killed her?" I question, picking up my burger.

"... Let's just hope it's there."

"But if it isn't? We have to plan for the worst, Heather," I caution. "This can't be our only plan, something always goes wrong. That's why they invented the backup plan."

"If it's not there, the store is our only hope. There has to be something there, something in the way they try to spook you... A clue fashioned from her own fears."

"... Well... there's a lot of blood," I offer. "And the suicides are almost all hangings."

"No, hanging isn't the answer. We already ruled that out," she sighs. "And I don't recall any witch that was sentenced to death by bleeding. There has to be something else."

"I'll keep an eye out for repetition tonight."

She looks down on her plate, stabbing her salad. I know what's going through her head, yet there's nothing I can say to soothe her. I need to find out as much as possible before my time is up. The rest of our meal is quiet, both of us lost in thought. When we're almost done, the wraith floats through the window beside us. I set a small plate of fries over in front of him.

"*I found the unit*," he offers. "*A leather bound book is locked inside a cabinet there. It looks like you described. The lock on it is special, though. I think it's sealed by magic. Someone didn't want it going anywhere.*"

"Perfect," I smile. "Now we just have to break in and take it."

"I don't know, Catori," Heather frowns. "Magic seals are super dangerous. They're only used on a couple occasions… one of which is to seal away harmful magic. This could very well be another demon locked up."

"… Should we chance it?" I wonder.

"Ask your dad why the lock is on there. I don't want to chance it if there's another demon. One is bad enough, this town can't handle a second."

It's not a thought full of rainbows and sunshine, but it's the truth. The first demon has done quite enough without adding a second. I'll have to pass by the house before heading to Heather's. If my dad is home, we might be able to get our answers faster. If not… it'll be yet another night of survival.

Chapter 20

After we finish eating, we head back over to the car. The security guard isn't there now. Once we're back on the road, there's really no place for us to go. Our only hope for answers is lying just out of reach. With nothing else to do, I just start driving.

"Nowhere to go?" Heather wonders.

"Dad doesn't get off work for a long while, the library won't tell us what we need, and the only clues we have won't be available until later," I sigh. "Do you have somewhere you'd like to go?"

"Out of town," she remarks. "Another state maybe. Across the globe. Anywhere but here."

"I wish," I laugh, humorless. "I can't leave without defeating that damn demon. Too many people are going to get hurt."

"Why'd you have to be such a good person?" she mutters, arms crossed over her chest. "Can't you just let the world burn?"

"Sorry, Heather, but you know the answer to that."

She sighs heavily, slouching in her seat. My father is likely sleeping at this hour. I don't want to wake him. With nothing else to do, I decide to take a whimsical trip. My mother should be at the hospital. Maybe I can convince her to hand over the key. When I turn in that direction, Heather sends me a curious gaze.

"Where are we going?" she asks.

"The hospital," I explain. "Mom should be there."

"You're going to try for the key?"

"Hell yes I am! I'm tired of this endless nightmare."

"We still have to talk to your dad."

"I know, but… we need something to do. I can't just sit still when my life hangs in the balance. Besides, having so many witnesses might benefit me. If she doesn't want me talking about it, then she sure as hell won't want people hearing about it."

"Smart," she smiles.

She sits back in her seat, happiness renewed, and I continue on my path. In the rear-view mirror, I can see our little fiery friend. He's just floating there, fires small in his content. The hospital isn't a long drive, so we're there in no time. When I park, I can see Heather is having second thoughts. My mother has a very strong, and opinionated, personality. It's no secret Heather ranks low on her list of preferable friends. Now that she knows where her bloodline is, she's going to be less friendly.

"If you want to stay here, I'll go in by myself," I offer.

"No, I can do this," she decides. "Let's go."

She exits the car, waiting for me to do the same. Together, we head up a small path that rounds the parking lot. The doors swish open for us, a blast of heat chasing the cold back outside. The smell of bleach is everywhere, drowning out all other scents. I always hated it.

Mom works on the third floor, so we have to take the elevator. As I wait for one to open, I listen to the nurses chatter. They've lost patience for some of the visitors. A ding turns my attention, the doors parting. We step in and I hit the button we need. As the doors starts to close, I get a sour feeling in my gut. It's too late to stop the elevator and get off.

"What's wrong?" Heather questions. "You look like you're going to puke."

"I think I want to," I mutter. "Something just hit me wrong. I think..."

I don't even get to finish, the lights going out. We're trapped between the second and third floor. Heather hums to herself, reaching over to hit the buttons a couple times. Nothing happens. With an exasperated sigh, she hits the speaker button. It's for emergencies only, so the nurses should be on the other end.

"Hey, can we get some help over here?" she wonders.

She's answered by static. I watch her frown, her lips turning down as her brows scrunch. Her finger hits the button again, yet nothing happens. I can only shrug when she looks my way. Once more, she hits the button.

"Hello? The elevator is stuck, can you help us out?" she asks again.

"*My apologies,*" an all too familiar voice comments. "*This delay won't take long, I promise. Due to supernatural malfunctions, the elevator has but one destination... the end. Thank you for playing, Catori. And thank you so much for giving me another soul to feed off of. I'll see you tomorrow for your first day of work. Until then.*"

The lights come back on and the elevator goes up, but it passes the third floor. Now I know that pit in my stomach wasn't my imagination. The numbers above the doors light up, progressing faster the higher we get. 5, 6, 7… the lines squealing as we're knocked to the floor with the velocity… 10, 11, 12. I swear I saw a little curl of smoke above us, slipping through the creases in the maintenance hatch door. At floor 20, Heather forces herself to crawl over to me. We're practically plastered to the floor. I hold her close, the two of us huddled in a corner. Finally, the elevator stops at floor 34.

"We sto...AHHHH!" Heather screams.

The elevator has suddenly dropped. The lights on the numbers are moving erratically, not even matching up with the floors at times. Our hearts are lurching, Heather's arms cutting off my airway. I feel weightlessness taking over, lifting us off the floor. We're pressed against the ceiling, gravity slamming against us in the fall. My only solace is that Heather is above me. I'll hit the floor first, hopefully breaking the majority of her fall in the process.

"Where's that overgrown firefly when you need him!" she shouts.

"I… I don't know," I frown. "I thought he was right behind us."

"I told you he was a ghost spy!"

"We should be getting close to… the end," I whisper. "Anything you want to get off your chest?"

"I love you!" Heather cries. "I wish I would've dragged you away from that damn store! I knew you shouldn't have gone in there! I'm so sorry I wasn't a more controlling girlfriend!"

"I love you, too!" I say, tears in my eyes as well. "I'm sorry I didn't listen to you before I went in! I never should've dragged you into my problems!"

We both scream, hugging each other tightly as we cry. I hear snapping cables and grinding metal as we near the bottom. I feel the impact, twisted metal screeching in my ears… and I'm still alive. Shocked, I open my eyes and look to Heather. Her eyes are closed tightly, nails digging into my skin. When I turn to look beneath me, I see a transparent mass of red. Confused, I try moving. It feels like I'm trapped in a circle of jelly.

"I think we're fine," I comment.

"W-what?" Heather squeaks out.

"We're still alive."

"We are? How?"

"She locked me out of the top floors, but she forgot the basement," Shadow remarks. *"I'm sorry you had to fall for me to save you, but I wasn't going to leave you... Never."*

The mass gets smaller, carefully moving us away from the ceiling. By this time, I can hear voices on the other side of the crushed doors. A crowbar hits the metal, the loud tap seeming to echo in my ears. When they're forced apart, a couple men look in.

"Oh my god!" one gasps. "There are people in here! They're still alive!"

"But, how? That was thirty-four floors!"

Ignoring the question, one of them reaches in for us. My legs are like jelly as I move toward the door. I support Heather, making sure she gets out first. As I crawl from the wreckage, I can't even look back. I know how bad it must look and I don't want to see it. If I do, my food isn't going to stay in my stomach. Cold washes over me, goosebumps tearing along my skin. It could be shock, or it could be the hand of Death hovering above me.

"Are you two okay?"

"Just shaken up," I assure.

"Hey, you're Gwen's daughter!" some states. "Oh my god, she's going to flip when she finds out. Come on, I'll take you upstairs."

I know the man from my past visits. He graduated medical school with my mom. Jase is a nice enough guy, but he's such a worrier. He's the type to check on a patient three times before they even know he's needed. Most of the elderly patients enjoy his company, but the younger ones find him a tad annoying.

As we climb the stairs, I can't help noticing the crackle of my friend. He's steamed, both figuratively and literally. I reach over and dare to touch the fire there. It's meant to be reassuring, but I'm not positive it got through to him. He's still sizzling when we step onto the third floor. Mom is standing by a reception desk, a clipboard in her hands.

"Gwen!" Jase calls out. "Your daughter is here."

"Catori? Is everything okay?"

"She nearly died in the elevator," he frowns. "Of course she's not okay. She's lucky to be alive."

"Thanks, Jase," I sigh. "I can handle this."

He walks away after patting me on the back. Heather takes a seat, nearly falling into it in her exhaustion. My mother takes note of that… and the sheet white that's taken over our faces. She pulls another chair over and motions for me to sit. I'm not about to complain, so I take the seat.

"What happened?" she asks. "Those elevators were just serviced, they should've been working perfectly."

"I'm not going to get into specifics with you, mom," I sigh. "You're not going to believe me, so I'd like to skip the upcoming fight."

"… Okay," she says warily. "What are you doing here?"

"I wanted to ask you for the key to dad's storage unit," I remark. "But at the moment, I just want to kiss the tiles and bawl in joy that I'm still alive. So, if you'll give me a minute to collect myself, we can start arguing after."

She glowers and stands perfectly straight, her arms crossed over her chest. I know that look, so stern and almost evil. She's not giving me anything but the boot. I lean back and groan, staring at the ceiling. One hand reaches over to grasp Heather's. I'm sure it's not lost on my mother.

"What do you need from there?" she asks.

"A book," I comment, tone weary. "Not to do any magic or anything. It's a history book."

"… I don't remember putting a history book in that unit," she says in suspicion.

"Did you even really look at the stuff you threw in that unit?" I challenge. "You don't strike me as the type to give a second glance to magic stuff. You wouldn't even get me a magician set as a kid."

"… What did your father say?"

"He said he was going to try and get the key from you," I offer. "But since I have nothing to do today, I figured I would at least try. If not, that's fine… I'll break into it later."

"Catori!" she gasps.

"Oh please, don't look so surprised," I remark. "It's not the first time I've picked a lock, you know that. You should be happy I'm telling you, instead of doing it and lying later."

She says nothing, yet doesn't go for the key right away. If she wants more of an explanation, I'm leaving. I don't have the patience for this, especially when I almost died. I've heard a situation like that can really change a person. Me? I'm two seconds away from driving to that damn store and torching it! How dare they try and hurt Heather! She's not part of this craziness, they should've left her alone.

"I've tried very hard to keep that out of our family," my mother states quietly. "You have no idea the strain it put between your father and myself. I certainly never planned on you finding out."

"Surprise," I say. "Can I have the key?"

"This isn't easy for me, Catori," she bites out. "Your father may not see this as wrong, but I do. Stuff like that doesn't exist, it's all pointless hopes and broken dreams. If you go in there, I'm afraid I'll lose you to that side of the family. I almost lost your dad, I can't lose you."

"I almost *died* five minutes ago," I glare. "And it wasn't a problem with maintenance. If you don't want to lose me permanently, I suggest giving me the key to that unit."

"You won't die because you can't enter that unit," she glowers back.

"I beg to differ. You might blind yourself to the supernatural world, but that doesn't make it go away! The ghosts will always be around you. You can keep ignoring them, I don't care, but I can't right now! So, you have two choices. Trust me and give me the key so I can win this morbid game, or keep it and let me die in a few days. I'm good either way, I came to terms with both outcomes."

"You better not have," Heather growls out, squeezing my hand.

"Catori, I don't have time for this nonsense," my mother huffs. "Go home. We'll talk about this later."

"And that's code for, 'your life means absolutely nothing to me'," I comment. "I told you. Let's go, Heather. Maybe there's still another way to find out how she died."

"I hope so," Heather states softly. "I can't lose you either."

We stand and walk toward the stairwell. I don't need much for our plan tonight, so I'm hoping to kill a bit more time. My father should be getting up around now. At least we'll find out why that cabinet is sealed. As we wander out to the car, a can feel a happy warmth on my back. Curious, I glance over at Shadow. Instead of hovering above my head, he's drifting in a lazy pattern.

"What's gotten you so happy?" I wonder.

"I have a key," he states, almost like a secret.

"Okay," I draw out. "Where did you get that?"

"*From around your mother's neck.*"

"No… way," Heather gawks. "You ghost thief… I'm so proud of you!"

"*I'm a spy and a thief!*"

I shake my head, chuckling at my friends. All of us enter the car and I start it up. As we drive away, the heavy feeling I felt in the hospital is left behind. The roads are clear, the sky slightly cloudy, and the air is cool. I usually love the autumn time, yet find myself wanting with all this craziness.

When we reach my house, my dad's car is in the garage. He's left the garage door open today. After parking, we get out of the car and walk in. My father is in the kitchen drinking a cup of coffee and reading the newspaper. At the sound of our footsteps, he glances up and waves in greeting. I sit across from him.

"Hey," I greet. "Quick question… why is the cabinet holding grandma's book sealed?"

"… Okay, now it's my turn," he frowns. "How do you know it's sealed?"

"*I'm a spy!*" Shadow states dramatically.

"He may have wandered in while we were eating lunch," Heather remarks, tone innocent. "We have no control over this one, he's just so stubborn."

With a roll of his head, he goes back to his paper. He doesn't seem nervous one bit. Shadow dares to get closer, curious about the news today. As he hovers just behind my father's shoulder, I wait for him to say something. Instead, he sets the paper in front of the chair next to him.

"There you go," he offers. "Page twelve has a rather good story on it. As for your question, I don't know. I noticed my mother had sealed the cabinet when I picked it up. She hadn't said anything about it, which is strange, but she kept a diary. I left it in the storage unit."

"What does it look like?" Heather wonders, hoping Shadow managed to see it.

"Um… a leather bound book decorated in feathers," he muses. "Real feathers. And there's a pretty round gem in the middle. I think I left it in a box on top of the cabinet. Did you talk to your mother?"

"I did," I frown. "She refused to help, so I told her I was going to break into the unit tonight. Then when we left, Shadow told me he 'found' a key. It was the one around mom's neck."

"Go figure," he chuckles. "Well, you have the key. Go find that diary and figure out why that cabinet is sealed. Be careful, guys."

"*I take good care of them*," Shadow states, tone proud.

"Someone needs to," my dad smirks. "They have no clue how to stay out of trouble."

We say goodbye and shuffle out. Back in the car, I can breathe easier. It's not the book we need, but at least it's a bit closer. I drive back to the storage area, walking into the office… and stopping. A splash of blood paints the back wall, just behind the counter. My body trembles as I step closer. I take a calming breath, leaning over to look behind the counter. The man from before is laying on the ground, his white shirt stained red from blood. There's a massive hole in his head, one eye blown straight from its socket, and brain matter is along one cheek.

That calming breath did nothing to help. I straighten out and walk back to Heather, ushering her back outside. I push her back in the car, telling her to stay put. Afterward, I search out the security guard. Steps slow and reluctant, I move along the side of the building. A storage unit is broken open. It's filled with tools and a few guns.

They're all pulled out and set on a table, bullets spilled all over the ground.

My heart beats like a drum in my ears. As I step around the corner I hear a bang. My body freezes, waiting for the bullet. All I feel is warm liquid splashing over my face and torso. I keep my eyes closed tightly, praying it's not what I think it is.

"Please don't be blood," I mutter after wiping my mouth. "Please, please don't be blood."

"Catori?" Heather calls out. "Catori! I heard a shot, are you..? Oh my god! Are you hurt? Where were you hit?"

"I wasn't," I remark. "How bad is it?"

"Uh… you… you've looked better. You're very red… I think there's some brains on you..."

"I thought so," I huff. "Is it the security guard?"

"… It is. He's much worse off than you."

I feel cloth on my face, wiping the blood off. When she's done, I open my eyes. Her sweater is a mess, her smaller frame shivering in the cold. I take off mine and put it over her shoulders. It was wrapped around my waist and didn't take any damage. The key is in the pocket.

"You take that key and go to the unit with Shadow," I say. "I'll call the police and wait here for them."

She nods, though hesitantly, and walks off with Shadow. As soon as they're out of sight, I dial the police and wait for the answer. The conversation isn't a long one. As I wait for them to arrive, the wind starts to bite into me. Warm liquid slowly cooling, leaving my clothes damp against the cold.

At the sound of sirens, I'm impressed at the speed. Just as before, I see my father's friend first. For a moment, I wonder just how bad this looks. I've just found three dead bodies in less than a week… it can't look too good. When Ray's standing before me, his expression is mirroring my thoughts.

"Are you going for a world record or something?" he wonders.

"Hell no," I frown. "You think I *like* looking like this? This is disgusting! If I could replace my blood with anti-bacterial soap right now, you know I would!"

"Okay, okay," he chuckles. "Simmer down. What happened this time?"

"Heather and I were here to get a couple books from dad's unit," I explain. "When we walked in, I noticed the blood spatter behind the counter. The manager is on the floor there. I couldn't imagine that happening with the security guard around, we had seen him as well earlier. That's when I found out I needed the key. I walked around the unit here, and there was a shot. Hence my awesome new style. I think he shot himself, but I wasn't looking. My head was turned before the shot, and I closed my eyes. I didn't open them again until Heather ran up. She's in dad's unit right now, those books are really important. I'm sorry I sent her in anyway. I didn't think it mattered when it wasn't the crime scene."

"It's okay, but I wish you both would've stayed here."

"You can check the security camera," I offer, pointing toward it. "You'll see we didn't touch anything. She cleaned my face up, but the sweater she used is right here. Mine didn't get dirty and she was freezing. I gave it to her to use."

"Thank you, Catori," he sighs. "And I still know where you live, so if I need you I'll be in touch."

"How is the investigation going on Sadie's death?" I wonder.

"… Just like you said it would," he whispers. "Everything you pointed out is right. I wonder if these two aren't connected to it as well."

"I didn't check," I admit. "But I think they are. I was just in here this morning, I can't believe it happened so fast."

"Don't worry, I'm sure it'll end soon."

"Yeah, I know that's right," I state softly. "I'm going to find Heather, if you don't mind."

"I'll want a statement from her as well."

"We'll swing by, I promise."

He lets me go and I search out Heather. As I walk, I can hear the footsteps of someone else. When I speed up, so do they. However, when I try and locate them… there's no one. Paranoia is eating at my mind. It follows me all the way to unit one thirty-two. When I enter the unit, Heather is sitting atop the cabinet. Not the very top, but the counter space. Shadow is snooping about the other boxes.

"Find anything?" I wonder.

"We found the diary," she grins. "Your grandma is a very adventurous woman. She's traveled all over the place!"

"Did she put anything about the cabinet?"

"She did. It says here that she came across a wraith that wouldn't cross over. It was the type that latches onto a person, not a place. Every person it latched onto found some really bad luck, eventually dying or losing everything. Your grandmother was called in to fix matters, so she sealed it away in a gem connected to her book's cover. You can see it right there," she says, pointing to the book. "When she knew her time was coming, she wrote out her will. She feared your mother would destroy her grimoire or set the wraith free, so she placed it in the cabinet and sealed it up."

"So… no go," I sigh.

"Well, I could try opening the book myself," Heather offers. "Like I said before, the dead are my forte. I know I can help it pass on. If I can't, Nana can. She could force the worst spirits to pass over. It'll take a few days, though."

"I have a few days," I smirk. "Let's get that book."

Heather nods and sets the diary down. Turning to balance on her knees, she presses her hands against the glass. It takes only a couple seconds to feel the static in the air. When the doors click open, she crawls back and drops to the floor. Petite hands pull the book down from its shelf.

"That was easy," she smiles. "I was expecting a much more difficult seal. Then again, it was for your mom… no offense."

"None taken," I scoff. "Come on, Ray wants to speak with you."

"Goodie."

The three of us head back, stopping at the office to speak with Ray. Like me, he goes through Heather's statement. Her statement mimics my own, and the security feed supports them. He tells me they had the same bruises as Sadie and the others, but the feed shows them a murder/suicide. When he has everything he needs, we get in the car and go to Heather's house.

It's getting late, but when I pulling into Heather's driveway… I turn off the car. There won't be a visit to the store tonight. The whole day was just exhausting and I can't risk dealing with the place. Not with the need for sleep so heavy. At first, Heather doesn't know what to say. It doesn't take long to brush that off, though. She hums happily as she follows me inside.

Chapter 21

The house is so quiet, bordering eerie, as we walk in. I pay no attention to it, dragging my feet through the living room. Heather is right behind me with Shadow. She takes a seat on the couch, but I collapse on it. I pull the blanket off the back, wrapping it around us. If left to my own devices, I would fall asleep right here.

"We should go to bed," Heather comments. "You head that way, and I'm going to put this down with Nana. She can study it while I sleep."

"I know 'study' is a code word for 'protect'," I comment. "You really think the demon would chance coming here for a stupid book we can't open?"

"Yes. Yes I do."

"*I'll keep a watch up here*," Shadow offers. "*You two can get some shut eye*."

"See you in the morning," I comment.

As Heather walks over to the basement door, I take a short stroll to the bedroom. For once, my mind isn't on the store. I'm just too tired to worry about nightmares and that demon. By the time Heather joins me, I'm in my pajamas and comfy beneath the blankets. I barely register her crawling into bed, already half asleep myself.

When the sun rises, I find myself alone. Not even Shadow lingers within the room. Confused, I get to my feet and wander to the living room. It's so quiet, the footsteps leave no sound upon the air. Just as I'm about to go to the front door, there's a massive boom. It deafens me. My hands cover my ears, a delayed attempt to save my hearing. The floor starts to tremble, knocking me off balance. Cracks travel along the walls.

"What the hell?" I state. "What's going on?"

I dodge the ceiling fan as it falls from above. The blades hit the floor and tear up the carpet. A crack moves along the floor as well. It rips apart, spreading as though it's on a fault. Without thinking, my body scrambles away. That side of the house crumbles, opening the way to see outside. Only… it's not 'outside'. I'm sitting in a dollhouse.

Completely stunned, I get to my feet and walk over to the edge. It's set upon a counter in store 1084. Blood drips from the roof, splashing in front of me. I gasp and back up, non too eager to repeat today. Something moves in the room outside my dollhouse. The figure is large and dark, gliding around as though on wheels. They don't seem to notice me.

A soft glow to my right catches my attention. I quietly move in that direction. I have to go back to the bedroom in order to see it, but when I get there… I'm shocked. A jar sits on a desk, filled with spirits begging to get out. Just to make sure I'm not hallucinating, I rub my eyes a few times and look again. Sure enough, there it sits. I notice a few faces I've encountered before. They're slamming their transparent fists upon the glass. All the others seem to be drifting in a haze.

A dark arm rests upon the counter, just beside the jar. It's the demon, sitting defeated at her desk. Without warning, she growls and her arm is flung my way. The entire dollhouse is sent flying. I try not to scream as I'm airborne. The house clatters to the floor and I ready myself for the impact. It doesn't come, my body slipping through an expanse of darkness.

I bolt upright in bed, heart hammering in my chest. Shadow is in the hallway, I can see his glow through the open door, and Heather is beside me in bed. It was all a nightmare. I breathe out in relief, covering my face with my hands. The mattress shifts beside me and a hand is on my shoulder.

"Are you okay?" Heather wonders, tone bleary with sleep.

"Just a bad dream," I assure. "Go back to sleep."

She pulls me back to the pillows and snuggles up against me. Although it takes me a rather long time, it's easier to relax like this. The store may reign in my nightmares, but it can't touch me in the house. Thanks to Shadow, I'm safe while I'm awake. Unfortunately, the warmth from Heather lures me back into the arms of slumber. Before I close my eyes, I can hear a voice in my head.

"It's pointless. It's never enough. It'll never *be* enough. No matter how much you give, she'll always want more. It'll never be enough... never enough..."

Chapter 22

The warm sun slips through the blinds, waking me from my slumber. Heather has long since left the bed. With a groan, I force myself to my feet. After a quick shower, I brush my teeth and head to the kitchen. Heather isn't there, so I assume she's downstairs. Although she's probably expecting me, food is first. With a large bowl of cereal, I sit down at the table.

"What are you doing up here?" Heather wonders. "You should be helping me with that book!"

"I'm eating."

"I can see that. But that book is going to save your life."

"Heather, I have no idea how to even use that damn book," I frown. "That's *your* area of expertise. You said you can open it, so open it. I'm going to enjoy my breakfast, and then figure out how to spend my day. I only have a couple left after all."

"Don't remind me," she mutters. "And I already told you, it'll take a couple days to break the seal."

"Then why do you need my help?"

"Well… it's more like… I need your *blood*."

"Grab a vial and cut me open."

She stares at me a moment, trying to decide if I'm joking or not. At the lack of smile, however, she sighs and walks over to the counter. She draws out a small pairing knife and a cup. For only a second, I wonder if the cup needs to be filled or not. No doubt it won't. If it did, she wouldn't have caved so easily.

As I eat, Heather takes my free hand. It's only a small cut, so it takes a little while to get the small cup's bottom covered. In all honesty, I thought it would be a lot more needed. When that's finished, she hands me a bandage and takes the cup downstairs. Not a moment later, she returns to me.

"What are you going to do today?" she asks quietly.

"No clue," I shrug, careless. "Maybe walk around a bit. I want to enjoy life while I can. You know... just in case."

"I wish you wouldn't talk that way."

"Heather, I need to be ready for any and all endings," I state, tone firm and soft. "As much as we hope I survive, there's always a chance I won't."

"You will... but I understand," she sighs. "Nana will study the book today. She's trying to understand what type of wraith is trapped there. When she knows, we can prepare ourselves to unleash it."

I nod, taking another bite of my breakfast. It isn't difficult to see the sorrow in her eyes. Although she's trying to think positively, it's getting harder with each passing day. Even my outlook is beginning to turn bleak. Unable to think of anything better to do, I decide the walk might be best. No speeding cars, no spontaneous fires, and no opportunity to murder me. Sounds good at the moment.

After I finish, I go brush my teeth and get dressed. When I walk back into the living room, Heather is waiting with my coat. After I put in on, she wraps her arms around my waist. After hugging her back, I head outside. The day is cool and crisp, the smell of dew rising from the grass. As I step out further, I can feel the warm rays of the sun on my face. There's a puddle on the sidewalk from late night rains.

The car is passed up. My feet taking me around the lawn and near the street. I'm not far from the house when I realize I'm no longer alone. Shadow drifts from the house, crossing the lawn to reach me. I pause only long enough for him to catch up.

"*You left without me*," he accuses.

"No I didn't," I smile. "You're always with me, remember?"

I hold up my hand to show him my ring. It warms with his happiness. My trek continues, leading me toward the bustling part of town. More cars moving through the street as I get closer, honking their horns at those in front of them. There's no traffic, only impatience. The library stands as a grim reminder of a friendship lost. I can't even look at it as I pass, so consumed with guilt.

A noise in the alleyway catches my attention, however I ignore it. Last time I checked the dark, I was assaulted with a jump scare. Just to be sure there won't be a repeat, I put a good distance between me and the darkness. Laughter fills the air and I look toward it. A small park sits just passed the library. It's filled with children at play, bringing a small smile to my lips. One of the boys kicks a soccer ball and it bounces past the fence. He chases it into the middle of the street… before a speeding car. So much for 'no speeding cars'. I take a deep breath and run after him.

Just as I reach him, I curl my body and somersault with him in my arms. I can feel the rush of wind over my back as the car passes. Eyes large and back wet from the tires' spray, I stand up and carry the boy back to the park.

"Be more careful," I comment quietly. "Look both ways before stepping into the street."

"I'm sorry," he cries.

"It's okay. No harm, no foul. Just, be more careful."

"Okay," he sobs.

"Go find your parents, okay?"

He nods, wiping tears and snot from his face. A woman is standing by the benches, face twisted in an expression of absolute horror. That must be his mother. He runs over to her, lifting his arms to be picked up. I don't wait for a 'thank you'.

There's a diner on the next corner. Not a restaurant, but fancier than fast food. At times I like to eat there. It'll be nice to sit down and enjoy my lunch. As I walk up to it, I can hear thunder in the distance. It's either incoming rain, or rain long passed. The diner has a few workers fixing the sign over the door. I don't think anything of it when I go to walk in.

I hear a twang overhead, and a loud creaking. Eyes sharp in preparation of defense, I look toward it. The sign breaks loose and swings toward me. A click on the door and I know it's been locked. Instead of rushing inside, I backtrack in a hurry. The sign swings past me, starting backward just as another twang sounds. The workers shout in panic as it falls to the cement. The edge hits and the sign falls toward me. There's no place to go but the street.

"Are you fucking kidding me?" I huff.

I bolt into the street, dodging a honking car and barely getting past a large truck. On the other side of the street, my breath is labored. I feel like the little digital frog that rarely ever makes it across. Shadow sinks to my eye level, a dark ball of fire.

"*Are you okay*?" he questions.

"Yeah, I'm fine," I sigh. "But now I'm even hungrier than before."

I can hear a faint chuckle from him as we start back. When I step up to the sign, I give it a wary glance and step over it. The door is unlocked now. A bell rings upon entry, alerting the waitress of another customer. She's there with a brilliant smile.

"Hello! Welcome," she remarks. "Let me show you to a seat."

She grabs a menu and leads me over to a small table. It's in the middle of the room, surrounded by other tables and lined by booths. It's two chairs, so I sit in one and Shadow floats above the other. I've been here so many times, I know the menu by heart. When she asks for my drink order, I just tell her the whole thing. It's scribbled into her notepad, and then she's walking away.

"*This place is so quiet.*"

"Yeah, that's one of the reasons I like it."

"*Do you think the store will call you tonight?*"

"Probably," I shrug. "By now, it's sort of expected. Why? Do you think it'll get me tonight?"

"*It's not funny,*" he scolds. "*That place is evil. I talked to my friend last time you went. She told me the demon is planning something... Something involving you.*"

I stop and look at him a moment. I remember him talking to Baby, but I can't imagine what could be happening. She always seems to know more than she lets on, though. Although the others are limited in knowledge there, she seems to be a wealth of it. With my contract with the demon, there isn't much left for her to twist about. The new development, however, feels very wrong.

"Really?" I frown. "I wonder how Baby found out."

"*Please, that girl has ears everywhere! If she don't know it, it doesn't exist. The point is, the demon knows you're going to die there... and she's happy about it.*"

"Isn't she happy about all the deaths there?" I question.

"*Not this happy,*" he warns. "*And I don't think it's about you dying. I think it's something more. I don't know what, but it's worse than death there.*"

"Hmm… I guess it's something to look into."

"*Something to look into very carefully.*"

My lunch is set before me and I put some french fries on a napkin, setting them before Shadow. The burger is large and kept together on a long toothpick. It has mushrooms and Swiss cheese. My stomach rumbles as I pick it up. For once, I don't hurry when I eat. Life is slowing down for me, preparing to stop at the end of this twisted path. I can slow down as well.

The pitter-patter of raindrops on the window sounds. A soft drizzle, nothing more. I sit and wait it out, slowly eating my french fries and drinking my pop. My mind tries to mull over the new information. What could the demon possibly want? Freedom might be one of those things. Baby did say as long as they were trapped, so was the demon. How could she achieve freedom? The train of thought gives me a headache. I pull out my cell phone and call on Heather.

"Hello?" she answers.

"Hey, Heather," I greet. "I was wondering… how could the demon achieve freedom from the store?"

"… Why?"

"Well, Shadow said Baby told him she was planning something. I was trying to figure out what she could want, but she already has a lot of power. The only other thing would be freedom, right?"

"It could be one thing," she offers. "She can never be satisfied when it comes to power, though. Greed in that area is common. As to freedom, though, it would need a compatible body. Those don't turn up often."

"… Would I be a compatible body?" I inquire.

"No, I don't think so," she states. "You don't practice, so your energies wouldn't match. You might be able to hold her, but the fight for dominance would tear you apart. One of you has to come out on top, but both of you are powerful. It would be too risky."

"Sometimes, the prospect of freedom is stronger than common sense," I remark. "Do you think she'll go for it anyway?"

"… I honestly don't know, Catori," she sighs. "Don't worry, though, okay? We almost know what we're dealing with. We'll know in time to save you."

"I trust you," I say. "I'll see you soon."

"… So you can go to that damn store," she bristles.

"I can't ignore it again tonight," I murmur. "My dreams are becoming too real. If I don't go tonight, I'll suffer another… and I don't know if I'll wake up from it."

"… Okay," she relents. "I'll have dinner ready when you get here. You can at least eat with me before going."

"Agreed. As soon as the rain let's up, I'll be home."

We say 'goodbye' and hang up. Shadow is quiet, but I can feel his focus. He was listening to the conversation. I can only imagine how angry he is. The dark fire he's made of turns red at the tips. I finish off my food and concentrate on my drink. Slowly, the rain falls into a light shower. It won't get any better.

I pay my bill and head outside. By now, the sign is placed and sturdy. Traveling the way I came, I pass the park and library. I'm wary of the street, as the roads are slick. The worse the weather, the more careless the driver. Since my attention is on the road, I miss the small stone that falls from overhead. Something crumbles and a dusting of stone hits my shoulder. I look up and gasp. The gargoyle perched upon the library is coming to life.

"Son of a bitch," I whisper.

"*You better get inside! Now!*" Shadow shouts.

I'm moving before he even finishes. Unfortunately, higher powers deem my life expendable. The doors are locked again. That demon is doing everything in her power to take me out… or drive me into her clutches. The gargoyle dives toward me, clawed hands reaching. Shadow gets between us, fires growing larger as he takes a more human form. Cloaked in flames and voicing his rage, he reaches for the stone monster.

It dodges the burst of fire that emits from his hand. I'm forced to take cover, crouching within the large paws of a lion. Probably not the best place to be, but that doesn't occur to me at the time. When one of those paws curls around me, however, I regret the decision. Before it can pin me down, I scramble from the large stone paw. Both lions are alive, moving to pursue me. The loud clunk of heavy paws on cement is deafening. Shadow, too busy with the flying threat, is knocked over by one feline.

"I can't get inside!" I call back, only inches ahead of the second. "I don't know what to do!"

"*I can tell you what not to do! Do not let them catch you!*"

"Gee, thanks for that. I was really thinking how nice it would be to play with a massive carnivore! How stupid do you think I am?"

I cry out when the paw reaches for me, putting a mailbox between us. It knocks it aside like a paperweight. It leaps and I roll beneath it, getting back on my feet and taking off. Shadow turns to face the second lion, leaving the gargoyle free. It zeros in on me. The gargoyle turns and dives once more. It's ahead of me and the lion is behind. I keep my path, narrowing my gaze in determination. When the stone gargoyle dives, I hit the ground… and it crashes into the lion. They both crumble and disappear. Shadow takes out the second lion, turning it to rubble.

As soon as those pieces vanish, I find them back where they started. Still and lifeless. My heart is hammering in my chest once again, threatening to finally stop. As I catch my breath, Shadow drifts over to me. He's back in his smaller form.

"Oh my fucking god!" I gasp out. "What the hell! I was just… they were all… how the hell..."

"*I did say she was powerful*," he offers.

"Will they come back to life?"

"*I don't know, but we should probably leave while we can.*"

"Good idea."

I hurry off, looking back a few times to be certain they're not moving. Eyes are everywhere, drilling into me from all directions. It's not just paranoia, not anymore. When I see Heather's house, I run through the lawn to reach the front door. I'm already soaked from the light shower, so a little more water won't hurt.

I fling the door open, slamming it shut behind me. As I lean against the door, trying to catch my breath, Shadow drifts through the wood. Heather is staring at us from the kitchen area. Her expression is torn between confusion and exasperation.

"What the hell happened to you?" she wonders.

"I was just attacked by two lions and a gargoyle," I inform. "It was crazy! I ran back here as fast as I could!"

"… Did they follow you? How did the lions get out? And where the hell did you find a gargoyle?"

"*Stone statues from the library*," Shadow comments.

"... Ah... right. So... hungry?"

"I'm starving! Dodging death uses a lot of energy."

She shakes her head, turning back to the stove. Two plates are made and set upon the table. It's getting late, but I promised to eat dinner with her. I sit down and smile at Heather. She sets a small plate of mashed potatoes and Salisbury steak at an empty seat. When Shadow is floating over his own chair, she takes her seat. A fourth plate is on the counter for Nana.

"What do you hope to learn tonight?" she wonders.

"I don't know," I answer honestly. "So far, all I've been learning is the way people die there. If I could just get into the larger office, I might find what I need."

"Are you sure?" Heather asks. "I mean, I don't think that demon is stupid. She knows what you're looking for. I doubt she would've given you free reign, if she thought you would find what you seek."

"I have to try," I sigh. "You have the book front covered, I need something to do in my spare time. Besides, Baby knows more than she's saying. I want to see if she'll tell me the rest."

"Maybe she's lying, have you thought of that?"

"*She's not the type to lie. She loves people, and she's done nothing but try to save them through the years. Baby, as you call her, has been trying to find a way to kill the demon. I think she's gotten a few ideas, but doesn't know how to go through with them. Catori can help her.*"

"Catori can barely help herself," Heather points out.

"Yeah, I think he's figured that out already," I smirk. "I'm nothing but trouble. If she has theories, though, I would like to hear them."

"And she'll tell you all this with the demon in the same building?"

"Last time I went in with Shadow, there was nothing. She didn't speak over the intercom, and I couldn't even feel her presence. I think she sealed herself in the large office. Maybe when she does that, it seals the store from her as well."

"Only one way to find out."

"Exactly!"

When I finish eating, I help her clean up the dishes. Afterward, I put on my coat and grab my keys. As I go out the door, I kiss Heather's cheek. She waits until I'm seated in my car before shutting the door. As I pull out, Shadow appears in the passenger seat. Together, we drive to the store we both loathe.

Chapter 23

When we get there, the sun has long since set. The moon now reigns over the night. When I stop in the parking lot, my engine suddenly dies. An ironic warning. With an irritated grumble, I put the car in park and get out. There's no sign of engine issues. I just got it looked at not long ago, so I know nothing is wrong with it.

"Damn store," I mutter. "Can't even leave my fucking car alone!"

"*I'm sure it'll start back up when you leave*," Shadow offers, drifting from the car. "*Just be happy it was the car and not you.*"

"… Come on," I sigh. "I need to get in there before I swear vengeance on that demon."

"*Haven't you already? I mean… you strike me as that type of person. Only… I picture you doing so internally, while giving a manic and insane cackle.*"

"You know me so well," I smirk. "Let's find Baby."

He follows me to the store's front door… or what's left of it. The rain has invaded the place, clinging to the fabrics close to the large windows. The tattered sign finally peels away and drifts to the ground. I step over it to enter, glass crunching beneath my feet.

The store seems deserted, yet holds an eerie feeling of eyes everywhere. I saw the amount of souls trapped here. They may not be the entire mass, but it was enough. I sit on a jewelry case, the one still mostly in tact, and Shadow drifts inside. The second he passes the front door, those eyes disappear. It's impressive, I have to admit. He settles against the case beside mine, taking a more human form. When he's finished, Baby appears behind the counters.

"*Back again, I see. You must really have a death wish.*"

"No more than usual," I smirk. "A little birdie told me you have the dirt on everyone here."

"*Oh did it,*" she comments, glaring over at Shadow. "*What else did that little bird tell you?*"

"That you know the master plan, or at least some of it. I can help you, you know," I point out. "I'm trying to stop that damn demon, too."

She huffs and leans on the counter, arms crossed over the fractured glass. I can still see the bruising around her slender throat, so dark against her pallor. As she attempts to mentally list pros and cons, I send my gaze out over the store. It's still worn and decrepit, however it lacks the threat of before. I can't see the children sneaking about today.

"*She wants you for something, but I haven't learned the whole plan,*" Baby confides. "*I've been trying to figure out how to kill her for good, but I know that witch tried before... it didn't work.*"

"I know," I inform. "My friend and I have been studying her as well. Heather told me a demon can be killed, but only in a specific manner."

"*How so?*" they ask in unison.

"A demon is a creature born of sin, so they used to be human. Obviously, not a very nice human. When they die, that death leaves a brand on their soul. When they return a demon, that demon can only be killed one way. The same way their human form was. Unfortunately, that history was botched. Our demon used to be a witch that used black magic. History has recorded that she was killed by hanging, but she wasn't. So when the witch of old attempted to kill it for good, she did it wrong."

"*So... We need to learn how she died,*" Baby states.

"That's about it. I don't suppose you managed to learn that, did you?"

"*No,*" she admits. "*You'd think that was the first thing I'd learn, but she's keeping most of her information close to the belt.*"

"It's okay, we'll figure something out," I sigh. "I've been all over this place looking for the answer, but no luck. If I can just get into that office."

"*There's nothing but glass jars up there,*" Baby scoffs. "*It's like a soul zoo. No one can get in, because that's the center of her power. We only know, because we're trapped there... so to speak. He's not, so he wouldn't know.*"

I stop at that, a flashback of my dream surfacing. If that's truly what lies behind that door, there's nothing there for me. Then again, if I can invade the center of her power, perhaps I can free some of the souls. That's sure to weaken her. I'm about to head up there when my cell phone rings. It's Heather, but I don't have time for a call now. Instead of answering it, I text her.

It's not what she's expecting, but she answers it anyway. I quickly relay what I've learned, and then what I'm planning. Unsurprisingly, she's not happy about it. I'm walking toward the stairs in the back, ready to attack that door with everything I can think of. That's when the floor begins to shake.

It knocks me off my feet with the violence. My body hits the tile, bruising my elbow in the process. I can hear the metal of the racks rattling. Above me, the ceiling cracks and falls. I roll away just in time. A larger piece comes down, one I can't dodge. Before I can close my eyes and embrace the end, something wraps around my ankle and yanks me out of harms way. I open my eyes and look toward it. It's a length of baby clothes, all knotted together just like Baby's noose.

"Thanks!" I call toward her.

"*Thank me by surviving, girl*!" she responds. "*Now move that ass*!"

I don't wait for another invitation, getting to my feet quickly. The clothes fall away from me and I run. The ceiling is crumbling, trying to take me out from above. With each chunk aimed at me, I manage to dodge. The door is in view, my feet pounding on the floor even as my heart races in my ears. Just as I'm about to pass through, one of the windows bursts. The glass is blown toward me. I shield my face with my arms, gasping as a few shards dig into my forearms.

Warm blood drips along my skin as I leap outside. The cool air burns at those cuts. I breath a sigh of relief, ignoring the pain through the adrenaline. With no other bandage on me, I'm forced to allow it to bleed into my sleeves. Although I don't want it all over my seats, I'll have to chance it. If Heather picks me up here, she'll flip out.

Shadow floats over to me, checking me over before drifting into the car. I know he's upset, as the fires around him burn white hot. With a reluctant sigh, I open the driver's side and sit down. The engine roars to life, just as he predicted. Damn store. With a shift into drive, the small car leaves the parking lot.

The roads are so empty tonight. An eerie feeling of paranoia weighs on my shoulders. It's almost expected at this point. Fog has come, laying heavily upon the streets. The sight reminds me of too many horror movies. With nothing on the road to kill me, I try to relax. Unfortunately, something is eating at the edges of my mind.

Just as I'm about to scold myself for letting her get to me, I see something in the mist. My heart literally stops. A long body barely arches over the top of the fog, like a treacherous serpent in the waters. It disappears into the murky fog once more. I slam on the breaks and put the car in park.

"If she ruins my car… I'm going to make her afterlife a living hell!" I growl out.

"What's wrong?"

"You didn't see that gigantic snake in the fog?" I ask, pointing in that direction.

"I wasn't paying attention."

"Well, it's there. I saw it right over there! I can't believe you didn't see it! What is it?"

"Um… I didn't see it," he responds.

I nearly hit the steering wheel with my head. Something moves alongside the car, bumping it from my side. I can't breathe anymore. The promise of long fangs and a crushing hold leaves goosebumps on my skin. In the rear view mirror, I see that body arch once more. Nothing comes to mind. I have no clue what to do. When the car is bumped one more time, I think I know what it's doing. That snake is wrapping around the car.

"We need to get out of here before it lifts us in the air… or crushes us."

"*So we're running willingly into it's mouth*?"

"Do you have a better idea?"

"… *No*," he admits.

"Then we're going with my plan!"

I throw the door open and bolt, heading for the nearest shelter. Unfortunately, it's only a gazebo in the town's square. With a silent curse, I gather my bearings there. Houses are everywhere, businesses a bit closer, but nothing is open. My car is rattled a little, however it stops. The serpent has abandoned the vehicle.

I climb up onto the railings, hoping to get a better view over the fog. Something glimmers beneath it. I thank the stars the moon is full tonight. Just as I'm wondering if it'll attack at all, it shoots heavenward. It towers over the gazebo, it's width half the size of my car. Atop it's head is a crown of long feathers, around it's neck… a necklace of human bones. It's mouth, a sharp beak dripping blood, opens as it screeches. When it moves, the glowing ebony scales shift. They're not attached to muscle, but to shadows. Those shadows escape between the scales to form extra limbs it didn't have before, as now it has large bone wings and short arms.

"What the fuck is that!" I scream in shock.

"*It looks like the love child of a snake and a chicken*," Shadow laughs.

"It's terrifying, don't laugh at it! You might insult it!"

"*It wants to kill you either way, so I'm gonna laugh at it. Maybe it'll get embarrassed and run away.*"

I groan at the comment. If only it were that easy. The snake lunges for the gazebo, my feet carrying me away just in time. It crashes into the wooden fixture, rolling onto the ground as I run. There aren't many choices for hiding places. I wind around a few trees, hoping to get it tangled. Although it gets banged up, it doesn't slow the pursuit. My legs are getting tired, still sore from the encounter with the store. I won't last much longer.

Shadow flies straight into the serpent's face, burning the scales there. Unfortunately, he's not very effective. He's just too little to cause damage to this thing. His wisp form rolls about the grass, leaving a trial of flames in his wake. The snake hesitates, so I know fire scares it. It's not enough though. Short of a direct attack, it's scales are too strong to harm it. It has to be on the inside… where the soft tissue is vulnerable. I won't let Shadow do that, though. He's good at setting fires, but we need an explosion. Close to my car, I trip over a loose shoe lace. I've never wanted to kick my ass as badly as now.

"*Catori! Look out!*" Shadow screams.

I turn just in time to see the monster looming. It's jaws open wide. Before a string of saliva can break loose, it darts toward me. I raise my hands, as though that's going to shield me. Everything stills. Or at least seems like it. Time has slowed down drastically, leaving me lost in the panic. A thought, as random as it is, infiltrates my mind. I really wish I could control fire like Shadow. My ring finger goes warm, that heat covering both my hands, and then… I'm lost in a haze of flames. It's resting between myself and the snake.

Jaws still gaping eagerly, I thoughtlessly push my hands forward. The fires move the way I motion. Time speeds up once more, the ball of flames shooting straight into the serpent's mouth. It swallows it, the sparks of flame glinting between its scales. My hands motion an explosion… and that pyre bursts outward. The scales are forced away from the shadows. Before they can smash me into the side of my car, it all stops… shivers… and disintegrates. The fog clears and Shadow comes over to me. I'm just too stunned to move.

"*Was that you?*" Shadow asks. "*I mean… I usually make the fires, but… I don't remember doing anything that big before.*"

"I think… I think that was me," I whisper out. "I… I need to… let's go…"

"*How about I drive back? You look like your brain broke or something. We'll have Heather repair it. Come on, crawl on in.*"

The front door, just to my right, swings open. Slow and steady, still completely baffled, I crawl into the front seat. That's where I still. Shadow hums to himself as he drifts into the car, my seat belt clips on its own. The engine starts, and then we're moving down the street. I don't really remember the ride. It all blurs together. I do notice, however, that my hands are too hot and the skin is singed. There was no spell. No incantation or runes drawn. It just… happened. Whatever I did… it wasn't Wicca magic.

Chapter 24

The front door doesn't open quietly. I don't even think I tried to open it quietly. All I wanted was to find Heather. Thankfully, she's relaxing on the couch. When she sees me, however, she's not on the couch much longer. My hair is a rat's nest, my clothes muddied from the attack, and my palms are nearly black.

"What happened to you?" she gasps, hurrying over. "Come sit on the couch, you look a wreck."

"I'm going to the bathroom," I say wearily. "I think I have to throw up, but I definitely know I need a bath."

She follows me, sending a curious gaze to Shadow. He has nothing to keep him occupied, so he looks for a distraction in the kitchen. When I get to the bathroom, I start the water. Normally, I love a nice hot bath. Recent surprises have me testing for lukewarm, though. Heather seats herself on the sink's edge, waiting for me to talk. It doesn't come fast enough.

"What happened at the store?" she wonders, tone soft and understanding.

"Just the normal shit," I shrug off.

"You *never* come home looking like that on a normal day," she points out. "What the hell happened there?"

"This didn't happen at the store. It happened on the way home. A giant snake manifested in the fog and attacked me."

"… Giant snake?" she asks in a squeak.

"Yep. It was half the size of my car, with a feather headdress, a necklace of human bones, and it was made of shadow and scales."

"How did you get away from it?"

"I blew it up," I frown, showing her my hands. "I have no idea how. I just… wanted to control fire and… it was there. No spells, no runes, no incantations. Heather… it wasn't witchcraft. What's happening to me?"

"I… I don't know," she sighs out. "But, I'll look into it. There might be something in Nana's notes about this. I mean, she's seen everything! She's had to of seen something like this."

"I hope so," I murmur. "I can't handle all this shit piling on top of me, I'm suffocating."

She's quiet for a long time, just waiting for the tub to fill with me. After a moment, she gets down and holds out her hands. I set mine on top of them. As she examines the proof of my insanity, I can only ask myself questions. If that demon can create something so sinister and massive… maybe it's too powerful to defeat. Can I really stop her? Am I enough?

"You're amazing, you know that?" Heather says quietly, a small smirk on her lips.

"How so?" I wonder.

"I bet you looked straight into that snake's eyes and blew it up. You know, like… cocky smirk and sinister glare. And you hardly seem as shaken as most would be."

"… I guess so."

"Was the first question in your mind, 'should I really go back to that store'?"

"No. But I had to ask myself if I could defeat her."

"You just blew up a massive serpent, with nothing more than your willpower," she laughs out. "And you're worried you can't defeat one little demon? You must be crazier than I thought."

I can't help the little smirk I give. Her positivity is so infectious sometimes. The water is turned off and Heather walks out, leaving me on my own. As I scrub the dirt off my skin, I breathe a sigh of relief. My hands still hurt, but the soot is beginning to disappear. The cause will never be forgotten, though. I'm almost positive my hands will never stop tingling.

The next morning, I'm less than ready to get out of bed. Thankfully, the principal is over the scare he suffered. I don't have to worry about keeping occupied when school is back in. I get ready and hurry to the kitchen. Heather is eating toast and oatmeal, a bowl already set out for me.

"How did you sleep?" she wonders.

"Oh my god, you have no idea," I sigh in bliss, sitting down to eat. "I haven't slept so good since this whole thing started. No nightmares or anything!"

"Good," she smiles. "Off to school then?"

"You bet! I'll bring you your assignments, don't worry. Can't have you sitting in the audience when I graduate after all."

I can feel her eyes roll. As soon as I down my breakfast, I rush out the door. At the sight of my car, I stop. There's a nasty scratch along the sides. My face goes hot with rage, hands balled into fists as I try to calm down. It took me forever to save for this car! My feet take me in a circle, like a boxer getting ready for the fight. I try to shake it off, murmuring to myself to vent the anger. When my head clears enough, I ignore the scratch and climb in. Shadow is already in the passenger seat.

"When did you get here?" I frown.

"Since Heather told me your school was open again," he offers. "You shouldn't go, you need to stay here. It's the fifth night, Catori, there are more important things to worry about."

"I appreciate the offer, but there's nothing I can do. My forte is investigating, I can't do that until night.

Heather is taking care of the magic stuff," I point out. "She should be able to open the book tonight… maybe tomorrow morning. There's nothing we can do until it's opened."

"*Still… don't you want to spend time with her before the end*?" he asks. "*You might never see her again*."

"I have faith in her," I inform. "If she says she can get something done, I'm not going to question her. I'll be fine, she won't allow anything else."

"*If you say so*," he sighs out.

I pull out of the driveway and head to the school. The roads aren't as busy as I expect and the parking lot is emptier than the norm. It's likely because the students haven't shaken off their encounter. Inside the building, I can see black sludge still staining the walls. A few faculty members are scrubbing hard to remove it. It's not helping. Doors are either missing or broken. Inside my first class, desks are tipped over and the dry erase board is littered with messages scratched into it by long nails.

Mr. Abott is trying to remove the calls for help. I have a sinking feeling school was let in… but we'll only be learning how to clean. It looks like a natural disaster shook this place. I walk over and clear my throat, waiting for him to take notice.

"Catori? I thought no one was coming today," he states in surprise.

"I had nothing better to do," I shrug. "You won't be able to scrub that off, they scratched it in. This board is junk now."

"… This whole school has fallen apart," he huffs. "What happened? Was it really the store's curse?"

"You wouldn't believe me if I told you," I wave off. "Come on, let's put the desks together first. At least that's doable."

He nods and we move over to the chairs scattered about. I feel awful, this is all my fault. Had I listened to Heather and stayed away from here, none of this would've happened. All I can do now is help clean it up. Shadow floats in, watching curiously before trying to help. A desk moves by Mr. Abott and he about jumps out of his skin.

"Don't worry, that one's friendly," I offer. "I call him Shadow, because he follows me everywhere."

"He's a… ghost?"

"Yep! He died in the old store," I explain. "They left him to burn in a fire. I couldn't just leave him, so… I brought him home with me. Ever since, he's protected me from that store's demon."

"Demon?"

"That's the curse. A demon had been slaying the workers there, trapping their souls within the store. She feeds off them, they're her power supply. When people wander in, she attaches herself to them in hopes of driving them to suicide. That's how the curse reached this place. I went in that store, and she attached herself to me. I should've known better than to come here."

"That's why all those people died? Committed suicide? It was that demon's fault?" he gasps out. "How are you still alive? I mean, they fell so quickly."

"I'm a *very* stubborn person and I love a good challenge," I smirk. "She put that challenge forth when she said I wouldn't survive… I'm going to prove her wrong."

"*Catori has lasted longer than any of the others,*" Shadow comments, righting a couple desks. "*She'll defeat the demon for sure! And I'm here in case she needs a good push.*"

He's quiet after that, taking in all the information given. This town has grown so used to the curse, it's overlooked. I'm sure it didn't start that way. It was probably a terrifying thought, just looking at it. I'm sure people passed the story along in hopes of dissuading trespass. Now, though, it's been forgotten why people steer clear of it. If luck stays with me, those stories won't need to be repeated.

Only a handful of the older students showed up, so classes were a mission to clean the school. Thankfully, most of those present have nothing better to do. Only a couple tables are filled at lunch. None of us wanted to sit alone, so we're all crammed between the two long tables. The faculty are eating with us as well, taking up a third.

"I can't believe we're back here," Wendy mutters. "I wasn't going to come either, but Brittany picked me up."

"I can't afford to miss any credits," Brittany frowns. "And neither can you."

"I know, but… this place is evil."

"It's not the school," I remark without thinking. "It's the store."

"You don't seriously believe that, do you?" Melissa scoffs.

"You guys just witnessed a massive haunting, and you're calling the store's curse a myth?" I point out. "I think you need to rethink your belief system, it's damaged somewhere."

She rolls her eyes, yet says nothing more on the matter. It's a silent win for me. As I pick up my sandwich, I notice something off about them. It's as though a silent question or two hangs in the air. As much as I don't want to know what it is, I can't stand the tension.

"What is it?" I frown.

"… Where's Heather?" Wendy asks quietly. "I haven't seen her all week, is she okay?"

"Yeah, she's fine," I wave off. "She's focusing on her studies at home right now."

"Are you really living with her now?" Melissa wonders, gossip mode on.

"No, I'm just staying with her for now. She was home alone and got hurt pretty badly, I didn't want it to happen again. Until her parents get back from their business trip, I'll be staying with her."

"Does she even *have* parents?" Wendy frowns.

"Everyone has parents," Brittany scoffs.

"We never see them! How can they exist if we never see them?"

"You never see *my* parents," I point out. "They're always working. Her parents are the same."

"… Must be lonely."

"… It is," I answer.

We're all distracted by our food now, unwilling to continue the conversation. When we're done, we all gather to clean the gymnasium. It's going to take a lot more than a bucket of water and a broom. The hardwood floor is cracked and broken in places, mostly from the hands reaching up from the ground. All the holes, however, are going to be difficult to mend. It'll take a professional crew for that. We do what we can in the meantime.

As I mop the floor by the stage, Wendy and Brittany are sweeping. After scaring Mr. Abott earlier, Shadow is hanging back. He wants to help, yet can't bring himself to scare another. Strangest ghost I've ever met. I plop the mop back in the bucket, lifting it up… and finding black goo on it. I groan in irritation.

"What's wrong, Catori?" Melissa asks.

"I have a feeling we're about to have a repeat of the other day," I sigh out.

"Why?"

I lift the mop again, showing her the goo. She's no fool, she hightails it for the door. As my friend gathers others to escape, I take my time. Once they're out of the gym, I start heading for the door. They're out of danger, that's all that matters. I keep going, dragging my feet just in case. The gym doors slam shut, my stomach dropping at the sound. Something is moving under the floor, coming straight for me.

"*Catori, over here! Get off the floor!*" Shadow calls from the stage.

I sprint over to him, breaking into a reckless run when the floorboards are bumped. They raise up, breaking as though a fin is surfacing in water. The second I reach the stage, I leap and climb upon it. There's no time to use the stairs, as a hand reaches for my ankle. It misses, though barely.

"*Now* what!" I scream. "What could I *possibly* have to deal with now? What is so *godawful* important you had to bother me while I'm *cleaning*?"

"*It's a wraith, like me,*" Shadow offers. "*Well... not completely like me. This one doesn't like people at all. It was feral when it died.*"

"Feral? Like… wolf boy, or something?" I ask.

"*Yep.*"

"Perfect. How am I supposed to beat it?"

"I'll try and deal with it, you just get outside. It's grave is beneath the gym, so it's reach won't include the front yard of the school."

I grumble in irritation, getting ready to make a break for the door. Although I have a feeling this won't work, I'm hoping it will. The wraith leaps for the stage, body leaving a trail of dirt. Shadow takes a human form, fires sizzling upon his being, and meets the wraith halfway. They lock in a grappling contest, so I dash for the door. When the wild boy, looking to be around my age, sees me he narrows his gaze. He throws his head back and howls. It echoes around the massive room, joined by many others. Wolves made of mist and shadow appear, eyes glowing red. I nearly puke at the sight, the hounds breaking into a run after me. As I reach the doors, they open without hassle. It worries me. That's when I hear Shadow's voice.

"Catori! The wolves aren't bound here, they can reach outside!"

"Perfect," I bristle. "Fine, let's play chase until I can figure out how to deal with you."

I bolt down the halls, zipping out the front doors and passing my friends. They call in question, yet fall into screaming when the dogs pass. All of them, teachers and students, call my name. I can't answer, though. My mind is too busy trying to form a plan. I made fire before, it should work now, too. As I run, I glance at my hands. I try everything I can to make a fire, cursing when it doesn't work.

"What's different from the snake?" I wonder aloud. "I was scared then, too. Why won't it work? What do I have to…"

I suck in a sharp breath when I trip. My body tumbles along the ground, ending with me on my back. As I sit up, I realize I'm surrounded. The snarling wolves step closer, snapping their jaws. I curl in on my self and listen to my heartbeat. It's the last time I'll get to hear it. My body starts to get warm, unbearably so, and sweat drips from my temple. I can envision a ring of fire around me, it's that warm. One of the wolves yip and I look up. Around me is the very ring of flames I saw in my mind. I sit up straight, hands touching the edge of the ring. With a calming breath, I push it outward. It rushes just like the fireball before, overcoming the wolves. By the time my friends reach me, the ghosts are gone.

"Oh my god! You look like you ran a marathon!" Brittany states. "Here, let me help you… Ouch! Fuck, you're burning up! Somebody bring some ice or something!"

"Where did that fire come from?" Wendy questions. "Did you get burned?"

"No, I'm fine," I state, tone soft and calm. "I think I need to go home, though. I need a shower something awful."

"Tell me about it," Melissa smirks. "You're sweating bullets. Reminds me of Heather when we showed her that Gardner snake."

I can't help but chuckle. Heather hates snakes with a passion. I force myself to my feet, stumbling only a moment. When Brittany tries to catch me, she flinches away at the heat that remains there. My palms, I notice, are once again singed. If this is going to be a frequent thing, I should look into getting gloves.

All around me, faculty are talking. Some are checking that I'm okay, others swearing the school is now cursed as well. It's all a rush of jumbled words to me. As I climb into my car, Melissa catches the light on the passenger seat. She gasps when the seat belt clips without my hand, the engine starting although I placed the key on the dash. Shadow pulls out of the parking space before she can say anything.

Back at Heather's, I enter the house and search for her. She's out back in her garden. I would've just jumped in the tub, but she heard my car. She's already hurry to enter the house. This time, she doesn't freak out when she sees me. Instead, she shakes her head and clicks her tongue.

"Girl, I'm beginning to get jealous," she remarks. "You spend more time with trouble than you do me. Should I be worried?"

"Not in the least," I laugh lightly. "In fact, I'm hoping you can scare trouble away."

"What happened this time?"

"Feral wraith with a wolf pack in the back pocket," I shrug. "Another fire incident. On the bright side, I think our friends are opening their eyes a bit more."

"Oh good, they can start gossiping about ghost business instead of our business."

She motions for me to follow her, taking me back toward the living room. There's a basket on one arm, filled with herbs. Instead of setting it in the kitchen, she carries it down to the basement. Nana is by her counter with my father's book. At the sight of me, her eyes grow large and she grins.

"*You have been a naughty girl, have you not?*" she asks. "*One should be careful playing with fire, Wanyecha.*"

"... Doesn't that mean 'Firefly' in Native American?" I frown.

"You know what's going on with Catori, Nana?" Heather wonders.

"*I know the energy,*" she comments. "*Though I have never witnessed it myself, I have heard the stories.*"

Heather sets the basket on the counter, waiting for her to continue. She, instead, looks to their grimoire. The cover opens and the pages flip in a blur. It settles on a page and sits open. I grab the book before Heather does, as she's distracted by separating herbs. As I take a seat on the stool there, I read aloud.

"I do not know her name," I state. "She had the shell of a human, but that she was not. From her fingertips, she could create water. The ocean fell to her whim, moving in such a way as she demanded. Never before have I seen a creature such as she. Neither human, nor witch. She was the sea, packed into a human shell and loosed upon the world. I thank the deities she had a heart of gold, for the world would perish had she not."

"So… this has happened before then," Heather frowns. "What is it? Do they have a name for it?"

"*No names, just the memory,*" Nana offers. "*Long ago there was one like Catori. There were others, too, though very few. I can count on one hand the rumors. And some may have been of the same person.*"

"Perfect, I'm an oddity to the witch community," I huff. "Why couldn't I be normal?"

"Because your mom wants you to be," Heather smirks. "Besides, crazy is a better color. It suits you."

"What are the herbs for?" I inquire, rolling my eyes.

"For the spell to release the wraith," she smiles. "I was going to do it after you leave for the store. You don't need to be here for it, and you've already faced one today."

I nod, grateful for that. When I'm sure the two are lost in their work, I head upstairs. So much is happening, I need to talk to someone around it. Maybe my father will know something from his mother. I jump in the shower to wash up. Afterward, I get dressed and pull on my shoes. Shadow follows me out to the car.

Thankfully, my father is at home. When I walk in, I find him making some grilled cheese sandwiches. One plate already sits on the counter. I don't even have to say anything and he's flipping the new sandwich onto another plate, setting them both at the table.

"About time you showed up," he comments, without looking to see who entered. "I've been waiting all day. Thought you would've come in a bit sooner, what with the wraith at your school."

"… Um… how did you..?"

"My strongest asset in my teachings is clairvoyance," he smirks.

"… That explains why I could never get away with anything," I grumble. "So… what do you know about spontaneously setting fires without magic?"

"… Okay, I didn't see that one coming," he admits. "Can you give me an example?"

"Well… you saw my school got attacked, but did you see how I took out the wolves?"

"I did not. My sight is limited."

I sit down and explain everything, including the entry in Heather's book. My dad seems flabbergasted. It takes him a long while to catch up, his jaw set and eyes focused the whole time. It's rather unnerving. Finally, he sighs and sets his chin in his hand.

"Mother used to tell me of humans that crawled from the earth," he informs. "She always said they were special. Forces that held the very essence of the elements within themselves. She said there were always four. None have ever been seen together. Each is a doorway to the afterlife, a focal point to help spirits pass on."

"So… mediums? Psychics?" I wonder. "I've never seen a psychic create fire with a thought."

"And they can't. Even clairvoyants like me can't. Those humans that crawled from the earth… they're far more than simple witches. My mother told me they were the earth itself. They were placed upon the earth to help the dead, to lead them to peace when they die with none. She said they were a gift from the elements, revered as demi-gods in a way."

"… I'm one of those things?" I gawk.

"Probably not, sweetheart," he admits. "You're just gifted in the fire element and your powers are surfacing. Fire is extremely hard to control, it's the only living element. If you're not strong enough, it'll destroy you. Try not to use it anymore, okay? Just until I have a chance to train you a bit in it."

"… Train me? Like… I'm gonna be a witch?"

"No, more like… you're gonna be able to control your abilities. If your mom thinks I'm making a witch out of you, she'll lock us both up. You'll get the asylum, but I'll get a jail cell."

"Gotcha. Don't tell mom."

He nods his head, relief settling on his features. I've never been married, but I'm pretty sure that's not healthy. A relationship is based on trust, yet he seems terrified of mom. Maybe she's a demon, too. I'll have to look into that when I'm done with the one I'm fighting.

Together we eat in a companionable silence. I tell him about the incident at school, more in detail this time. As we laugh and joke, Shadow stays above my head. He's wary of my father, though I don't know why. They seem to be at a stalemate right now. Tolerating each other simply because they're attached to me. I'll have to fix that later.

The hours grow long and my dad has to get some sleep. As he heads upstairs, the front door opens. I turn to see my mother, weary from work, walking in. She looks like a zombie. When she sees me, she's confused for only a moment. As soon as recognition hits her, she mumbles a 'hello' and continues to the living room.

"Hard day, mom?" I ask.

"Too hard," she sighs out. "I swear I didn't get five minutes to sit down. There was a nasty pile up today, five critical and two fatalities. All were rushed to our hospital. It was hectic all day. What brings you here?"

"Heather had stuff to do and I didn't," I shrug off. "I figured I'd turn up here and see how you two were doing. Dad had a rather boring day, or so he said. He just went up to nap before work."

"What will you be planning for tonight?" she questions. "That store again? People are beginning to say it's too dangerous to be around, honey. I think you should stay away from it."

"I can't, my investigation isn't over yet," I respond. "But if it makes you feel better, it'll be over in a couple days."

"Good. I don't want you getting hurt."

"I know, mom," I smile. "I'll see you later, okay? Go get some rest."

She nods, though I doubt she heard me, and I head for the door. Heather is busy with her vengeful spirit, so I'll be driving to the bane of my existence. Once more, I have to ignore the scratches along the side of my car. The engine rattles, though it quiets after the initial start. I grumble under my breath as I pull out.

The drive is uneventful for once, allowing me a small moment to relax. It's a golden silence. The information I've learned from my father rests at the back of my mind. Unfortunately, I can't focus on it right now. Inside that store is evil incarnate, I need to focus on that. One wrong step, and I'm yet another victim.

<u>Chapter 25</u>

Like a titan that's weathered too much, the store stands. Tattered and decrepit, but very much alive. It's like a showdown, me outside... and that demon watching from behind concrete and glass. Her rage is static upon the air. It leaves a feeling of satisfaction within. One more night and I'm in the clear. I can't help the grin that breaks out on my face. Just one more night and it's all over.

Prepared for anything the store can throw at me, I step through the threshold. Shadow is locked out almost immediately. I know I should be worried, but something deep inside is calm. A cloud of shadows barrels from the door at the back corner, giving a shrill shriek as it races toward me. The demon reaches for me from the smoke, yet doesn't touch me. After her fit, the smoke disperses. She's glaring for all she's worth.

"So are you gonna fix my car, or pay me for the damage?" I wonder.

"*You are an infuriating human, aren't you*?" she growls out.

"Only one more night after this," I point out. "Feeling worried yet? I'm not. I told you I would survive and that's what I'm gonna do."

"*Your end will come before the contract is up*," the demon bristles. "*Tonight is your night to die*!"

"After you," I smirk.

She utters a scream of anger, shaking the building with the mere sound. After that, she disappears. The store is still for a drawn out moment. I hear a switch getting flipped, the lights turning off one after the next. The inky black washes over me. For just a second, a chill runs down my spine.

A dim pale yellow light comes to life. It covers the store, yet barely illuminates it. Carefully, I walk forward. There are no laughing children, no curious spirits… just me in a deserted building. Near the back, by the stairs that go up to the offices, I hear a sink running. Opening one of the other doors, I realize it's a bathroom. As I heard, both sinks are running. With a sigh, my hand reaches out to turn the knobs off… but it doesn't stop. The sinks fill up and the water races to the floor.

I hum in question, my eyes catching more water from under the stalls. With a shiver of disgust, I slowly open one of them. The toilet is crammed with paper, traces of feces still coating the walls. I gag at the mere thought, the stench as bad as decayed bodies. Water is flowing over the bowls, dirtying the tiled floor even more. This room is best left alone. I hurry out before my vomit joins the rest of the mess. By now, it's beginning to pool in the easily overlooked divots.

Water splashes as I step through them, heading to the back room. The second I swing them open, I hear the pipes bursting. Liquid showers the room. On edge with the amount of water, I back up and start for high ground. On the stairs, I let out a breath of relief. At least the water is staying downstairs. My feet take me up the steps, skipping a few on the way. Unable to think of anything more to do, I search out the 'pretty lady'.

The larger room is empty. I sigh and try to open the fire escape there. It doesn't budge, though it's no surprise. The sound of running water freezes the blood in my veins. It's not like downstairs, not as plentiful, so I'm not panicking yet. Not more than I am, anyway. I walk over to the smaller room. The blood that poured from the snack machines is still there, as are the reaching hands in the bloodied microwave. The sink, however, is running.

It's spray is small, poor water pressure, so it's hasn't even filled it's bowl yet.

"Thank the stars," I murmur.

I don't even try to turn it off, knowing it'll be useless. Just as I'm calming my racing heart, the blood in the machines stops… and water pours out instead. The sink's pressure suddenly triples, nearly busting the spout. Instead of pulling out my hair, I groan in annoyance. It's merely hiding my fear. Running toward the stairs, I look over in time to see a wave bursting from the bathrooms. There's no time to get away. It overcomes me, washing me down the steps and onto the floor.

My body rolls away from it, just in time to get swept up in another wave. This one comes from the bathrooms downstairs. I gag at the smell of the liquid. The second I'm on my feet, I hurry for the front door. As I pass them, sprinklers burst. My heart speeds up as the water reaches my knees. None of the many holes leading outside are releasing it.

I don't understand why, but this demon cares little for the laws of science. Near the shelves of broken figures, I slip and take a fall. The water tries to swallow me up, yet I'm quick to get on my feet. It's like it has a mind of its own. Although my eyes search for a familiar face, my hope plummets. I'll receive no help here, but that doesn't mean I'm going to die easy. Determined to shove failure in the demon's face, I try to think of a way out. There may be many holes to slip through, but there are no exits available. If the water can't get out, neither can I. That means I have to break out. How can I find a weak point, though? My only choice is to get to the front and search as best I can.

The closer I get to the exit, the further the water reaches. Soon, I'm swimming to the broken doors. Taking a deep breath, I dive beneath the cold waters. As I come up to the hole I typically use to get out, my hand presses flat against a force field. I swim back to the surface, my foot knocking against the jewelry counter. The room is about halfway filled.

I pick up a broom floating near me, diving down to try breaking the window. It doesn't work. I'll need to find something heavier. In a store like this, there should be a thousand things to use. Back at the surface, I try to think. There must've been something I saw in an earlier visit I can use.

A fire extinguisher was over by the book shelves! I swim over and dive for it. Once it's in my hands, I return to the window. The red cylinder is slammed against the glass, yet doesn't even make a crack. I let it fall to the side of the jewelry counter. At the top, I'm already able to touch the ceiling. Any longer, and there won't be room for me to breathe.

"I could really some help here," I mutter. "Maybe even a route out of here."

"*Sorry, girlie*," Baby calls, though I can't see her. "*We're all sealed up. You're on your own. Don't let her get the best of you, or I'll kick your ass for the rest of your afterlife!*"

"… Perfect."

On my own, I rethink my approach. A flash of light catches my eye. Shadow is outside, trying his best to break through the demon's field. He's managed a small crack, but nothing more. If I can hit from the inside, at the same time, we might be able to shatter it. Then again, I would need to weaken it from this side.

Beneath my feet, I see a glimmer. There are rings left in the case. If one of them is a diamond, I can use it to weaken the glass. Under the water, I grab up as many as I can. When I next surface, my head is nearly to the ceiling.

Ignoring it, my focus is on the rings. A few look like diamonds, so I drop the others and approach the glass. By the crack Shadow has managed, I draw an 'X' with one of the rings. Two don't work, but the third is perfect. It cuts into the thick surface like a knife through warm butter.

With that finished, I swim over to the clothes racks. I grab a loose bar and swim back. As Shadow hits the outside, I slam the pole into the glass. The blow comes too slowly for success. Unsure how to make it fast underwater, I have to gather myself above.

Back at the surface, my eyes lock onto a glint of red. It's the fire extinguisher I used before. An idea pops into my mind, and it's retrieve it from beside the jewelry case. I grab a few floating shirts as well. With the shirts, I tie the fire extinguisher to the rod. When I'm finished, I dive back down. Waiting for the right moment, I yank the pin. Since the clothes are already holding down the handle, the extinguisher bursts forth with a good speed. It shatters the glass and the water pours out. I cough up some water on the concrete outside.

"*Are you okay*?" Shadow asks.

"Yeah, I'm fine. I wasn't expecting that."

"*Neither was I! You must really be trying her last nerve, she's never gotten that desperate before*!"

"And here I thought we were coming to an understanding," I smirk.

"*Good thing you knew how to get out.*"

"It was a complete fluke. I watch too many movies," I wave off. "If that hadn't of worked, I highly doubt I would've gotten out."

"... *Good thing you're luckier than most*," he deadpans.

"Let's get back to Heather before I go back inside."

"*Why the hell would you go back inside after that*?" he asks in disbelief.

"She wrecked my car, damn it!" I bite out. "She's gonna pay for that!"

I just know he's shaking his head as he floats away. With nothing better to keep my attention, I get in the car. I have one whole day to map out her torture. For now, however, I need to check on Heather. If that wraith is gone, she'll know how to defeat the demon. Tomorrow night, I'll end this once and for all.

Chapter 26

When I pull into the driveway, lights are flashing like a rave is being held. I frown and shut off the car. As I come upon the front door, it opens by itself. Curious, I step through the threshold and into the hall. Shadow is behind me as we join Heather in the living room. Furniture is floating about the room, cabinets slamming open and shut loudly, and something is wailing like a banshee.

"Hey, did I miss the party?" I wonder over the noise.

"No," she frowns. "This wraith is stronger than I anticipated. I've been at it for hours, but it's just not giving in! I don't know what to do."

"Does Nana have an idea?"

"No, she doesn't either. She tried earlier, but the wraith just won't listen to reason."

"… It's a vengeful spirit, honey, they don't think with reason. Maybe it just needs a night to settle down."

"You think you can sleep with this racket?"

"You have no idea. Come on, let it go tonight. As long as it doesn't try to kill us in our sleep, let it be."

She's hesitant at first, yet nods in agreement. I can see the weariness in her eyes. I lead the way to the room, pushing a chair away as it floats too close. It slams down on the floor, leaving a gouge in the wood. We both get ready for bed and crawl beneath the covers. As I start to get comfortable, Heather turns to face me.

"Why were you dripping wet when you walked in?"

"Uh… Let's not worry about that right now."

"… Okay, but tomorrow morning you better explain."

"Deal."

We close our eyes and I listen to the clattering cabinets and banging furniture. The wail slowly lessens. I peek an eye open, staring straight into the face of a child. Tears of blood stain his cheeks, his visible body littered with marks. From cigarette burns to bruises, cuts to ligatures. Pale skin is charred black in some places, telling me they likely died in a fire like Shadow. I can't wrap my head around this little thing being the wraith. He can't be more than seven years old. Then again, scared children can throw the best tantrums. I reach a hand out to him, waiting until he moves. Slowly, almost mistrusting, the child sets his hand in mine. I smile warmly, just holding that small hand. Afterward, I close my eyes once more and fall asleep.

In the morning, I'm the first to wake. I realize my hand is still being held. The boy from last night is still watching me, his fingers wrapped around my own in a tight grip. It's almost desperate. Since Heather is still sleeping, I slip out of bed and lead him to the living room. Shadow is hanging back, not willing to scare the other wraith. I thank him silently for the opportunity, knowing he's right there if I need him. In the living room, I sit down and smile at him.

"Hello," I state. "My name is Catori. Do you remember yours?"

"... *No*," he offers quietly.

"That's okay, I can give you one," I say, tone kind and caring. "How would you like that? Do you want a name?"

He doesn't say anything, eyes glancing away. I can tell he was shy in life. After a moment of patience, he nods his head. It's very minute; I almost missed it. At the permission granted, I look heavenward in thought.

"How about... Aden?" I muse. "That's a nice name."

Once more I get no words, just a nod. I count it as progress. Something is making this child ground himself in this world, and I need to find out what. The faster I resolve his unfinished business, the faster I can help him be at peace.

"So, Aden, what *do* you remember?" I venture.

"... *I lived in an old house and... I got hurt a lot*," he attempts. "*So I hurt them back*."

"How?"

"... *I don't remember*," he replies. "*I just remember it was really warm*."

It breaks my heart. This poor boy had a violent life… and a bloodier afterlife, if my grandmother's notes are correct. My free hand reaches over. It's slow, in case he wants to pull away. He flinches, yet doesn't move, and I caress his cheek. Bloody tears are gathering in his eyes. It's not fear, nor is it anger. I'm probably the first person to ever show him kindness.

"How did you come to be here?"

"*I lost something*," he frowns. "*When I was looking for it, people tried to hurt me... so I hurt them*."

"I'm so sorry," I offer. "That's not right. They should've tried to help you."

"... *One person did*," he states quietly. "*She was an old lady, but... she was nice. She wanted to help me find what I lost. She told me she was going to seal me up in a book!*

She said it was just until she found what I lost. And she never let me out."

"That old lady was my grandmother," I smile. "And she didn't forget about you… She died."

"*Wh-what?*" he gasps. "*She… she's gone?*"

"She is. She left her book with my father, so she probably expected him to pick up the search. My mother, though… she took it away and put it in a storage unit. I'll help you, okay? I don't want you to stay miserable forever, that's just not fair."

"… *O-okay.*"

"What did you lose?"

"*It was something I wore… something around my neck,*" he frowns. "*I don't remember what it looks like, but… I know it was always around my neck.*"

"Okay, that's a start," I smile. "I'll get my friend to help me. We'll search through some history books and newspaper clippings. I'm sure we'll find a picture of you, so it might show what it is you lost. You have to be patient, though. I might be gone before I can find it, but Heather will finish the search for me."

He takes a moment, yet nods his understanding. For now, he'll have to stay in Nana's company. I can't risk him finding a mugger and killing more people. By the time we're finished talking, I can hear movement from the bedroom. Aden hears it, too, as he disappears in a blink.

Heather walks in, yawning as she stretches. She doesn't notice me at first. I can see her eyes warily searching the room. No doubt, she's confused as to why all the noise stopped. The last thing we need is for Aden to get out of the house. Finally, she sees where I'm sitting.

"How long has it been quiet?" she whispers.

"All night," I shrug. "I'm pretty sure Aden didn't move."

"… Aden?"

"The wraith," I explain. "I named him Aden."

"… You know it's a man?"

"It's a boy," I inform. "I saw him at our beside last night. I think he held my hand all night long. Then when I woke up, I brought him out here so we could talk. I didn't want to wake you up."

She's flabbergasted, I can see it on her face. As she works to form words, she flails her arms about dramatically. I understand completely. Her forte is spirits and I haven't an inkling how to handle this magic stuff. Yet here I am, getting a wraith to talk before her.

"How is that even *possible*?" she finally states. "I tried to calm him down all fucking day! He didn't even sit still long enough to take form!"

"I guess I just have a way with wraiths," I frown. "Point is, Aden is looking for something. He said it's important to him, so he can't leave without it. My grandmother started looking for him, but died before she found the object. I told him I would take up the search."

"And what are we looking for?"

"Something that he wears around his neck."

"What does it look like?"

"He can't remember, but I have a plan. To the library!"

She hangs her head in defeat. The second we're dressed and fed, we hurry to my car. Shadow is already there. We drive over to the library, fighting for a parking spot. On the way to the doors, I give the statues a wary look. They came to life once, I don't want it happening again. Especially with Heather here.

Thankfully, we pass without issue. It's slow inside, silent like the grave. I don't even have to ask for the keys anymore, as the librarian has them ready. With a quiet 'thank you' I take the keys and head for the archives. My heart sinks with every step, though. I can't help thinking of the life lost because of me.

"Where do we start looking?" Heather wonders.

"House fires," I answer. "He looks like he burned alive. His clothes, though, were more recent. And he said my grandmother was already an old lady. She died a few years ago, so it's likely he died not long before then."

"Okay, I'll get on the computer. You check out the shelves. Maybe there was a case done on it."

"While we look, I'll call dad. He might be able to narrow down our search."

Heather nods and we split up. The dust has gathered another five layers, so I have to dust off some of the books. Grimacing at the mess on my hands, I wipe them on my pant legs. My cellphone is taken from my pocket, the contact list providing a quick call option. It only takes a few rings and my dad answers.

"How's the investigation going?" he wonders, tone distracted.

"Interesting. How's the paper?" I answer.

"Boring, as per usual. What help do you need? Did you get that book open?"

"The book has been open, but the wraith is a strong one. Heather can't force it to pass, so we have to help it find what it lost."

"I've never been good at finding things, Catori," he says, uncertain. "I don't know how much help I'll be. My forte has always been people or pets, not objects."

"Don't worry, we have a place to start. Grandma started helping him before she died. Did she say anything to you? Maybe she was focusing on a certain place at the time?"

There's silence from the other end, but I know he's thinking. As I await his answer, I flip through a few files. There are a few suicides, a couple murders, but no house fires. Setting the file back where it belongs, my fingers pull out another. Nothing interesting there either. Finally, my father begins to speak.

"Well… she was spending a lot of time in the police station," he says. "And she asked a bunch of questions about an old farm house at the edge of town. There was a nasty fire that brought it down, but that case wasn't assigned to me."

"A house fire?" I ask. "Who had the case? Do you know?"

"Yeah, my buddy did. Ray Hagan. It was just before we were put on the same detail."

"Great! Will he be working today? I really need to talk to him about it."

"He gets off for lunch around eleven-thirty, likes to go to that little sandwich place you like."

"Thanks, dad! I really appreciate it," I convey happily. "I'll talk to you later, okay?"

"You better. Tonight is the sixth night, Catori," he reminds me. "If you don't call me at one in the morning, I'm tearing that place to the ground myself."

We hang up after that. A skip in my step, I find Heather at the computers. She's nearly asleep on the keyboard. I try to sneak out, yet I can't bring myself to… not after what happened to Sadie. With a reluctant sigh, I shake her awake.

"We're going to eat lunch," I state. "Maybe we'll manage to get answers there as well."

"So… you have a specific place in mind?"

"Yep. Hey… where's Shadow?" I wonder.

"I don't know. He was here a minute ago, kept complaining about hearing someone cry. I told him it was probably from upstairs, but he insisted it was here."

Before I can run back and investigate, I see his little fire floating toward us. He doesn't give an explanation, nor do I ask for one. Instead, we all leave the archives. The keys are dropped off at the desk before we go. In the car, Heather's curious about our next stop. Unfortunately, I'm too focused on questions I want to ask. Her questions and guesses go unnoticed by me.

By the time we reach my favorite sandwich place, a patrol car is pulling into a parking spot. Ray Hagan gets out of the driver's side. We follow him inside and take a seat in his booth. He's surprised at first, yet notices the sense of urgency surrounding us.

"... Can I help you?" he wonders.

"As a matter of fact, you just might be able to," I smirk.

"He can?" Heather whispers. "Are you sure? I mean, I really don't think he's qualified to take on the dead."

"Not like that, Heather," I frown. "He was assigned a case a few years ago... involving a house fire... on a remote edge of town... Sound familiar?"

"... Oh!" she draws out. "Yeah, he might be able to help out."

I roll my eyes and shake my head. Sometimes she's a little dense, but it just makes me love her all the more. Before I can get into my questioning, the waitress wanders over to take our orders. We all choose something to eat, plus a plate of fries for Shadow, and she leaves. I at least wait until we have our drinks before speaking.

"That house fire... can you tell me about the case?"

"... Why?" he asks, brow raised in question.

"Well... I don't think you'd believe me if..."

"My house is haunted by a wraith!" Heather says enthusiastically. "It's a little boy that died in a house fire! Catori thinks it was in that house, because her grandmother was trying to free his soul from our plain! So to help his cross over, we have to find the object he lost!"

"…"

He just stares at us. It's about that time Heather thinks her statement over. A blush eats up her face and she hangs her head.

"I'll just let Catori talk now," she murmurs. "Obviously, we come from different worlds."

"Don't worry about it," he shakes off. "I've heard way worse in my day, trust me. I think there was a guy that accused big foot of beating up his girlfriend. Needless to say, he was five sheets to the wind at the time."

"Seriously, though, we need to learn about the family," I sigh. "It's really important. I wouldn't be asking you if it wasn't."

"I know, Catori, I know. I remember your grandmother coming to me, she was talking of ghosts, too. I'm not saying I don't believe… I just don't know a lot on the subject."

"We just need to learn about the family. Specifically, a little boy… around seven in age," I provide.

He nods and sits back, breathing in deep before releasing it. It's a calming breath. My father uses them all the time, before speaking of a topic that unnerves him. He always told me it came with the job. Whatever happened in this case, it left a scar on Officer Hagan. Our sandwiches come and we thank the waitress. The second she's gone, he seems to come unraveled. I can see the lines of age appear, making him look older than he actually is.

"That case was a hard one," he says, voice quiet. "That family was always very private, and the children had a tendency to lash out. I arrested their oldest on charges of arson a few times in the past. They never stuck, though. In total, the two had three children… a boy and two girls."

"No, there was another boy," I point out.

"They adopted him a year or two prior to the fire," he informs. "I was the officer that took him there… I'll never forget that kid. His name was Lewis Keaton, a little kid born to a drug addicted mother and a drunk father. They weren't bad people when they were clear-headed, you know… just had problems they couldn't kick. Children services took him away from them, he ended up in the system. Five houses took him in, but they all sent him back. He had connection issues, couldn't see them as his parents."

"So this last place kept him?" Heather asks.

"This last place killed him," he states.

"Wait… what?" I wonder in surprise. "When? He told me they hurt him, not that they killed him!"

"Took half a year," he sighs out, ashamed and regretful. "He called me a couple times, I left my number with him. Every time I went out to check on him, I didn't find anything wrong. He always wore jeans and long sleeve shirts, even in the dead of summer, but some people are like that. By the time I realized what was happening, it was too late. He was beaten to death in their cellar… where they locked him up at night. I found a blanket and pillow stuffed under a table there. That's where he slept."

"Oh my god, that's horrible!" Heather gasps. "No wonder the poor thing turned into a wraith!"

"Please continue," I prompt softly. "It might do you some good to get it out."

He nods, yet doesn't continue right away. I can tell he's been carrying this burden for years. For a moment, I wonder if he's talked to my father about all this. From what I remember, Ray was a rookie during all this. It would've been his first big failure, something he'd never get rid of. He's fighting back tears, too stubborn to let them fall. After he clears his throat, he starts up once more.

"Lewis was a quiet kid," he states. "They beat him every day… and he wasn't the first. The family had been adopting for years before him. All their children came up missing, but they were spaced so far apart no one suspected the parents. Lewis was just another adopted runaway… Until the fire, anyway."

"How did the fire start?"

"The fire department investigated it. They said it started in the cellar… right where his body was buried. In fact, they said the scorch pattern there was the outline of his body. It was all curled up, looked like he was sleeping. Creepy."

"Did he have anything of value?"

"Well, not really. Not monetary, but… there was a necklace he showed me. He loved that necklace, his birth mother gave it to him. It was so he'd never forget his birth parents. They were trying so hard to clean up their act. They were going to get him back, come hell or high water. When they learned of his death, they fell apart. His mother overdosed, his father shot himself after her death. Most tragic story I've ever investigated in my career."

"What happened to the necklace? Do you know?"

"Well, he had it when I dropped him off there. Next I saw him, he told me someone took it away. His foster parents said he lost it outside somewhere. It didn't really settle right with me, but kids lose stuff all the time. Besides, he was working the fields with his siblings. Seemed like an easy place to lose something."

"Thank you so much, I really appreciate this," I state. "I owe you one."

"You owe me a couple, but who's counting," he chuckles. "Stay out of trouble, Catori. I don't need to hear from your dad you got yourself in too deep."

"I'm always over my head, it's how I learn to stand tall," I offer. "See you later, Ray! Come on, Heather, time to leave."

"I'm not going anywhere until we've finished our meals," she glares. "Now sit down and eat."

I hesitate only a moment, and then heave a sigh. I haven't touched my sandwich at all. Sending Ray an apologetic glance I sit back down. He laughs at that, obviously enjoying my discomfort. I scoot close to Heather, leaving room for Shadow on the booth seat. It's not much, but it's something. As we eat, Ray notices neither of us are touching the fries. They're set on the table beside me, forgotten.

"Why get the order of fries if you aren't going to eat them?" he asks.

"They weren't for us," I shrug. "They were for Shadow."

"Shadow? Who's that? Oh, god, please tell me you don't have an imaginary friend. I thought you outgrew that phase! I *rejoiced* you outgrew that phase!"

"… Why?" Heather wonders.

"Do you have any idea how many times that girl wound up at the station, because 'her friend made her do it'?"

"Golden," Heather laughs. "I always got in trouble, too. But my excuse, was 'a ghost possessed me'."

"It's not an imaginary friend," I bristle. "Shadow is a wraith from the store. Well… he *was* a wraith. He's not so hostile anymore… does that mean he's no longer considered a wraith? Are you still considered a wraith?"

I direct the last question to the empty spot beside me. In answer, his fires glow green. I take that as a 'yes'. Ray can only stare again. He squints his eyes, trying hard to see what we see. Heather reaches over the table, setting her hand on his. The second she touches him, I can see a change in his expression. It goes from searching to disbelief. He can see what we see now.

"That's a ghost?" he whispers. "Do they all look like that? Are there more?"

"There are spirits all over the world," Heather smiles. "Some are full body, some shadows, some light… and some that change shape."

"Shadow can change shape," I offer. "He stays a ball of light for the most part, but in the store he takes a more human form."

"… Can he do anything? Like move furniture, or something?"

"He can do a lot of stuff. He can move things, set stuff on fire, possess other people… maybe more. He has a friend at the store that can manipulate cloth, too."

"Unbelievable," he murmurs, sitting back against his seat. "Simply unbelievable. But… why the food?"

"It's polite to offer the dead food in some countries, I just always liked the idea," I shrug.

He nods, going quiet again. When Heather pulls her hand away, he starts to squint again. This time, however, he gives off a disappointed air. Seems the gift was only temporary. We all eat our food in silence, Ray leaving before us. His break is up and he has to return to the station. We offer him a 'goodbye', finishing up ourselves.

Chapter 27

Back on the road, I call dad for the address of the old farm. The second I have it, we're headed straight for it. That necklace has to be there somewhere. As I drive, Heather searches her phone for information. The second she finds a picture, she shouts in joy. I only swerve a little bit.

"Sorry," she blushes. "I found his picture. He wore his necklace on the outside, so now we know what it looks like!"

"Perfect," I smile. "Almost there."

"… What if it isn't there?" she wonders.

"Then we check the field."

"… And if it isn't *there*?"

"I don't know," I shrug. "I mean, they probably took it from him. So we can ask around at pawn shops or something. Maybe they used it to keep him from running away, or talking to people. You know, like, 'if you say anything we'll destroy it'. It was his most prized possession, I've no doubt he would've taken the punishment to keep it."

"Maybe you're right. The way Officer Hagan told it, they were likely serial killers. They would've kept his only possession as a trophy, wouldn't they?"

"That's exactly what I'm thinking."

I slow down at the end of a long gravel drive. The house is a mere skeleton now, charred 'bones' standing up to the weather. Not very well, though. Only about two corners and a few scattered posts stand. A staircase leads the way to a section of second floor, not yet fallen thanks to a support beam. There's also a chimney reaching for the sky. The rest is a pile of ash and forgotten rubble. Further away is a barn, still standing and untouched. Weeds have run rampant, the fields beyond filled with dying crops, and a broken down tractor is stuck in some mud.

"Lovely," Heather mutters. "Someday, I'm sure we'll have a house just as beautiful."

"How can you say that without throwing up in your mouth?"

"… It's extremely difficult."

I turn off the car and get out. I'm halfway to the front door when Heather's door slams shut. I wait, though I don't have to. In a place this dilapidated, we need to stay within sight. The second she's beside me, I go to enter once more.

"No, let's check the fields while we have light," she says. "No telling when it'll go dark out here… or how long this search will take."

"Good idea," I relent. "After that, we'll check the barn. It's on the way back to the house."

"Perfect."

The path to the fields is hard to make out. As it was highly traveled, there's a little dip in the ground. I almost trip over a couple planks hidden in the overgrowth. When we get to the rotting crops, we split up. Shadow is in the corn field, but Heather and I search the smaller garden before it. It has tomatoes and squash, plants lower to the ground.

Prodding around all the stench is turning my stomach. I try to breath through my mouth, yet the taste is just as bad. As I dig about, I come across soil that's fallen in a little. I glance back at Heather, who's watching me in confusion.

"Did you find a dip in the earth, too?" I question.

"… Yes," she nearly squeaks out. "Do you know what it is?"

"No, but..."

"It's a shallow grave," she whispers, just loud enough for me to hear. "We're kneeling on a cemetery!"

I'm stunned, there's no other word for it. You would think the police would've searched here. Then again, Ray said there was no reason to suspect anything but runaways. It may have been deemed unimportant, or Lewis was thought to be the only death. I can't bare to dig beneath the earth. There's still a chance the necklace was dropped here, though, and we continue to search. We'll apologize afterward and call the authorities when we're done.

Nothing comes up in the gardens, not even for Shadow. He does, however, find a couple bodies lost there. How they could've been missed I'll never know. By his account, they're very little skeletons. I pray they were already dead when they were placed there, but I highly doubt it. With nothing to show, we head to the barn.

The second we're standing inside it, we both turn to walk out. Knives and blades of all types hang from the ceiling. Blood is wiped upon the walls, and a couple carcasses hang on thick hooks. The smell is unbelievable. My senses are probably damaged for life.

"Fucking sickos!" Heather yells outside.

"Heather, some people actually do butcher their own meat," I sigh. "Let's just hope that's all they butchered."

"I am *not* going back in there!" she huffs.

"Okay, stay out here," I sigh. "I'll go in and look. Shadow, can you take the hayloft?"

"Of course."

We head back inside, Heather hot on my heels. The only thing worse than going in, is staying outside alone. The barn is most definitely a butcher shop. There are shelves filled with canning salts, a diagram to the different cuts, and a large slab to carry out the task.

We look through the cans on the shelves, hoping to find a hidden cache. There's nothing here. Up in the hayloft, we watch Shadow's light float about. I head over to the carcass, wondering if they would be sick enough to hide it there… I can totally see that. Again, there's nothing.

"*Nothing here!*" Shadow calls down.

"Looks like we're searching the house," Heather sighs reluctantly."

We trudge back up to the house, daylight still holding strong. It is late, though, and I have my doubts as to getting back in time. All that is placed aside, as Lewis's eternal peace is more important than mine. Standing before the great mass of fire damage, I take a deep breath. It reminds me of the store when the threshold passed, though it's not as dreary. The spirits have long since passed from here. The ash is no longer flaky, as it rained not long ago, so our shoes sink into it. The kitchen, once white, is nearly black with the fire damage. I draw one of the drawers out, yet it tumbles to the floor.

Glancing back, I can't see Heather or Shadow. Before I can search for them, I hear her yelp. In the room over, the living room from the tattered furniture, she's pulling herself off the floor. Shadow is laughing at her from a couple steps away.

"It's not funny!" she gripes. "Now I'm filthy!"

"*Who wears white to a ghost hunt anyway?*" he snickers.

"Someone that doesn't know she's going to an ash-filled gateway to hell!"

"Guys, calm down," I sigh. "If there still is a spirit around here, I don't want to wake them. I'm sorry you got dirty, Heather, I'll buy you a new outfit tomorrow."

"… Okay," she murmurs. "Where should we start?"

"I was going to check the kitchen," I frown. "My mother has, like, ten hiding places in our kitchen. Maybe this mom thought the same way."

"Okay, I'll take the left," she says. "Shadow, try looking under the floor and in the ceiling that survived."

"*No problem.*"

We split up, though not very far, and rummage around the kitchen. I can remember some of my mother's hiding places, so I search in those. The freezer, long since turned off, has nothing but a couple ice trays full of stale water. There's also a couple melted ice cream containers. Odd, considering places like this are usually cleaned up. With the eerie burn patterns, the fire fighters and police likely let it go. They say they aren't superstitious around here, but I've seen quite a few moments that dispute that.

With the freezer a no-go, I try in the back of a cupboard. Moldy and stale food is still within them, though burnt to a crisp in some areas. I move aside some brittle boxes, sucking in a sharp breath when a mouse runs out. After catching my breath, I move the last box. Nothing is in the back. My last resort is the top of the fridge. Mom usually has a cookie jar or coffee can up there. Standing on the counter, I can see a jar… but it only has a mess of rotten candy.

"No luck here," I huffs. "You?"

"*Nope*," Shadow calls.

"No. Just a lot of rotten food and mice."

"Cellar?" I question, wary.

"Looks like it," she sighs. "I'll go. You and Shadow check upstairs. Have him go first, though. I don't trust those stairs."

"I don't want you to be alone."

"I'll be fine, I promise. Go look upstairs. Try sifting through the ash down here while he goes, it may have fallen during the fire."

My gut wrenches so hard as she walks away, I think I might vomit. Something isn't right, I just know it. I trust her, though, and shake off the feeling. Shadow floats along the rickety stairway, and I grab the metal sifter from the cabinet. As he rummages upstairs, I scoop up a bunch of ash and sift through it. The first bunch leaves me with a couple coins… and a few human teeth. I gag at the sight, shivering in disgust. The sifter goes in again, hitting something large on the couch. Carefully, the ash is dusted away to reveal a skull.

"Seriously?" I mutter. "Shouldn't they have gathered all these bones."

Ignoring the discoveries, I continue with my task. I don't really notice as the night approaches. Time just seems to pass so slowly. The floor groans beneath my sneakers, my heart stopping a moment. Carefully, I move away from my spot. Shadow floats back down, having only gone up a few minutes ago. The drive must've been longer than I anticipated.

"*I found it*," he says proudly. "*It's in a jar they hung on the inside of the chimney!*"

"Great job, Shadow!" I grin. "Let's get Heather before we go up to get it."

I step forward… and the floor cracks. I only have time to gasp before the floor is gone beneath my feet. Shadow catches me rather quickly, but I'm not worried about me. In the cellar, beneath the rubble of burned posts and wooden planks, is a piece of fabric. It's the same color as Heather's jacket. Heather, my Heather, has been crushed.

Chapter 28

My heart breaks, I swear it does. Warm blood trickles from between my lips. At first, I think it really is from my broken heart. Then I feel the pain in my tongue. I bit it when Shadow stopped my descent abruptly. Tears gather in my eyes, the sight beneath me forever burned into my retinas.

"Heather!" I scream out. "No!"

I can hear the echoic laughter of the demon. This is her doing, and she'll pay for it. Shadow gently puts me on the ground, helping me pull the beams away. I can barely see what I'm going, tears blurring my vision. My heart aches so much, I could be dying right this very moment. I can barely breathe as mucus clogs my airways, yet I still manage to reach Heather. Carefully, I pull her into my arms. My eyes go wide, however, when I hear her groan.

"Son of a bitch," she mutters. "That fucking hurt."

"You're alive!" I state in shock. "Oh my god! I can't believe you're alive! You're one lucky son of a bitch!"

"No," she smirks, though in pain. "I'm a daughter of a witch. Get it right."

I can't help but laugh, both relieved and agonized. If I had lost her, truly lost her, I would've lain down my life at that damn store. I felt as though my soul had been crushed. Perhaps there's no soul to give to the store anymore. Perhaps I already signed it over to my Heather. I help her to her feet, holding her close. The only reason I don't crush her against me, is the pained groan she gives.

"Let's get out of here," I remark, sniffling in an attempt to control my emotions. "I need to get you to the hospital."

"No, just get me home," she argues.

"Absolutely not! You're going to the hospital!"

"Then… at least let me get the book," she attempts. "And we have to give Lewis is necklace… We didn't find the necklace! We can't leave without it! I'll never find out how to save you!"

"*I found it,*" Shadow informs. "*I can knock it down for you.*"

We're both lifted off the ground. He sets us back on the floor, floating upstairs by the chimney. I set Heather on the couch, after moving the skull, and rush to the fireplace. A small jar comes crashing down, shattering on the stone. The necklace tumbles over and stops at my foot. I grab it, heedless of the shards, and run back to Heather. It's deposited into her hand, and then I'm lifting her up.

As soon as she's safe in the car, I climb in the driver's side. Shadow barely has time to get settled in the back, and I'm darting down the drive. I know I shouldn't be speeding, but it's so hard not to. Heather is in pain and she needs medical attention. The road is a blur, though not from the speed we're traveling. My mind isn't clear right now, the near loss still controlling me. By the time we reach her house, I'm ready to tear apart that store.

"Okay, stay here," I say. "I'll run in and grab the book..."

"Catori, I'm going inside," Heather states. "I know I was hurt, but Nana can heal me better than any hospital. Trust me, okay? I wouldn't be saying this if it weren't true."

"But..."

"Look into my eyes, Catori," she bristles. "Do I look like I'm lying to you? Look, my arm's bruise is already nearly gone. Okay?"

"But… how?" I wonder, dumbstruck.

"My element is water," she smiles. "Water is a healing element, therefore, I heal faster than most. I'll be fine, okay? Let me go inside and you go to the store. I'll call you when I find the answer we seek."

"… I want to send Lewis off with you."

She nods in understanding. The two of us go inside, yet Shadow waits in the car. He knows I won't be long. When we walk into the house, Nana is scolding our new wraith. The living room is a complete mess. It looks like someone came in with the intent to rob, yet couldn't find what they were looking for. Lewis is pouting on the couch, the only piece of furniture untouched, and Nana is shaking her finger at him.

"Hey, Nana!" I smile. "Guess what we found!"

"*A paddle I can use on ghosts would be wonderful*," she huffs.

"Uh… no, we didn't find that. I don't even think that exists. But… We found his name!" I cheer. "Your name is Lewis Keaton, and the object you were looking for… is a necklace your birth mother gave you."

"*I… I remember! I remember my mother*!" he cries out, tears gathering in his eyes. "*My mother was going to find me! I have to go to her and my father*!"

"Lewis, honey, they died," I inform softly. "After you were killed. They already passed over, I think. You'll find them on the other side."

"*But… I didn't find mother's necklace…*"

"Then it's a good thing we did," Heather grins, holding it out to him.

"*Good lord, child*!" Nana gasps. "*What trouble were you into*?"

"I'll tell you later," she offers, sheepish.

She hands the necklace over to Lewis, his small hands reaching for it. As he takes it from her, a bright light begins to outline him. He's sobbing with a large smile on his face. His form begins to disappear slowly. For a moment, my heart swells with his happiness. The boy looks between his necklace and his transparent hands. A spectral one has appeared around his neck now, yet the real one can't be taken with him. Lewis holds it out to me.

"*I want you to have it, I know you'll take care of it,*" he says through tears. "*I'll never forget you and I don't want you to forget me! Thank you so much!*"

"I will," I smile. "And I'll never forget you, Lewis, I promise."

I take the silver chain from him, watching him pass over with a sense of pride. It feels so good to help him. I can only imagine what freeing the store's souls will feel like. Once he's gone, I kiss Heather on her cheek and head for the door. Nothing needs to be said, we both know I'm going to win this.

As I climb into the car, I have a soft smile on my lips. Shadow is now in the passenger seat. He seems happy as well, so I assume it's because another wraith was freed. A lump grows in my throat, yet I turn to him anyway.

"You can pass over as well, you know," I offer.

"*No. I'm going to stay with you,*" he says, tone happy and determined. "*I'm going to protect you.*"

"Someday, I'm sure you'll be ready," I say. "I'll be okay with that. You need peace just like every other soul."

"*After the hell I was trapped in, everyday here is peace,*" he comments, soft and sad. "*That's what it is, you know... Being a wraith. It's being trapped in a vengeful hell. I was already set free, already put at peace, when you took me from that. I will always be grateful, Catori. Thank you.*"

"You're more than welcome."

The car purrs to life before backing out of the drive. It's already late, but that's okay. I've freed a soul tonight, and I'm about to free a whole lot more. When nothing happens on the way to the store, I get a little nervous. Something always happens, and she should be trying like hell to kill me tonight. After I park and get out, I expect something... anything... but there's nothing.

"Okay, now I'm worried," I murmur.

"*No one has ever made it this long,*" Shadow explains. "*She's thrown everything she's used before at you. There's a good chance she'll need to think of something new.*"

Shrugging it off, I head inside. At the threshold, in the process of entering, I hear Baby screaming from inside. She's calling for me to stop, but it's too late. I'm already inside. Behind me, I feel that force field go up again. Once more, Shadow is locked outside. I don't really understand why, other than the fact he protects me.

The lights are dimmer this time around. It sets off every alarm bell in my mind, yet I refuse to panic. I escaped from a near drowning, there isn't much more she can do to me. A mass of shadow races from the back of the store, tendrils dancing like a mess of serpents. It stops just before me.

"*Welcome to the last night of your life,*" the demon cackles.

"What are you planning on doing tonight?" I wonder. "I mean, you've already tried so much and I'm not dead yet. I'm curious to know what's next."

"*Absolutely nothing,*" she laughs. "*You'll end your own life, I promise you that. Unless, of course, you'd like to make a deal.*"

"I already made a deal with you," I point out. "I'm about to win said bargain."

"*If the night ends,*" she corrects.

"Every night ends," I frown. "This one won't be any different."

"*But it will be, as it will never end. You're going to be trapped here, with no food or water, until you succumb to insanity... just like all the rest.*"

"So… the night is just going to restart at the end?"

"*That's right,*" she grins, sick and twisted.

"… Okay," I smirk. "Let's play."

"*Why aren't you making a deal? You're going to starve to death, every night, for the rest of eternity*!" she screams. "*Is that what you want?*"

"The best part about being me, is the fact I'm always prepared," I say, one hand patting my backpack.

I thank every god in existence I bring it out of habit. This one was already packed and sitting in my backseat. I never go anywhere without one. The only thing I never remember to pack… is a first aide kit. After Heather's accident, I've not doubt that'll be the first item I pack. With a screech of rage, the demon lashes out at me. Her sharp claws are barely dodged.

"Uncalled for," I scold. "Stop throwing little temper tantrums! You're too old for that!"

"*You'll either kill yourself here, or you'll become my new vessel*!" she shrieks. "*The choice is yours, but there is no escape*!"

"You think very little of me," I frown. "I guarantee you, I'll be walking out of here in the end. And it won't be because I'm your new vessel."

She shrieks once more, blasting upward and into the ceiling. Some of the tiles there are shaken loose. I step away before they can hit me. My bag is set atop the jewelry counter before I pull myself up. A light grows near me, taking the form of Baby. She watches me pull a granola bar from my bag.

"*... You really are prepared, aren't you?*" she smirks.

"You know it."

"*I found out her plan just before you entered, I'm sorry I couldn't warn you faster*," she says sadly. "*But, the night is almost over now. You won't have to wait long for it to loop.*"

"That may prove irritating, though," I sigh. "I've no need to travel about, Heather has the book now. I just have to wait for her call."

"*You won't get it,*" Baby informs. "*She'll block all the calls coming in. However… the contract ends at midnight. The loop won't start until one, so you'll have an hour to think up a way out. That's all I can give you, though. I'm so sorry I can't do more.*"

"That's more than enough, thank you."

It's almost midnight now, according to my phone's clock. By now, I know I won't be getting home to see Heather. I managed to break out before, but that's only because of oversight. She didn't expect me to be so resourceful. This time, she'll have planned for it. I'll spend the rest of my life here… dead or alive. Whereas I would love to spend it alive, I've made up my mind. This bitch is going to pay before I'm dead.

Chapter 29

I walk over to the window, breathing on the glass pane. Carefully, I write a message backward for Shadow. He's darting along the length of the building, in a panic and unable to reach me. With a soft smile, I wave at him. A short goodbye before I'm gone. Maybe I'll have unresolved business and we'll see each other again, who knows.

I wander through the store, taking a seat in the center of it. I set an alarm on my phone before setting it next to me. My body relaxes and I close my eyes, concentrating with all I am. There's something inside me, something great and locked away. I need it now. I search through myself, meditating like I used to do long ago. My father meditated a lot when I was younger, so I used to do it with him. Once I hit pre-teens, however, life was too hectic to relax. Now, I have nothing better to do.

Just as the alarm starts to buzz beside me, I find what I'm looking for. My mind is surrounded by fire. Everywhere within my subconscious, bursts of flames envelope the world. With a smirk, I imagine the store going up in flames. A more satisfying sight I will never see. When I open my eyes, I can feel tears of bittersweet sorrow on my cheeks. The fires are everywhere, eating up the store like a child with a candy bar. Baby is standing in the kids' section, a smile on her face greater than any I've ever seen.

From above, likely the large office, I can hear the demon screeching. I can't decide if it's in pain or anger. I just don't care anymore. The mass of shadows arrives once more, charging straight for me. This time, however, she doesn't stop. I'm knocked backwards by the force, staring up at the ceiling in shock. Within me, something is fighting for control. It's such a strange sensation, being pulled in two directions mentally. Instead of feeling fear, however, I feel nothing but rage. I glance down at a puddle near my foot, but my reflection is not my own.

Pain tears through my psyche, my head thrown back with it. Fingers curl as I try to fight it off. How do you fight off something in your mind, though? My breathing quickens, limbs falling numb as she pushes control. Heather's words surface through my haze. Our energies aren't compatible. The other witch she first possessed was from her own clan, but I'm not. Her clan is an earth element, and I'm fire… which also happens to be how she died. If the way she's fighting is any indication. I'm stronger than her.

I fight with all I am, drawing upon the bullheadedness I was born with. The fires in me burn hotter, touching her even though it's all mental. She starts slipping up, losing ground. Warmth trickles from my nose, likely blood from the stress on my mind. Heather did say it could tear me apart. Finally, I can almost taste victory. I can feel my limbs again. That's all I need to open my mouth and talk.

"How *dare* you!" I hiss. "How *dare* you try to control me! *Me*! You won't win with this fight any more than you have the others!"

"*You idiot! You'll kill yourself as well!*" I yell, though it's not me speaking. "*What will your precious Heather think then*?"

"I guess we'll never know, will we?" I spit out. "And by the way… the contract is over, I won. Your store is trying to kill me. You know what that means, don't you?"

My voice is smug and venomous. I can hear the scream within me, so strong I open my own lips to allow escape. The shadows exit through my parted lips, gathering in the air. It wrenches about in pain, fires sparking within it. Just like the serpent she sent for me, the demon bursts outward… and disappears. Her power, however, has sealed me inside this place.

I sit back down, waiting for the end. Although the fires have grown hotter with my rage, I'm not yet sweating. The spell locking me in won't likely leave until one. I'll be long gone by then. If not by fire, then by smoke inhalation. Coughing every now and then, I feel the weight of sleep on my shoulders. Just as I'm about to succumb, a spectral hand slaps me across my face. I'm startled to attention by Baby.

"*No you don't!*" she bites out. "*I didn't protect you all this time, just for you to give up! Now you wake your ass up! You're not dying tonight!*"

"I don't think you've noticed, but the store is in flames," I point out calmly. "There's no escape... not this time."

"*That's why I'm gonna help you, stupid!*" she says with a smile, though her eyes are sad. "*You need a shield, and I can only give you one... but it's worth it.*"

I'm confused, yet I don't convey it through more than a look. I can hear something crumbling in the back room. Slowly, I get to my feet and walk that way. The fires seem to make a path, letting me pass by. When I'm finally in the back, I see a skeletal hand break through the concrete. A mostly decayed body crawls from the earth. Baby drifts over to it, connecting to it's form. It's muscle and tissue start to grow once more. It doesn't completely change, only enough to recognize it. Baby's body has turned into a zombie-like creature. I can see her soul lighting up it's eyes as it walks over. Her jaw opens and closes, teeth grinding as she speaks. With no lips, it simply looks like she's a puppet… which she might as well be.

"*This is my body*," she says. "*I will sacrifice my remains to protect you. You saved us, but I won't let you join us without trying everything to save you.*"

I can't even speak as she steps forward, curling around me in an attempt to protect me. The fires have started to invade this room as well. I can see from beneath her living corpse as it spreads. Something in the pile I found Shadow in moves. His body also stands and wanders over, eyes lit up like search lights. He's not in the building, but that's not stopping him.

"*I can't keep this form moving, but I only need to get it to you*," he says, his body reanimating like Baby's.

The second he's close enough, he covers us in his larger form. The larger man goes still around us. More crumbling concrete echoes in the room, more corpses crawling from unknown graves. Over by the compactor, I can see Carrie. She's calling out to the others, rallying them to protect their savior. She doesn't have a body, as hers was simply blown up, but she's ready to do her part.

Tears drip from my eyes. Such a heartfelt atmosphere suffocates me. All the bodies brought here to strengthen the demon, are being used to protect her 'killer'. So many circle around me, piling up to keep the fires from reaching me. I can't even pay attention to the smell of decay. The sobs I let out are overjoyed and hopeful. Their efforts are so sincere, but pointless… my life is already over.

The flames crackle outside my shield of death. I can hear a beam fall, one of those surrounding me gasping in pain. Just as I'm about to close my eyes and succumb, a strange energy fills the room. It's not the demon, but it's strong like her. Only now do I wonder if she was working for someone. The bodies lift and move, making way for this new creature. When Baby and Shadow are moved away from me, I'm left with a hand in front of my face.

Hesitantly, I set my hand in theirs. As they lift me from the ground, my eyes travel the appendage. A light silver armor covers their arm, only slivers of skin showing. There's heavy boots and more armor, a naked belly, and intricate breast plate. She reminds me of a Valkyrie. Finally, I look into her face.

"… Heather?" I gasp.

"Catori," she smiles. "You're so lucky you didn't die, I would've killed you."

"… Heather, you're in armor," I gape. "And… is that a scythe? Are you kidding me? What the hell!"

"I guess I should explain myself," she blushes. "But I would like to do that outside of this fire, if you don't mind."

I can only nod, jaw still hanging open in shock. She takes her long scythe, waving it toward the wall. A hole in the force field opens. Just as I'm stepping outside, she whispers a 'thank you', and taps the floor with the pole of her scythe. The spirits leave their corpses, lifting into the sky. A glowing portal opens for them, allowing them passage to the other side. When the last of them enters, Baby stopping before waving goodbye, it closes tight. Heather faces me and the world around us melts away. It's replaced by the living room of her house.

"Catori, I'm an envoy for the dead," she informs. "It's my job to help the dead pass over. Unfortunately, demons do exist and they feed off trapped souls. I'm unable to break the hold over them. I needed you to do that for me. Not you specifically… but… well… one of the Roots."

"… Roots?"

"That's what you're called, or… people like you. People that harness an element without magic. You don't use magic, because you *are* that element. Born in a human shell, but capable of so much more!"

I can only flop back on the couch. By now, Nana has come up from the basement. Her spirit form melts away, leaving an older version of Heather. So much is going through my head right now, I just can't focus. The woman I love is an envoy to the dead… Does that make her dead as well?

"Nana?" I whisper.

"My name is Jade," she offers. "I'm Heather's mother and teacher. I didn't expect to meet a Root here, but I'm glad you arrived. That demon was too powerful for us. I'm sorry we had to put you in that situation, but… you were the only one that could stop her."

"I… you… I can't… what the hell..?"

"I'm sorry I didn't tell you, Catori. I wanted to, I really did. I almost blew it in that damn elevator!" Heather mutters. "I just… I wasn't supposed to get attached to anyone. After a mission… I disappear. I mean, well, I don't literally disappear… I just… this life… this identity… it doesn't really exist. My name is really Nixie Pranet. Tomorrow morning, no one will remember me… Not even you. I'm so sorry, Catori. It breaks my heart to leave you behind, but… it's for the best. My job is just too dangerous to keep you near. This is why I said my life was complicated."

She's in tears now, sobbing in pain and sorrow. Her mother sets a hand on her back. Unable to contain myself, I get up and wrap her in a hug. It feels strange to hold her while she's dressed in armor. Both of us cry at the loss. If I don't remember her upon waking, what will I do? I can't lose her, it just hurts too much.

"I'm truly sorry, Catori," Jade sighs out. "I am. Envoys live forever, it makes it impossible to be with a human. You would only suffer… It's just better this way. Please understand."

"I don't want..."

"I know, honey, I know. But you won't remember this in the morning. It'll all just be a vivid nightmare, that's all. I promise."

Before I can say anything more, she touches my shoulder… and I'm lost in darkness. It hits so quickly, I know my knees buckled. I can feel my body falling to the floor. At the same time, I can feel Heather slipping from my hands.

Epilogue

The sun shines through my blinds, waking me from my sleep. I yawn and stretch. The sound of my back popping is wonderful. It's Friday, which means it's a school day. So close to graduation, I'm tempted to stay home and fake sick. The place was victim to an explosion anyway, the students probably won't be flocking to the doors after that. Unfortunately, I know they'll be needing help with the clean up. I'm always a sucker for extra credit.

I dress and head downstairs, where my mother is making breakfast. I stop at the smell of eggs and bacon, tilting my head to the side in question. She can see it in my expression. When the plate is at the table, I sit down and start to eat. Something keeps nibbling at my mind, though. It really bothers me, like that *one thing* you know you forgot and can't remember.

"What's wrong, honey?"

"I don't know," I comment. "I just… feel like I forgot something."

"I'm sure it's not important, dear," she smiles. "Eat your breakfast. I've no doubt you'll have a long day at school today."

"No kidding," I snort in humor.

After breakfast, I hurry outside. My car sits in wait for me, though something is different about it. I check the side of it, looking for scratches. Nothing. Humming to myself, I sit behind the wheel and start it up. For only a second, I swear I see a fire in the backseat. When I turn around, it's not there.

"I must be losing my damn mind," I mutter.

The car starts up and I back out. As I head to school, I can't stop the annoyance in the back of my mind. Something isn't right! I pass a house on the way, one that looks so familiar. I can picture the inside of it, every room, and can't understand why. I've never been in that place. Shrugging it off, I continue to drive past it. It isn't until I park at school that it hits me. My eyes land on the ring I wear, noting the strange symbols etched there. The symbol of fire locks on my gaze. Something inside clicks and I can see flames all around me.

"Heather!" I cry out.

"About time, girl. I thought you'd never remember!" Shadow states from the passenger seat.

"What the fuck!" I scream in surprise, nearly falling out of the car.

"Oh, so you remember her, but not me?" he bristles. "I'm insulted."

"I remember you, Shadow, I just wasn't expecting you to be *right there*," I remark. "How do I remember all that? Heather and Jade said I wouldn't..."

"You're one of the Roots," he provides. "All magic comes from you, so it doesn't really affect you like humans. Your stunt at the store unlocked your bloodline, so it burned away the spell used to make you forget."

"... How do you know all this?"

"I was listening to them talk after you got knocked out. They didn't take into consideration I would stick around, they thought I crossed over with the rest."

"And why did you stick around?"

"I already told you I would. Now get to class, you're going to be late."

I do as told, mind still on the fact I can remember the whole ordeal. I don't know whether to be thankful, or angry. In class, I test the waters. Dropping Heather's name leaves confused faces, just as I thought. No one remembers her but me. The day drags on slowly, but thanks to the explosion, this is the last day. I blow through my tests with ease, leaving as soon as I'm done.

Back home, no one is home. I can already feel the emptiness left behind. So used to seeing Heather when I come home, the loss is hitting hard. Depression sets in as I head to my room. When I open the door, I'm shocked once more. Heather, or Nixie, is standing there dressed in her armor... with a bouquet of roses.

"You just couldn't stay out of trouble, could you?" she chuckles.

"You know me," I wave off, already teary-eyed. "If I'm not in trouble, I'm not living."

She opens her arms and I rush to them. The second we hug, everything rushes back. So much happened in the past week or two. Every heartache, panic attack, and bout of anger is overwhelming. Nixie just hugs me closer, her tears of happiness soaking into my cheek. This may be the end, or it may be the beginning. With a new girlfriend and an unlocked ability, there's a lot to learn. If she stands by my side, though, I'm willing to take on anything. This is where we belong and I'm okay with that.

Made in the USA
Middletown, DE
15 May 2023